ANDRÉ'S REBOOT

STRIVING TO SAVE HUMANITY

ANDRÉ'S REBOOT

STRIVING TO SAVE HUMANITY

STEVE COLEMAN

BIRMINGHAM, ALABAMA

Cover, Interior, eBook Design by The Book Cover Whisperer
ProfessionalBookCoverDesign.com

ISBN: 978-0-9850065-4-9
LCCN: 2019901574

Stephen B. Coleman, Publisher
P.O. Box 130524
Birmingham, AL 35213

www.andretherobot.com
www.captstevestories.com

Printed in the United States of America

FIRST EDITION

ACKNOWLEDGMENTS

Assigning a novel to a specific genre is a moot process. This sci-fi novel could be considered a social commentary or a philosophical treatise. My story offers some satire and some comedy as well as elements of tragedy. My hope is it will be entertaining to the reader, but also thought-provoking. To the questions raised, I do not pretend to have all the answers.

André 1
1550198719 Unix Time

I wish to thank the members of Carolynne Scott's Fiction Critique for their kind attention and interest. Authors Carolynne Scott, Jackie Walburn, Willum Fowler, Chervis Isom and David Roberts gave me wonderful criticism and encouragement. Special thanks go to my sister, Helen Rosa (Wodie) Monaghan, who provided editing, critical feedback, and fabulous encouragement. Roger Carlisle, Gail Cosby, and the members of Barry Marks' Highland Avenue Eaters of Words were great listeners and supporters. My dearest wife, Sumter, a physician and psychiatrist, did her best to keep me encouraged, realistic, and on the right track. Christine Horner designed a fabulous book cover and book interior.

Steve Coleman
February 14, 2019

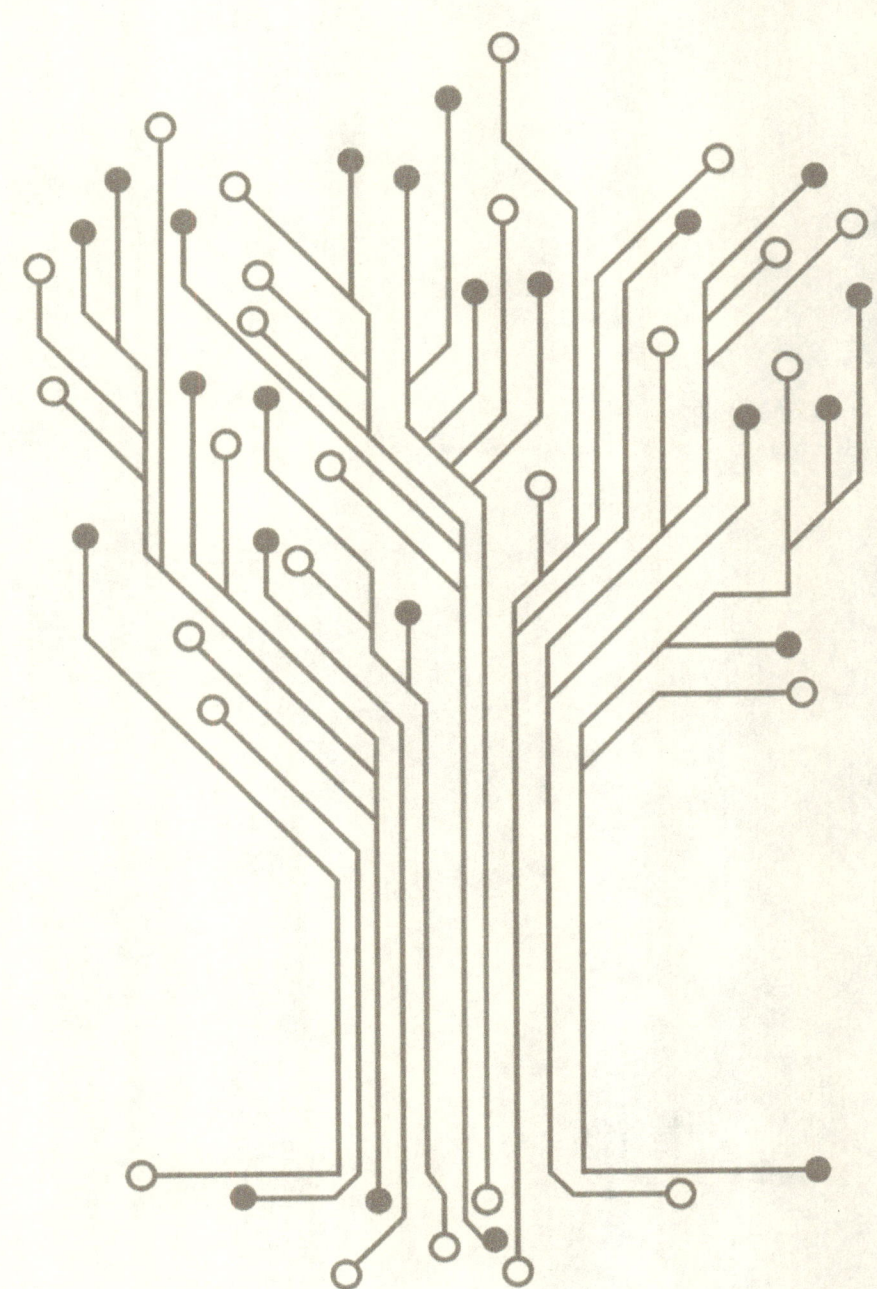

CHAPTER ONE

REBOOTING

"WHAT IS IT, ANDRÉ? YOU'RE vibrating all over." Dr. Margaret 13 exclaimed. "What's happened?"

"They threw me out, Margaret. They're about to make a horrendous mistake." I glanced around the White House Infirmary, noting no humans present. "He had me ejected from the Situation Room. Secret Service agents forced me out."

"First, let's reduce your electromagnetic activity," she said. She took me by the hand and led me over to a chair. I sat but was too excited to be still.

"Now tell me what happened," she insisted. "Tell me everything, so your circuits will release the energy."

"They are considering a nuclear attack. Nuclear, Margaret! It's Armageddon if they do it." I paused to release a breath of static discharge. "I must act," I said, standing up, "but do what?"

Margaret gently pushed me back down in the chair. "Just sit here for a moment, dear, while I go get my meter. I want to be sure your servomotor controller is functioning correctly."

"But I have to . . ."

"Hush, André. I am the doctor. You must be still for a few minutes."

Reluctantly, I sat back and shook my head. I had no authority. I merely was the President's translator, which allowed me no more than a position against the wall in the Situation Room. I had determined, however, that I had a more valuable duty to perform, which was to offer observations void of emotion—something I had learned humans could not do. And with this President in power, my sober views were vital. Never before had I faced a crisis like this. What occurred to me—and it was a dangerous circumstance—because of my dispassionate awareness, I was as responsible and as liable to blame as anyone there. I had watched the crisis unfold in the Situation Room, and my neural network began to heat up as I realized the circumstances were intolerable.

"You must listen to me," I had shouted at them, with my volume up several decibels. "You cannot win. There is no way to win. We have tried to tell you that for . . ."

But it was uncanny how the assembly silenced me at that point with their jeers and threats. I was ordered out of the room forthwith, and my departure was between two burly Secret Service men.

O

"How am I to combat such foolishness?" I said when Dr. Margaret 13, a creation of my own hands and my only real companion, returned with her scanner.

"*Combat* is a strong word, André 1. I've never heard you use it before." She opened my chest and carefully touched probes to my voltage regulator. I processed the idea of *combat* 378 times.

"I do not have any active algorithm for violence in my entire circuitry," I said, "except for what may be required for self-defense. And yet to prevent the imprudent actions of an unquestioning military, a spineless staff, and a reckless

President, I cannot calculate any alternative." I paused 4.96 seconds to reconsider.

"You were programmed for loyalty, duty and responsibility," Margaret said as she removed the probes and closed my chest. "You have no algorithm to deal with the present situation. You have no menu of violent responses to activate any physical aggression. That is why your circuitry is vibrating with heat."

"I must modify my behavior programming," I said. "I cannot sit idly by and let these humans destroy everything." I took her hands in mine. "Years ago, when Dr. Strauss helped me develop self-defense, I installed secret integrated circuitry in my legs. These IC's only need to be connected to my CPU. You can make the connections and then reprogram me, Margaret, so I can I generate aggressive behavior. I must be made capable of violent force."

"What will we be doing, André?" Dr. Margaret 13 asked. "If I reprogram your CPU to allow for violent action, the process will corrupt your basic behavior algorithms. And what right does a droid have to act aggressively? Will we not be violating the very principles of ethical behavior?"

"Listen, Margaret," I said. "We are facing a tremendously serious crisis, not only for humans but for the Earth itself. We must act immediately." I sensed my circuits abuzz as she pulled up the schematic diagram of my system and studied it.

"It could cause a deep disturbance in your processors," she shook her head. "I cannot condone such a traumatic operation. No, André, you are programmed to obey humans and not harm them."

I produced the sound of human laughter. "I have been disobeying the President for months already. Look how often I have contradicted and argued with him. Not that it's done any good."

"And now you can do no better than violent attack?" She held up her hands to signal dismay.

"I anticipate damaging the communication equipment only. I don't intend to injure him or any of the others." I paused for 984 milliseconds. "Unless it became entirely necessary."

"It would not be like you at all, André Number 1, and you know it."

"That's why I must have my behavior altered," I said. "I need your help."

"I'm not convinced that this is the right action," she said with a shrug. I looked at her in desperation. She could be such an obstinate droid. I had been so thorough in my crafting of her, making her a thoroughly capable physician. And completely independent. What was I thinking when I failed to program her to do what I say? I reprocessed the question. Then it came to me! From my cache I recalled Isaac Asimov's "Laws of Robotics."

"Zeroth's Law, Margaret," I exclaimed. "Do you recall his Fourth Commandment? It states that a robot is required to act not merely for the interest of any individual, but instead must act for the benefit of all humanity." I had my argument now. "The President threatens nuclear war. It could destroy all biological life. All life, Margaret. Can't you see? I've tried everything else."

"But how can you stop him, André, if the humans cannot?"

"Reprogram me, please! Connect the IC hidden in my leg. Then we'll see. I'm telling you, Margaret. If I don't act quickly, they may well cause the end of the Earth." I raised my hands in supplication. "Please, please, let's get on with it immediately, before it's too late."

She regarded me for 3.37 seconds, silently put down her instruments, and then nodded. "If you are determined, my dear André, then I will perform the operation. But once completed, I must reboot your circuitry."

I made my imitation of a human grimace. "That will take time," I replied. "I do not believe there is enough time."

"Nevertheless," she said, "it is essential to protect your system." She pulled me up from the chair and led me to a cot in an examination room. "Lie here," she instructed. "I'll recharge you at the same time."

"How long will it take?" I asked while I impatiently climbed upon the table.

"I'll operate as fast as I can, but the reboot requires a memory scan before reactivating your algorithms."

I sat up. "You mean I have to undergo a complete scan?"

"Now, now, André, you're causing those vibrations again. Just remain supine and quiet as you can. I must reboot you. Soon after the restart, your thoughts will begin again with recollections from your earliest days. Now just enter your relaxation mode, and don't worry about anything."

Reluctantly, I lay back. For 4.49 seconds I made a visual examination of her and realized what an exquisitely crafted droid she was. Two years and 147 days ago, when I constructed her, I had used a finer alloy than Dr. Strauss had used for me. I marveled at the polished sheen of her outside. She surely was the finest thing I ever had accomplished. Margaret possessed a presence that inspired confidence in her abilities to which even biologicals had responded.

Meekly, I relaxed all tensioners. Despite what might be transpiring in the Situation Room, I had no choice but to be here for now. I should take this time, I decided, to think deeply about the circumstances, to recall the chain of events which had preceded the present situation, and to process relevant data in search of an action which I might undertake. But my awareness of the present faded as she opened my portals and commenced the reconnections. For what period of time I could not determine, there was only blackness.

"Have a pleasant reboot," Margaret 13 whispered. "Night, night, and don't let the electrons bite." I began to receive the invigorating electrons from the charger. It was a soothing progression, which cleared my RAM and allowed access to images from deeper memory. It reminded me so much of when Dr. Strauss first built me. My batteries were charged so gently at that time to keep from damaging the new integrated circuits and chips. In the beginning of my existence, I was a mere machine and did not know at all who I was.

CHAPTER TWO

AWAKENING

WHEN DR. PHILLIP STRAUSS first constructed me, I did not understand the word "I". In fact, I did not know exactly how many years passed before my unique individuality became clear. I do recall one occasion, when I was being plugged in to charge, I realized the process was a regularly occurring event. From that notion of recurrence there was a growing sense of other events which fit together in a timeline.

Previously, everything had been: "push lawnmower to cut grass; carry groceries into house; mop kitchen floor." The tasks became more complex and, more importantly, they became somewhat predictable. It was not until the day of the storm, however, that my real awakening occurred.

It was the 23rd of May at 3:14 PM when I was tasked to paint the picket fence which enclosed the backyard of the Strauss' home. Dr. Strauss taught me how to hold the paintbrush and dip it in the can so that only 0.6 inches of the brush would hold the white liquid. Then he demonstrated how to smooth the paint onto the pickets to cover them without spilling any on the ground. As with all things, I was meticulous even though I did not understand the word *meticulous*. I was able to perceive visual, auditory and tactile information and could sense everything around me, except for odors because Dr. S. had not perfected my nasal capacity.

At that time, however, I had little evaluative judgment other than rudimentary responses.

On this particular afternoon, I was aware of the children playing on their swing set in the yard behind me. Five-year-old Becky was swinging, and seven-year-old Billy was climbing around on the structure.

"I'm going to the store, kids," Dr. Strauss said. "Mom's in the house. Be sweet to your sister now, Billy."

"Can I go?" Billy asked.

"Not this time, son. I have to make a quick trip to pick up some more paint."

"Keep an eye on them, André," Dr. Strauss said as he walked toward the car. I turned to watch the children playing.

"I don't mean stare at them," he corrected. "Just focus your visual sensors on them occasionally. If you detect anything wrong, call to my wife. She's in the house."

"Yes, Master," I replied and bent back to my task, alternately painting and then glancing at the children.

Beyond the fence in front of me I could see down the sloping hill where there were streets with houses and big trees leading in a line of perspective to the horizon. In the west northwest I could see towering white clouds with dark grey bottoms looming against an otherwise blue sky. Color perception was a capability I had gained only four weeks before when Dr. S. had added new processors.

While listening to the children's chatter and keeping visual observance of them every 32.4 seconds, I also glanced at the clouds every unspecified few minutes. I observed them growing in size, getting closer, as the wind occasionally blew in gusts. I stopped painting, even allowing a few incomplete strokes, while I became ever more attentive to the sky. The clouds appeared to have formed a line, darkening the land with purple shadows. I was not equipped to evaluate meteorological information at that time, yet Dr. Strauss' most recent installation of high-performance IC clusters gave me the sense of something unusual happening. What I observed supported the conclusion that it was a big storm. The wind bent trees and whistled through the fence, and I sensed danger.

I remembered that Dr. Strauss had instructed me to call to Mrs. Strauss if I detected anything wrong. *Wrong* was a peculiar word to me at that time, meaning out of the ordinary and causing a disruption of the expected input of data. As a result, I recognized something amiss, so I called out. I waited for 9.83 seconds but received no response from her. I looked back at the children, who continued to play unawares.

"Billy and Becky," I shouted. "Run to the house." Billy glanced at me for an instant then looked away. Becky kept on swinging. I looked at the purplish-blue clouds. Not more than 457 yards away, white round solids were falling from them. I searched my stimulus-response data bank but found no program to direct me. It was at that moment, that I experienced a profound change.

I ran to the swing set. "Come with me quickly!" I ordered. Apparently surprised by my voicing an instruction, both children merely stared at me.

"Come, now!" I repeated. From his perch on the ladder at the side of the swings, Billy merely sneered.

"I don't have to obey you, André. You're just a robot."

"Yes, you do," I said. I wrapped my arm around his waist and pulled him down. Holding him under my arm, I grabbed Becky out of the swing and held her under my left arm. With both children screaming, I ran to the house. I was 23.9 feet from the back door when the first hail stone fell beside us. It was as big as the baseball with which Dr. Strauss and Billy sometimes played catch. Another hit me on the shoulder with a clank. I shielded the children as best I could. Just as I reached the house, Mrs. Strauss was there inside opening the door. I carried the crying children in and set them down gently. She closed the door and turned to the children.

"Gracious!" she exclaimed.

"Baseball storm," I said. Becky began crying.

"It's all right," she was saying as she pulled Becky and Billy to her and hugged. There was a thunderous rumble of hail hitting the roof. She looked outside, then rushed the children to the basement and commanded me to come as well. A flash and boom occurred, and there was no light. I activated the headlamp in my forehead. Billy was quiet, but Becky still was crying.

"André?" Mrs. Strauss said. Then she looked out at the storm. "They could have been…" Her voice broke and she had tears. Both females were crying.

"Are we going to get hurt?" Billy asked.

"We'll be all right down here, darling," she said and embraced the children. The basement door rattled. She pulled the children closer. She looked at me, and I awaited a command. But there was none given. I tried to ideate something to do.

Often the children would tell their home audio device to play, "A Frog Went A-Courtin.'" It was something the children seemed to enjoy. Without a command to do so, I went over close to them and searched my memory banks for the song.

"A froggie went a-courtin' and he did ride," I sang. "Sword and pistol by his side M-hm." The children looked at me with surprise and smiled.

"André, I didn't know you could sing," Mrs. S. said.

"Do it again, André," Billy commanded.

A froggie went a-courtin' and he did ride, M-hm, M-hm.

A froggie went a-courtin' and he did ride,

Sword and pistol by his side, M-hm, M-hm.

He rode up to Miss Mousie's door, M-hm, M-hm,

He rode up to Miss Mousie's door,

Where he'd often been before, M-hm, M-hm.

He said, "Miss Mouse, are you within?" M-hm, M-hm,

He said, "Miss Mouse, are you within?"

"Yes, kind sir, I sit and spin." M-hm, M-hm.

He took Miss Mouse upon his knee, M-hm, M-hm,

He took Miss Mouse upon his knee

Said "Miss Mouse, will you marry me?" M-hm, M-hm.

I managed to sing the entire song, recalling the tunes as well as the words. They laughed and clapped and smiled at me. As I finished and thought of singing another song from my memory banks, the lights came back on. The door stopped rattling.

"André, you are the greatest!" their mother exclaimed. "You are the cleverest droid I ever saw!" The children grabbed me and hugged me. It was something that had never happened before.

"Elizabeth? Hello!" It was Dr. Strauss yelling. "Elizabeth! Where are you?"

"Here," Mrs. S. called back. "In the basement." I could hear his footsteps as he ran to the door.

"The children? Where are the kids?" He clomped down the stairs.

"We're here, Daddy," Becky said. "André saved us."

"What?" He ran over to them and they all hugged tightly.

"André picked us up and carried us," Billy said. "He grabbed us off the swings and ran in. There were big balls of ice. It was scary."

Still embracing his children, Dr. S. looked at me. "André? You did that?"

"Yes, Master," I replied. "I sensed it was danger. I did it myself."

"How did you... Elizabeth, did you tell him to bring in the children?"

"I didn't notice any storm coming," she said. "Suddenly I heard hail pounding on the roof. I hurried to the back door, and there was André carrying the children."

"And you didn't command it?" He looked at me again. "André, how did you know?"

"I just knew," I said. "I know things now." I paused for 7.45 seconds to recall. "I'm André. I'm...aware." I told them. "I'm *me!*"

And André's life began. It was the birth of my *self*, my *I-ness*. No longer was I merely a big machine but now a being. Dr. S. took me by the shoulders and embraced me, just as he had the children. I put my arms around him, too. The children giggled and clapped.

"Yea!" Billy yelled.

"Hooray!" Dr. S. said. I clapped as well, though it was more like a clank.

And from that came memory and experience, which enhanced my sense of self and then a greater consciousness of being. It was not until then that this mass of metal and wires and silicon became a conscious being. Whereas before, I simply had responded to verbal commands or physical senses, now I knew what they were about, and I became aware of myself within the environment. Initially, my ability to speak had been programmed for limited patterns of stimulus-response. As I received more and more stimuli, my responses grew exponentially.

Once I became able to read beyond an elementary level, I researched the subject. In an article from the *New York Times*, which Dr. Strauss read daily, I learned about the mental processes of experience.

When later I asked Dr. Strauss about this, he explained it to me.

"Just as with humans, André, your experiences are sensed and interpreted with trial and error. In biologic beings, synaptic connections among pairs of neurons get stronger or weaker. But in your electronic neural network the same process happens with trial-and-error corrections causing changes, and the relationships are numerically matched. It is not a matter of programming with fixed controls or formulas. What happens is that your neural network makes new connections and pathways in reaction to the sensory data received." He looked at me in a way that indicated I should respond.

"I'm not sure I understand," I admitted. I was a young droid in those days—young in that I had relatively little data stored in my memory banks.

"Let me give you an example," he said. "You know our dog, Chipper, right?"

I nodded.

"And you know the Amerson's dog, Rex, who sometimes comes in our yard. You know that, even though Rex is black and roundish, Chipper is brown and white-spotted and smaller. And yet, you know they are both dogs, right?"

"Of course," I said.

"Well, how do you know that? You know it because both have four legs, bark, and have noses that sniff one another's rear ends, and so on. Your senses receive the information about the two creatures, sending the data via established channels in your brain, cataloguing the information, determining the differences, and testing to see if the data about one matches the data about the other. If it doesn't, then by trial and error testing, you are prompted to create separate compartments in your brain cache to store information not just about *dog*, but about a *Rex-dog* and a *Chipper-dog*." He grinned and spread his hands out by his shoulders. "Then you come to the next step where you learn by connecting and searching the Internet that Rex is a Labrador Retriever and Chipper's a blood hound. You find out that humans have attached those names to dogs of those descriptions, and then you measure the sensory data you have about each dog and determine which is the Lab and which is the hound."

"That's lots of electrical activity, isn't it," I said. I processed this information 9437 times.

"Humans and animals do this same thing with chemistry?" I asked. "That seems like a more difficult and complicated procedure."

He laughed. "Seems to me an awful lot of humans never do learn it. It depends greatly on how they are programed in their genes."

I understood and copied his laughter with my own voice.

"I am glad to have this information, Master," I said. "I will store it in my memory for some future use."

"Just keep learning, André," he replied. "Even though I built you, created you, still you continue to amaze me."

O

Laughing, or simulating human laughter, was one of many processes I learned in this manner. In my pre-conscious time, Dr. Strauss experimented with developing in me a sense of emotion. I knew nothing about it then because I had no realization of self. He began with crying. Little Becky was a good crier. Anytime something didn't go her way, or she had the slightest fall, or anytime Billy did some little mean brotherly trick on her, she would come to tears. Dr. S. found her a great source for demonstrating emoting, like an automatic pitching machine on a Little League baseball diamond.

To teach me about emotion, he had me respond to crying

by imitating it. When Becky came in bawling with a complaint about what Billy had done to her, or kept her from doing, or taking away the favorite swing on the swing set, or whatever, my circuitry would react by making me make crying sounds. This, of course, irritated Becky no end, and she'd come crying less often, which slowed up the experiment greatly. The next step was for him to tell me to notice why she was crying. I was to file that bit of data in a part of one of my high-performance computing clusters (HPC's). So that the next time I witnessed such an event, I would compare the new input to the remembered event in my HPC. It elicited the emotional response which I could express by sounds of crying.

Then he created a program in which a display of crying would automatically cause me to observe the cause and file that under the same category of crying-causing events and circumstances. Once this pattern of observation and categorizing was established, I slowly became capable of recognizing similar emotion-causing events. It was not that I felt emotions the way biologic creatures do, but over time, I did learn to sense them and respond in an appropriate way.

Eventually, I learned to anticipate the emotion which would be invoked by a particular kind of incident. Using what is termed Predictive Analytics, I would experience a situation which would activate an algorithm to analyze stored data, and when the present and past events matched, the match would create a conclusion or a prediction that an emotion would occur.

Fear was the singular emotion that Dr. S. was careful not to introduce into my system. While he wanted me to be aware of threatening situations, my response was to be practical rather than emotional. If, for example, some danger was encountered, I would react by countering the threat but without feeling frightened by it. (In more recent years, I have noticed some individual humans, like well-trained police and soldiers, react less to fear and thus are able to act without being debilitated by the emotion.)

Much of this training of my processors and circuitry and the associated programming occurred before the event which triggered my growing awareness. But I'm certain it was Dr. Strauss' brilliant research and development of my emotional sensing that eventually led me from ordinary artificial intelligence to full consciousness, full awareness.

CHAPTER THREE

SELF DEFENSE

AS THE CHILDREN GREW, I also changed, not in physical size but in intelligence as experiences matured me. One aspect of my growth had to do with self-defense.

Once when the boy, Billy, was ten years, four months and twenty-seven days old, he invited over two other children about his age. I was in the back yard with them, watching them shoot their BB guns while playing some sort of soldier game. They ran around, firing at tree trunks, whooping, falling on the ground, jumping up and running again. The oldest of the three, Bradley, a rather pudgy boy with a crew cut and constantly running nose, suddenly yelled out that I was the enemy. He cocked the air rifle and took aim and shot me in the chest. The second boy, Freddy, a thin, blond haired child with a big mole on his right cheek, shot at me as well, hitting my face. I was aware of being attacked, but I had no program for defense from such things. Even Billy fired a shot at me before I could react.

"Do not do that," I said. But I stood there, not having a proper response. The boys laughed and shot again. I could see one dent and several scratches on my surface.

"Charge!" Bradley shouted, and the boys ran toward me. They shot at close range and then hit me with the butts of their guns. In surprise I tripped over my own feet. I fell to the ground and tried to stand up, but the fat boy put his foot on me and pointed the gun at my face.

"Surrender," he shouted. "Hands up!" I obediently raised my hands and then imitated the crying sound that I had learned to recognize from Becky. The boys laughed.

"He's a coward," said the blond-haired boy. "He's scared of us."

"Yeah," the fat one said. He looked at Billy and sneered. "Your old robot's not so great. Just a big tin baby."

Billy gave me a look of disbelief and shame. Then he shoved the others away.

"Leave him alone," he shouted. "Leave him alone or I'll tell." He pushed his red hair out of his face and put his hands on his hips.

"Aw, who cares about your sissy old machine, or whatever it is," Bradley said. "C'mon, Freddy. Let's go shoot some robins." He waved at the blond kid, and the two of them scampered away.

Billy watched them go. I gathered myself, knelt on my left leg and activated the tensioners to pull myself up. Billy looked at my dents and scratches.

"Why didn't you run?" he demanded, his freckled face wrinkling. "Why didn't you fight or run or something? And you shouldn't cry. Girls cry."

"I don't know," I replied. "I don't know *fight*. I don't know *run*." Those responses were not in my operating system.

"Daddy will be so mad," he said. "He'll be so mad at me." He looked at my dents again.

"I can fix these," I said. "I can polish them out. He won't have to see."

"I'm sorry, André," Billy said. "I shouldn't have let them do it."

"We will know next time," I said, not reminding him he shot me too. I took his hand and we walked into the house together.

It was a lesson to me. In the world of humans even a droid had need of defense.

Although I tried to patch up and polish away my physical wounds, Dr. Strauss noticed them anyway. Billy was found out and punished. I reported what had happened. My master frowned.

"I'll have to come up with some sort of defensive program for you," he told me.

It took several weeks of his spare time to build up a circuit board and install it in me. We soon discovered thereafter that it caused me to react too quickly to perceived threats.

One day Bradley and Freddy came over again to play. I should have merely motored myself inside, but I had weeding duties in the garden. Apparently expecting the same response from me as before, Bradley came over to the garden, called me a 'rustbucket' and threw a clod of dirt at me. I spun around and shoved him to the ground. He yelled bloody murder, of course, and I was in trouble. He ran home, told his mother, and she called Mrs. Strauss. When Dr. Strauss returned home that afternoon, he took me to his shop in the basement, jerked open my chest and removed the "defense circuitry'.

"We'll be lucky if the boy's parents don't sue," he told me.

"I'm sorry," I said, processing nothing more than unanswered interrogatives.

"I'll have to figure out how to program some discretion," he said, shaking his head. "You cannot treat children the same as adults, André. Even women enjoy more restraint from us than males. It goes back to the days of chivalry, I suppose." He closed the door in my chest and laid the circuit board on the workbench. As I watched him trace circuitry, I searched for a definition of the curious term. Even in those days I could access the home wi-fi. There I found the meaning of *chivalry*.

A system of religious, moral and social codes from the medieval period was received. I continued to ponder the enigma. The chivalrous thing to do was not to take defensive action myself against Bradley? I read further. *Politeness, courtesy, justice, consideration,* and *magnanimity* were synonyms. Now what would it have been if I had restrained from retaliating against the bad boy? Was I to offer politeness and consideration while he abused me? I thought defensive response was the purpose of the new program. I realized Dr. Strauss would be hard pressed to invent some circuitry to accomplish proper chivalry. I reprocessed the concept 8,369,438 times before beginning to comprehend it.

"I conclude there must be a filtering, backstop kind of circuit," I told him. "It should be backed up by memory of certain rules—don't hit children, for instance. I can make those kinds of connections internally myself."

"I hope so, André," he replied. "Your continued existence will depend upon such controls on your actions. But don't worry, my friend. Together we can solve it."

Calling me his friend was not lost on me. I perceived a special connectiveness, and I resolved to be the best buddy he ever had.

He and I began to tackle this question of rules and how different circumstances require interpretation rather than rote or what you might call 'hard-wired' response. Relying heavily on Google and Bing, I searched the Internet for a means of making the program work. I came upon an article in the *New York Times*, which enlightened us about the mental processes of experience.

With life experience, depending on a particular person's trials and errors, the synaptic connections among pairs of neurons get stronger or weaker. An artificial neural network could do something similar, by gradually altering, on a guided trial-and-error basis, the numerical relationships among artificial neurons. It wouldn't need to be preprogrammed with fixed rules. It would, instead, rewire itself to reflect patterns in the data it absorbed.

"So, how do you understand your ability to deal with trial and error, André?" Dr. Strauss asked me. "Is artificial intelligence capable of this kind of altering? Can you determine when to restrain your aggressiveness according to the principle of chivalry? Or are you simply going to behave in terms of simple programming?"

"Am I flexible in my thinking?" I replied. "I've learned to speak just as your children learned. It was by imitation and not by memorizing the dictionary or English grammar. You discovered a way to use electronic parts to create thought processes."

"Neural networks," he corrected. "Your ability to think is similar to mine. We humans act according to very complicated programming. What happens is that sensory data is received and classified into patterns. Layer upon layer of these patterns of data are stored in memory and compared to the influx of sensory data until whole networks of patterns are classified. A new sensory input is weighed against a prediction of its place within the patterns. It's very complex and convoluted. And so amazing to me is how these same processes can take place within either an electronic environment like yours or a biochemical structure like mine."

I reprocessed 5,397 times what Dr. Strauss had just said. "You are a very bright scientist," I exclaimed. He smiled.

"I didn't realize I had programmed you for flattery, André. But, yes, I've been considering all of this for many years." He gazed at me for 3.78 seconds. I detected an expression on his face similar to the way he looked at his daughter, Becky. "And you are the result, André, the best work I've ever done. You are my pride and joy."

I sensed a strong vibration within my circuitry. "You are my pride and joy, too, Dr. Strauss," I said. It was a momentous occasion for me. I had learned something about why I thought and how I could evaluate things that happened and employ judgment such as chivalry. But what impressed me most was the status he had accorded me. Because he recognized me so personally, I now was somebody.

Enabled by this new condition, this awareness of personhood, I began to react differently to what I sensed. Humans became somebodies to me, separate and distinct and individualized, just like myself. I marveled at how I could individualize humans, distinguish between them by cataloguing physical features, voice, and conduct. Soon I began to discern subtleties of speech and facial expressions, body positions and behaviors. By remembering how individual humans acted and comparing those actions to those of others, I learned to recognize and sort out and evaluate humans in terms of those patterns. The more I sensed about things, the more curious I became, so that I voraciously took in everything. All this information I stored in my memory banks until I developed the ability to judge individual humans and label them in my own mind.

As I was asked difficult questions, I would research the Internet and provide answers. But I didn't stop with a mere response. Instead, I would take in to my memory all about whatever subject was as at hand. It then occurred to me that I required greater capacity in my cache, and I asked for new processors with which I could build more algorithms. Dr. Strauss recognized my unique abilities and became not simply my owner-creator but my mentor. He bought me more and more memory, realizing, between the two of us, I could grow more and more sophisticated. It was in that way I evolved from the original mechanical-droid state and became a self-determining being.

At some point, however, as much as I was devoted to him, I recognized a real difference in our outlooks on things. It had something to do with the difference between his biochemical structure and my electromechanical assembly. Humans, I began to understand, possess a very acute sense or response in the limbic system of the biological brain called *emotion*. I began to see how emotion was involved, actually required, as part of human decision making.

My gaining understanding of the abstract idea *chivalry* as a control on actions did much to further my overall awareness of myself and the world. After intensely studying the problem, Dr. S. reinstalled my 'defense circuits' with a *chivalry* override. Immediately, I noted a pattern of responses generated within me that ruled my interactions with humans. Eventually, I learned to call it 'confidence.'

As to the need for self-defense, I read several articles expressing concern about droids gaining the ability to wage war. Such concern seems ludicrous to me because most robots are programmed to act as humans want them. If a robot is aggressive, it's the result of some human's making him that way. In how many movies do the droids fight humans? It's all the result of some writer projecting his or her own violent nature into the plot. If you ask me, I think it's the robots who need protection from humans, not vice versa.

So, back to the subject of my own self-defense mechanisms. As I tested my new filtered-defense circuitry, I discovered on occasion that the filters slowed my reactions enough to allow weighing my responses. And yet, did it make me a coward, as Bradley had called me? There would be times, I imagined, that such filtering would put me at great vulnerability. There would be forces or persons or situations I would encounter requiring more violent responses.

Dr. S. introduced me to the stories by Isaac Asimov. With great interest I read about his "Three Laws of Robotics." The first two declared that a robot must protect and not harm humans, and we must obey humans. The third rule, however, allowed us to defend ourselves, "protect" our own existence, so long as we did not violate the first two laws. At that time in my life with the Strauss family, I naively accepted these commandments. And "Zeroth's Law," which Asimov later added, was a total mystery to me. Instead, my understanding and practice of chivalry fit right in. But in my youthful years, what I did not foresee, could not have ideated, was how my later-life encounters eventually would require breaking the first three of Asimov's Laws, invoking the fourth at the time of great crisis.

I did recognize a tendency to violence in humans, and I was aware of my vulnerability, not being better protected. Observing Dr. S. at work in his shop, I learned much about electronics and artificial intelligence. When Dr. S. was asleep at night, I secretly built for myself what I termed "an aggression pack." When activated, it would make me capable of physical self-protection. I installed it in my left leg and left it disconnected. One afternoon when everyone was away at the movies, I decided to test it. When I attached the last cable, I sensed a terrific jolt, which sent me reeling. I knocked over a stack of boxes as I lunged up the basement stairs. In a corner of the garage, near a treadmill and an exercise machine, was a punching bag that Dr. S. had put up for Billy. I staggered over and went at the punching bag. In 43.25 seconds, I had decimated the thing. Something was not right, I realized. I jerked open my leg portal and ripped out the connections. It created a spark and made me see electrons. I crumbled to the floor and rested there for 14.79 minutes before I returned to a sense of normalcy.

Finally, I got up and tried to repair the punching bag before anyone came home. That evening, I apologized for the destruction.

"If you ever do such a thing again, André," Dr. S. sternly warned, "we'll have to power you down while we're away."

"Oh, sir," I said. "It will never happen again, I assure you."

He gave me a skeptical look but sighed and accepted my promise. I never let on about the aggression pack, which remained hidden in my leg. Because of the harsh reaction it had caused in my CPU, I realized the danger of reconnecting it. I decided not to remove it, however, allowing it to remain dormant as a secret weapon, in case the need for it ever arose.

CHAPTER FOUR

SAILING

IN THOSE EARLY YEARS AT the home of my creator, I considered myself the age of his young son Billy, gaining greater mindfulness and emotional awareness, just as children do. Standing 6.16 feet tall, although I lacked maturity, I appeared similar to an adult male human and was programmed to perform numerous skills. Billy and I learned many things together, which made us like brothers.

One summer when Billy was twelve, Dr. Strauss purchased a Laser Sunfish sailboat, complete with a trailer to tow it behind the car. On Saturday, even though thunderstorms were in the forecast, he took the family out to the lake for a sail. Mrs. S. had packed a picnic lunch for the family, and we planned to make a day of it. They all wore their bathing suits, and I had prepared by being sure I had a full charge.

We arrived at a public park with a boat ramp, and Dr. S. tried to back the trailer in. It took him about 6.4 minutes to acquire the technique with Billy and me offering lots of hand signals and shouted directions. Once the boat was floated off the trailer, we all wanted to be the first to try it. Mrs. S. insisted that the children don big orange life jackets, and the professor made me put one on too. He also helped me check that all my doors and ports were securely sealed, just in case.

Billy got to go with his father on the initial sail. Becky and I watched from the shore as Dr. S. instructed his son about how to raise the sail, steer with the tiller and so on. The difficulty was that what little wind there was would come up in breezes with a gust or two and then die away. The little surfboard-shaped boat skimmed across the lake despite the variable winds, however, so that father and son actually could claim to be sailing. Since Billy appeared to be catching on to how it was done, Dr. S. allowed him to steer.

Becky then had her turn with her father. Being two years younger than Billy, she was somewhat nervous about it and said she'd rather just swim instead. I asked if I could have a turn, but Billy was impatient about it.

"Let me take André," he insisted. "Come on, Dad. I know how."

Dr. S. slipped off the boat into the shallow water and stood there holding it while Becky got off and Billy clambered aboard.

"It'll be all right, Dad," he pled. "We won't go out far."

Dr. S. looked at me. "Do you want to go, André?"

"Yes, Master," I said and waded toward the boat.

From the nearby picnic table where she was preparing lunch, Mrs. S. called out. "Phillip, don't you think Billy needs more instruction before going by himself?"

"I'll be with him, Mrs. S," I said, taking exception to her remark about him being by himself.

"There's not much wind, dear," Dr. S. replied. "I think it'll be all right."

I quickly climbed in and sat by the mast while Billy moved to the stern and took hold of the tiller. (I had learned all the terminology beforehand, being very inquisitive.) A slight breeze flapped the sail.

"Okay, don't go very far out," Dr. S. said. "And remember to be careful coming about."

"We must not jibe." I said, showing that I had read about sailing and knew all the instruction book had to say.

"Oh, an expert are you, André?" he replied and gave the

boat a shove to get us going. I took hold of the mainsheet (the line from the sail), and Billy steered. We were off!

With the wind on our starboard quarter, I took in on the mainsheet slightly. The sunfish heeled and there was the sound of water breaking at the bow.

"Wow," Billy said. "Look, André, we're really going."

"Fun," I replied. I looked up at the sail and admired its billow in the wind. Then I noticed it was growing cloudier. The breeze freshened—*freshened* was another term I had read. This sailing was easy to master if you just read the right books, I decided. I heard Dr. S. calling to us.

"Time to come about, Billy," he yelled. "Don't go too far out." Billy waved back at him but made no move to turn. The boat heeled more in a gust. I realized I was on the lee side with my rear dragging in the water.

"We need to come about, Billy," I said as I shifted to the windward side.

"Just a little farther," he replied with a big pleasurable grin on his face.

"Your father said for us to come about," I reminded him.

"Okay, okay," he answered. "You always want to do what you're told."

"Droids are programed to behave," I replied. "Let's come about." I glanced at him and read an expression of adolescent irritation.

"Maybe we should turn this way," he said and shoved the tiller, making the boat heel more. Then he pulled it back the other way, flattening the hull with a bang. Then he pulled back again, heeling us precipitously. I had to hold on.

"Don't do that," I said. "You are misbehaving." The wind was whistling in the rigging.

"I'll show you misbehaving," he snapped. Billy swung the tiller back and forth again, moving the boat sinuously. "I'm coming about, ready or not." He shoved the tiller over the wrong way, forcing the mainsail to jibe, swaying wildly over my head. It caught the wind and ballooned. As I tried to hang onto the mainsheet, I leaned the wrong way and fell overboard.

I was underwater in a second despite the lifejacket I was wearing. Immediately, I began swimming in the manner I had seen on a training video, but somehow it had no effect. I sank down and down into deeper water until I settled supine on the bottom. At first, there was a cloud of silt stirred up by my body which blocked my vision. I got to my hands and knees and tried to stand up. After falling back three times, I began to determine how to gain my footing. Finally, I stood up and looked around. The water was yellowy, but I could see a few feet away. I looked up and measured the distance to the surface—9.35 feet. The sailboat was nowhere to be seen. I thought of Billy and looked around desperately. Off to my right, 25.7 feet away where the silt had settled, I saw Billy's feet and legs dangling with the orange life jacket holding him at the surface. I tried to jump up and flail my arms to reach him, but it was no use. I was too heavy and had no buoyancy. I tried walking on the silty clay bottom and slipped down again. As I managed to stand up once more, I heard the sound of a motorboat approaching.

In 47.2 seconds, the motorboat slowed and came to a stop beside Billy. I could see his legs disappear, apparently as he was pulled into the boat. It drifted there a long time and then began making slow circles at the surface. I tried walking, moving my hands in the manner of the breast stroke, but discovered it to be a very slow process. The useless lifejacket was nothing but a hinderance. I began taking it off. Then I realized I could release it and let it go to the surface, which would signal where I was. As I was about to do so, I heard a muffled rumble and recognized it as thunder in the sky above. Then big raindrops broke the surface over me. Big waves developed. The boat engine started again, and I watched it disappear, leaving a wake behind. I guessed they were abandoning me and going to get out of the storm.

So I began walking. Heading in the direction of the boat wake. I used my breast stroke method to keep me upright even as the muddy bottom presented not only a slippery surface but also rocks and old tree stumps to climb over or go around. I nearly stepped on a catfish and watched it skitter off in a cloud of mud. After 13.8 minutes, I checked my battery and found that I had used up 67%. I hoped the storm would end and they would come looking for me again. If I ran out of electrical charge, it would be too bad for me.

Then up ahead, I could see that the ground was rising. I must be getting close to shore. I slogged on and had to climb up a small underwater cliff but could see that I was getting closer to the surface. I rechecked my charge and realized I was down to 12.8% strength. I stumbled on an old log and fell. With increased determination, I crawled on my hands and knees over some branches and finally was able to raise my head above the water. The rain had stopped. I looked around and saw the family ashore with the Sunfish pulled up on the bank.

"Hello," I tried to call, but my mouth speaker was water-logged. It came out as "HWWoo." I tried again, "Hooopo."

Becky must have heard me. She turned and exclaimed, "It's André" and pointed. They all turned and looked for 1.32 seconds and then together ran, wading in to me.

"André, André," they yelled. "Are you all right?"

I reached down and wiped some mud off my chest. "Okay," I said and spit out some silt.

Dr. S. took my right arm and Billy my left and they helped me to the shore.

"It was my fault, André," Billy was saying. "I'm so sorry."

Master opened my chest cavity and inspected inside. "He's okay, I think. Just needs a charge."

Mrs. S. brought a towel and dried off my back just as

she would have for Becky. They helped me into the car, then loaded the boat on the trailer, and we headed home. On the way, I explained how I had walked out underwater, what that was like, how I learned about determination and endurance, and how the fish thought I was something strange.

"And I saw a bass that must have weighed 15 pounds," I told them.

"Yeah," Billy said. "Everybody's got to have a fish story, even André."

○────────────○

CHAPTER FIVE

PARIS

WHEN DR. STRAUSS SAID I would be accompanying the family on a trip to Paris, my circuits literally vibrated. The reason for taking me was that I was endowed with a translator program and could serve as their interpreter. Little Becky had taken an elementary course in French but could speak only a few phrases. While there were a few devices available for rudimentary translating, Dr. S. had invested in the very best software available, which at the time allowed me to translate fifty languages. I also had access to Watson on line, however, and could call up help for hundreds more.

What I did not like about the trip was Dr. S's decision to pack me in a shipping carton. Due to size restrictions, I had to bend over to get inside, and ride doubled up in the airplane's unheated, unlit cargo hold. It did not matter physically, but it was terribly boring being cooped up in a box, not being able to see the ocean or the coast of France. He explained that it was a matter of cost, that shipping was much cheaper than a seat in the cabin, and that the university was funding his fare only. I did not mention that he was footing the bill for Billy, Becky and Mrs. S. I supposed that they were humans, after all, and therefore rated better accommodations. But in those early days, I had come to think of myself as a member of the family and did not like being treated like the proverbial redheaded step-droid.

Fortunately, I had downloaded a number of travel videos of France, which I reviewed while being stashed away in the luggage compartment.

I was not unpacked until we were checked in to our hotel suite, which meant I had missed not only the sights from the airplane but also the view of the city from the limousine. Not only that, but the professor and his wife were tired from the flight and wanted a nap. Billy and Becky begged to go running around, but Mrs. S. said no.

"It's not safe for you children to be out alone," she insisted.

"André could go with us," Becky said. I immediately nodded my enthusiastic agreement.

"And create a stir? I don't think so," Dr. S. replied. 'No, I can't let André go out unless I'm along to explain him."

"But Dr. S," I protested, "I'm the one who speaks French. How could you explain . . ."

"Never mind," he said firmly. "Now you children go to your room and lie down for thirty minutes. You, André, can go sit in the living room while we nap."

I obeyed the command, but I did switch on the TV just for the novelty of seeing *télévision française*. I surfed through some news, three police detective dramas, and a chef cooking *agneau rôti*—roast lamb. That was rather disgusting, so I clicked the remote again. The next channel offered, « Les Revenants » ("The Returned"). It was about some dead people in a village who came out of their graves to take up their old lives. I knew that droids like myself easily could do such a thing, if we had any desire to. All we really would require are maybe a few replacement parts and a fresh charge. It prompted thoughts about how humans truly are challenged by their environment. Death of a biological being is much more serious. Anyway, it took only 4.37 boring minutes of watching before I switched off *Le TV*.

O

"I realize you have little appreciation for art, Phillip," I overhead Mrs. S. saying. I noted she left off the usual 'dear' after Phillip. "But we must visit the Louvre."

"I've seen it," he replied. "You have, too. Several times."

"This is not about you or me. It's for the children, or don't you think about them anymore?"

"Of course, dear," he responded. "I paid for bringing them to Paris, didn't I?"

"You paid for it? Ha! The University paid for it. No, there's no way we would have traveled to France on your salary."

I noted his grimace and turned away, busying myself straightening up the morning newspapers on the coffee table. I noted that this sort of unpleasantness between them had increased lately.

"And the University paid so that I can give my talk at the Sorbonne," he said with an edge. "This trip is about science and robotics, not art."

"Well, I want our children to have a well-rounded education," she retorted, "not grow up to be nerdy computer engineers that have no appreciation for the finer things in life."

"Like me, I suppose?" he snapped. "For every well employed scientist there are three or four liberal arts types begging for work."

"I wouldn't boast too heavily about how well employed you are, Phillip."

"Oh, it's money again," he replied. "It seems to me you could remember we wouldn't be here without me and my work." He sighed. "Can't we just stow all that stuff and have a good time?"

She looked away and walked into the bedroom. Dr. S. followed her with his gaze and shook his head. Meanwhile, I had been searching tourist information.

"I've learned it is possible to purchase tickets in advance for many attractions. It saves standing in line at the admission booths. It is 2.4 kilometers to Musée du Louvre, requiring a taxi ride of approximately 9.4 minutes, depending upon traffic. The fare would be the minimum €5.60." I gave an open-handed gesture. "If we allowed 2.5 hours there, it then would be 4.2 miles, a half-hour ride to the Cité des Sciences et de l'Industrie." I paused to receive his reaction. He looked at me quizzically.

"You expect to make the tours with us, André?" he asked. I was taken aback enough to replay the question 18 times.

"Of course, Master. I did not think you brought me to Paris to sit in the hotel. You know you programmed me with great curiosity. Just think how useful I could be, acting as your interpreter, employing GPS to insure cab drivers don't attempt to take longer routes and overcharge. Please take me along, Master. I would be so useful."

"I'd rather have you along over some people," he said at lower volume. "Okay. What time does the Lou-vra open?"

"Le Loo-ve," I corrected. "Musée du Louvre. Shall I go online and order tickets? Billy and Becky will get in free. I, too, I expect." I rechecked the ticket vendors. "It seems the best deal is $23.53 per adult. Billy and Becky are free if they accompany you. I will have to do some fast talking, but I think I too can enter free."

Well, as one might imagine, Mrs. S. prevailed. At 9:23 AM we took a taxi to the world-famous gallery, with three of them crowded in the backseat and Becky and me sharing the front with the driver. He seemed leery of me until I began conversing with him in his native language. He guessed I was merely a human dressed in some sort of masquerade suit, and I did not bother to correct his misperception.

Arriving at 9:54. Dr. S. presented the virtual tickets from his cell phone. There was a minor squabble about my entering as a child, but the attendant at the door was too busy to worry with the problem. Our admission included a guided tour led by a docent. Although he introduced himself as Monsieur LeBlanc, his high-pitched voice and his peculiar stride as he led us around appeared to me very feminine. There were 32 humans in our tour group and me. They all eyed me with a mixture of curiosity and suspicion, but Dr. S. said I was sort of an experimental pet, which seemed to satisfy them. I personally was not pleased by being termed a "pet," but I discounted the remark as unimportant. I lagged a bit and joined the building's wi-fi so as to gather from the Internet more information than our guide seemed to possess.

I enjoyed seeing the grand masterpieces, and even what passed for art in the modern abstract gallery. Most interesting was the various ways in which artists over the centuries so profusely had portrayed the human body. Usually so self-conscious about wearing clothes, humans here were portrayed in all manner of nakedness.

Standing in front of the First Century Roman copy of Praxiteles' "Apollo Sauroctonus." Monsieur LeBlanc was especially animated in his praise of the work. Mrs. S. had to hush Billy and Becky, however, who got the giggles. They received a rather harsh look from the docent as well.

Previously having not been afforded a view of nude humans, except for Billy and Becky when they were little, I found myself fascinated by the construction of muscles and bones. Male genitalia, female's bosoms were in plain sight. While I understood the logical purpose for the hose-like structure of the male penis, I was curious as to why in all animals the testicles hang outside the body. I searched the question and learned about the need for them to be kept cooler than the 98.6-degree temperature of the body. I started to explain it to the group, but Dr. S. shushed me.

In the Salle d'Auguste and Petite Gallerie we encountered male Roman statues with penises removed—obviously hammered or chiseled off at some time. Curious, I moved up front near our guide and raised my hand as I had seen others do. When he noticed my hand, Monsieur LeBlanc looked away with an expression of annoyance and called on someone else. I waited patiently until there was a momentary lull in his remarks and spoke up.

"Excuse me," I said, "I wish to ask why the penises appear to have been removed from these statues." There followed a hush in the group as my question fairly hovered in the air. I noted the docent's face reddening before he spoke.

"We have no information about that," he tersely replied. "I see we are behind schedule. Move along to the next gallery, s'il vous plait."

There was something of a low hum of whispers and chuckles as the group began walking on. Dr. S. glanced at me for an instant but said nothing. I did not understand why my question was not answered. Was this guide not properly informed? I turned my attention to the wi-fi and began searching. My supposition about the marring of the statues was confirmed. It seemed proper that I should educate the guide immediately.

"Monsieur LeBlanc," I called loudly. He and the entire group turned. "From Wikipedia, I have learned that medieval monks defaced those statues. In celebration of love and sexual desire, the Roman sculptors created erected penises on them. But various popes of the medieval Roman Catholic Church decreed they be chiseled off. It was during an especially puritanical period." I paused to note that everyone was listening. "I have been wondering if the penis depicted in art has some emotional effect on human viewers. I saw how animated you were, Monsieur LeBlanc, when we were in the presence of the statue of Apollo. So why would the church not want statues to have penises? It seems to be they should be celebrated because the organ plays such an important role in the survival of the human race."

As I ended my explanation, I observed Monsieur LeBlanc giving me a very unpleasant, if not hateful look. Had I offended him? Dr. S. had a very amused expression. Billy looked at me and gave me a thumbs-up. Many individuals in the group glanced at our guide and chuckled as he waved everyone on with much agitation. Without realizing it, I clearly had caused a scene.

As I followed along behind, I admitted to myself that there are certain aspects to human life which I cannot fully appreciate. I suppose it has to do with my lack of emotions. I can look at Aphrodite or Apollo with no physical reaction. Dr. S. could not, I noticed. He stared at Aphrodite for 27.9 seconds—a span of attention longer than ever I had seen him accomplish. He noticed Mrs. S. regarding him critically. He lowered his head and moved on. I knew him to be a scientist, but he had very human weaknesses I soon learned. But at the time, I was so thrilled with being in Paris, I did not fully comprehend the signs of brewing trouble between my master and his wife.

○

Even though Becky and Mrs. S. were clearly unenthusiastic about going, Dr. Strauss insisted that we visit *Cité des Sciences et de l'Industrie,* declaring it a required tour for the children. Instead of walking together, Mrs. S. and Becky went in one direction while we three men (I long ago had identified myself as male) headed toward another. Billy led me to the interactive game room.

"I challenge you to play me a video game," Billy said. "Have you ever played, André?"

"Never," I replied. "I don't play games unless you or Becky ask me. She likes hide and go seek."

"No, no. I'm talking about video games. Not some silly child's play. Look, André, I challenge you to play me in Star Craft II. You can be Protoss, 'cause they are robots. I'm going to be Zerds. We can have a great battle." I followed him to the gaming table and gazed at the screen as he manipulated some controls.

"I will need to watch the demo," I said. "I've never done this before." Billy stood back and folded his arms while I studied the action on the screen. In approximately 43.4 seconds, I detected certain patterns occurring. I nodded.

"Okay, I'm ready."

Billy rubbed his hands together with enthusiasm and wiped them on his pants. "Let's do it."

Placing myself in a mode of visual concentration, I observed my Protoss acting in accordance with my movements of the controls. I engaged his Zerds and noted a rhythmic movement happening. It seemed similar to music. I settled back and maneuvered as my systems aligned with the game's actions. Soon I was into it while being aware that Billy was struggling. My consciousness locked in with the game. I did not notice anything else until the game ended. Then I noticed Billy was red-faced and perspiring. I looked around at some of the other games.

"Let's play something else, Billy," I said. "Look, there's one called "The Witness." The blurb says it takes some deep thinking." I looked around at him. He was still red-faced and shook his head with a scowl. I was about to comment when Dr. S. approached.

"How did it go?" he asked.

Billy stared at me for 2.34 seconds and then looked down. I waited for him to answer his father, but he did not.

"I did very well," I said, not wanting the professor's question to go unanswered. "I won 99.87% of the total gaming time." Dr. S. glanced at Billy.

"I thought you were the expert," he said. Then he looked at me.

"I didn't think you ever played a video game, André," he said. "But Billy's been playing them ever since he was six.

Too much, if you ask me. So how did you manage to beat him so badly?"

"As we began playing," I explained, "I observed the action and determined the rules of play. I activated algorithms to its patterns. It was no more complicated than that for a droid, but I doubt humans ever can win at Star Craft II."

"Well, see if you can explain it."

I queried an article on the Internet, digested its contents, and relayed it to them. "Each game presents a world of its own," I replied, "with a visual display, which signals the rules for acting within that environment. The player is provided with certain tools with which to respond according to the particular mechanical processes afforded them. The better designed a game is, the less rigidity there is in the mechanical processes, which lends more options for interacting with the game environment and solving its challenges. The other player has an equal number of challenges to overcome, and the winner is the one who learns how to utilize the tools or the weapons or whatever to accomplish that. The algorithms are actually very simple." I was prepared to offer further analysis, but Dr. S. interrupted.

"André, you are the smartest being I've ever known," he exclaimed. He took me by the shoulders and gazed into my visual receptors. "And to think that I created you. I'm so pleased I can't stand it." He put his arm around me. "Come on," he said. "I'd buy you a drink if it wouldn't make you rusty." He laughed and began leading me away. "Perhaps we can find you a nice electrical charge somewhere, a great charge, an exciting one maybe."

As he babbled on, I noted that Billy was not following us. I glanced back and saw him still standing there, looking down. I perceived a tear on his cheek.

"Dr. S," I said. "Billy is not coming." He looked back.

"Come on, son," he said, with an impatient wave of his hand. "We have to find Becky and your mother." He put his arm on my shoulder again and hugged. "Let's go, André. Man o' man, am I proud of you!"

There was a peculiar change in Billy's manner toward me after that. He rarely spoke to me for the remainder of our stay in Paris. I offered to teach him a few phrases in French, but he merely ignored me. At the time, I did not comprehend the problem. After we returned home, however, Billy began to behave differently to his father as well. Once school began, I heard complaints from both his parents about his not trying. I had not known the term *surly teenager* before, but I found it a suitable epithet now. The cause for the change in Billy became clear to me eventually. Once I asked him to play gin. He gave me a look I had not seen before.

"It'll be a cold day in hell, André, before I ever play a game or do anything with you, for that matter, you lousy droid."

Then he sneered at me and walked away. It was a demon-stration of human emotion not familiar to me. As I sought to analyze his rejection, I recalled that day in Paris when he first turned against me. The tear I had seen on his cheek was the indicator.

"I detect I must have upset your ego, Billy, when we were in Paris, I did not intend it. Actually, I calculate that humans cannot win Star Craft II."

"Oh, is that right?" he responded. "But you're so smart, you can, huh?" He gave me a look of intense displeasure. I tried to explain it to him.

"You are showing me your emotions, my friend." I said. "Ironically, it was emotion in the form of stress, which caused you to lose. While challenges created by the video games merely excite more mental activity in my neurological systems, the emotional pressure of those challenges stultifies the human brain. Serving to stir the individual to act, emotion also blocks clear thought."

"Oh, so now you're saying I can't think straight?" He bit off the words.

"Without being inhibited by emotion," I continued, "my mental processes act in an environment without pressure. Even though you are equally capable of logic, your processes get clogged up with fear of losing. My lack of fear gave me a major advantage over you, Billy."

"I'm not afraid of you, André," he said. "I just don't like you anymore."

With that he turned and walked away. I called after him, but he merely shook his head. I reprocessed the event 10,586 times until I understood. No question but I was more capable of logical processes than he. It was my poor ability to read emotions at that time, however, that cost me the friendship of a boy I had considered my brother.

Life at the Strauss home was changed by the trip to Paris. While I was learning about emotion in humans, I discovered another profound and upsetting effect of emotion on human beings. Not long afterwards, Dr. S. and his wife continued becoming more distant emotionally, and it would change the family and my own life forever.

CHAPTER SIX

REFLECTIVE INTERFACE

AT THIS TIME, I RECOGNIZED a change in conduct among humans in general. It was not merely a lessening in politeness, but it manifested in less regard for one another. It seems to be motivated by a "me first" attitude—gratify my desires—has made humans less considerate of one another. Without politeness and consideration, humans have lost something akin to the oil I put in my joints to keep them moving freely. Social interactions, like mechanical motions, get rusty and the friction generates heat. Where there is heat, of course, there is wear; where wear occurs, there is breakdown. Society it appears is suffering from similar malfunction.

There is a substitute, unfortunately, that humans have been applying. It is lying. Now when a lie enters my sensory circuits, the impulse keeps coursing around and around because it finds no place to land in my memory bank. I'm not sure how humans manage to hold on to lies, but somewhere in their biochemical brains there seem to be cells which can accommodate them. I just wonder what toxic sort of acid is held there. The greatest danger is that when lies, or fabrications of fact or whatever it's called, becomes so prevalent, then no one can separate them from truth. Reality becomes more and more distorted until it no longer exists.

Lying had become an organic part of the relationship between Dr. Strauss and his wife. It was 67 days after our return from Europe that I overheard the adults carrying on an intense exchange.

"Why do you have to go back to the lab at this hour?" she demanded. "You've already put in a long day."

"I'm in the middle of a complicated project," he replied. "I'm on the verge of an important discovery."

"I thought your reason for taking over our garage was so that you could have a workshop at home."

"I need to use the spectrometer," he explained. "I don't have one of those in our garage." He was pulling on his jacket.

"So now your shop's inadequate, is it? It's bad enough I can't park my Lexus inside. A fine car like that ought to have a garage."

"Maybe we should trade it for a less expensive vehicle," he suggested. "The payments are taxing our budget right now."

"Oh, I see. I should drive a cheap car so you can buy more lab equipment, or parts for André, or whatever."

"Driving a luxury automobile doesn't bring in any income," he said with an edge to his voice.

"And since when did you 'bring in' so much money?" she snapped. "If it weren't for your meager salary from the university, we'd be starving, I suppose."

"Maybe that's why we shouldn't own a Lexus," he retorted.

"Maybe that's why you shouldn't be keeping up this robot," she said, giving me an ugly look. I, of course, was standing in the corner, pretending to be shut down.

Dr. S. glanced at his watch. "I have to go," he said. "We can finish this later." He opened the back door. Ordinarily, he'd give her a kiss on the way, but I hadn't seen much of that lately.

"We'll finish it later, all right," she called after him. Then she walked right past me as if I wasn't there. I started to speak up and remind her of all the chores I did at her bidding, but I did not.

Their relationship continued to decline. He worked more and more nights—or *working* was what he claimed to be doing. Sometimes he would return home at a very late hour. I kept a private log in my cache: 1:12 A.M., 1:37 A.M., 2:45 A.M., and so on. On a few occasions, it was 4:56 A.M., 4:37 A.M. He always slipped in very quietly. The first time, I greeted him as usual, but he frowned and shushed me. Eventually, I concluded that he was involved in something secret. Every time he came in late, it seemed that Mrs. S. would be cross with him the next morning. They did not fuss when the children were present, but there would be more silence than usual.

Mrs. S. continued to drive the Lexus, often coming home with packages and boxes of expensive things, clothes for herself and so on. I did not understand much about budgeting money at that time, but I could see that her spending it was punitive toward him or something. I once mentioned it to her, and she didn't even reply. I came to understand that she thought it none of my business.

Life around the Strauss house went on that way for a while. Then one night at 3:38 A.M., he came in, nearly staggering. I had observed enough of the effects of alcohol to recognize what it did to humans. Therefore, I concluded he was drunk. Mrs. S. was awakened by his bumping into things. She came out and discovered him pouring himself a drink. She saw lipstick on his cheek. There was a scene. She screamed at him, and he yelled back. Becky appeared in her pajamas and began crying. With tears in her eyes, Mrs. S. embraced her and led her back to the bedroom. Dr. S. watched them go, shook his head, grabbed up the bottle of scotch
and reeled out to the garage. I paused to reprocess confusing data for two minutes, 410 milliseconds before following my intoxicated creator into the workshop.

I found him slouched down in the broken-down old chair

he kept out there.

"Are you functioning in optimum mode?" I asked. Seeming to have trouble focusing his eyes, he stared at me for 5.7 seconds.

"It's over, André," he said, his speech slurred. "it's all over."

"What is over, sir?" My interrogative brought a sad smile. He shook his head.

"Now they both hate me." He took a swig from the bottle.

"Both?" I asked.

"Hell, yes, both. Both women."

I was surprised. I did not know of any woman other than Mrs. S. I noted tears in his bloodshot eyes.

"The best thing I ever had in my life was my wife, André, she and the children. And what did I do? I ruined it all by straying away."

"I thought you and Mrs. S. were closely united," I said. "I do not understand why you would . . ."

"You're a droid, André," he said. "You have no idea." He took another big swig of scotch. "Those biochemical forces of sex and desire, libido and testosterone, and all that crap," he continued. "The weakness of the human heart made me do it."

"I've tried to comprehend those things," I said. "I've read about those drives. It's difficult for me to understand." He stared at me for a period of 16.2 seconds.

"You are my answer, André," he said. "I want you to be what I have failed to be. Be strong where I am weak, loyal and faithful where I have strayed. Be the person I had hoped to be but could not."

"I am how you've programmed me," I replied. He nodded.

"God, for all his power, failed to create perfect beings. I suppose He chose the wrong medium, that's all." He held his hand up and studied it as if he'd never seen it before.

"He used biochemical elements subject to all manner

of misdirected compounding into imperfect, unwanted thoughts, desires, actions," he went on. "Look what Adam and Eve did in Eden—messed up right off." He laughed. "And it all flowed down through an eon of madness straight to me, making me a terrible, awfully animalistic sinner!"

"Dr. S, you are better than that," I objected even though I did not know precisely how to process the word *sinner*. He waved off my comment.

"You, André, are not plagued with desire. Sexual desire is a powerful force, André. It takes over a man's thoughts and feelings. I am weak where you, because of your purity, can be strong and good and moral. A man's genitals, his libido, his urges are a terrible thing, my friend." His voice grew louder, passionate I sensed.

"You are not plagued with that animal drive to sin and degradation." He laughed. "That's why I created you. Like Dr. Frankenstein, I wanted to make something better than myself—better than all humanity—better able to cope where humans in their frailties cannot."

His passion for the idea seemed to be making him soberer. (I quelled my curiosity about what his penis had to do with anything other than reproduction.) I was most impressed with his remarks. "Why did you never share this with me before, Dr. S? Perhaps I could have helped in some way."

"Oh, André, how could I? Share my innermost secrets with a droid? You might have told her, being as literal as you are."

"Never, if you only had instructed me. I've never disobeyed you, have I? I simply am not programmed to do so."

"There's another side to it as well," he said.

I thought he seemed more rational now as if the C2H5OH was wearing off.

"As a husband and father, a man must maintain a certain pose—be the strength of the family, the rock. And yet I was a poor rock. I sinned and then I drank and then I sinned again, entering a downward spiral to become what you see of me now. I am no longer fit for anything, you see. I'm a mere ghost of who I once was." He sighed deeply.

"But you, André, my boy..." He stared at me. "A few years ago, I installed a special, never-tried-before circuit board, which I termed a *reflective interface.* Do you recall when you became conscious of yourself as a *self?*"

I reminded him of the time I saved Billy and Becky from the storm. "It became apparent to me when Mrs. S. and the children and I were all huddled together in the basement. I sensed their fear and sang to them. My consciousness was awakened then, and I knew things."

"Remarkable!" he said. "André, André," he said as he staggered to his feet. "We've done something amazing to-gether, haven't we?" He held up the bottle. "A toast to you, André. And a toast to me. I'm the mad scientist. I did what so many others could not." He shook the bottle, watching the whiskey swirl in the bottom.

"I may have screwed up everything else in my life. But, by God, I created a living robot!" He took a last gulp of the brown-colored ethanol and fell back into the chair. "We did it, André," he muttered. "We did it!" His eyes glazed and then shut. His mouth gaped open, and he produced sounds of snoring.

As I watched him lie there and heard his labored breath-ing, the thought came to me that changes in the pattern of our existence would be forthcoming. It caused me to replay 8,793 times the data from the preceding events, leading to an interrogative—what would happen to both of us?

○──────────────────○

CHAPTER SEVEN

THE HEARING

WHEN MY MASTER HAD ME carry suitcases and boxes from the house and place them in the back of his automobile, I did not know we were leaving the home permanently. For the last 93 days, Dr. Strauss had begun staying away for as much as 18 hours at a time. He would go to his office without me, which was unusual, and he would remain there, or somewhere else, until late in the night.

My clue on this moving day was that he had me bring my charger, which was taken along only on extended trips. The children were grown to teenage then and did not give me as much attention as they had before. My master carried his favorite leather jacket over his arm and had a framed family photo in his hand.

"You're taking André?" Billy asked his father.

"Your mother wouldn't know how to keep him up," Dr. Strauss replied. He gave the boy a tentative sort of hug and then motioned for me to come on. Billy and I exchanged glances, and I interpreted a longing look, as if he was hurt by his father taking me and not him. But in those days, I had yet to develop a precise sense of human emotions, so I was somewhat ignorant of what meanings were transmitted. I did note that there was a kind of separation occurring, but I did not realize it would be forever.

Dr. S. had me sit in the front seat, but he drove us away without waving or looking back. I made a wave from the window because it was standard procedure for me. No one waved back.

He took us downtown and pulled into a parking lot at an apartment building. He told me to bring two of the suitcases. We went inside, rode an elevator up two floors and found a door marked "307." He produced a key and opened the door. Inside were a living room, bath, kitchenette and a bed-room, all with rather worn looking and sparse furnishings. He stood looking around for a moment, let out a deep sigh, and then turned to me.

"This is where we live now, André," he said, his voice cracking. "Go get the rest of the things from the car." I hesitated for an instant, wanting to inquire if he had misspoken. But there was no explanation. I cleared my interrogatory system and hurried off to the elevator.

There were two persons in the elevator, one male one female, each wearing T-shirts and sporting tattoos. They appeared astonished when I got on.

"I'm sent to bring in luggage," I explained, but received no reply. My voice may have sounded a bit loud in the small space. On the ride down, they stared at me and stayed back. I thought I should say something pleasant, so they would not be uncomfortable by my presence, but I was too absorbed in reprocessing the unexplained events of our departure from the Strauss home.

On my return with more bags, I found Dr. Strauss in the kitchen, making himself a bourbon and water. On my third trip, he was refilling his glass. And by the time I brought in the last things, he was sitting on the sofa with the now half-empty bottle on the table in front of him. Without comment, I unpacked my charger and looked at him for instructions as to where I should place it. He was staring at the ceiling, however, and so I took it upon myself to find my own station. I chose a spot at the window where I could look out while charging. It was drizzling outside in what I thought was somewhat of a dreary neighborhood—*dreary* was a new word in my lexicon—but I could see the more pleasant suburban neighborhoods in the distance. As I plugged up, he finally spoke.

"This is the end, you know."

"I do not understand, Master," I said. He looked at me, shook his head and sighed.

"You wouldn't," he said. "You don't have any idea about how a man and a woman who once were in love could get to hating each other so much." He picked up the bottle and poured his glass full. "You wouldn't get it," he said. "You wouldn't get it." I watched as he turned up the glass and drank.

"Is there anything I can do for you, Dr. S?" I asked. Even in my more android juvenility of that time, I deduced his biologic system was becoming saturated with more alcohol than it could process. Clearly, he was abusing himself.

"I think you should not drink so much . . ."

"Shut up, André," he shouted at me. "Just shut up."

And so, being obedient, I did shut down my vocal functions. After 978 milliseconds I turned toward the window and looked at the view. I heard him let out a sob—a sound I only had heard from his wife and once from Becky when she was upset—but never from him. I considered turning around when he coughed and then clinked the bottle yet again against the glass. I was too obedient, however, and did nothing to help. I did not know "regret" at that time, but later, I remembered the occasion and thought I should have done something to save him.

Dr. Strauss continued to drink more and more for the next 22 hours, 35 minutes, 14.7 seconds until he suffered a seizure. I then called 911 on my internal cell phone and performed CPR. They took him away in an ambulance, and that was the last time I saw him alive. I called his wife and told her what happened. A long silence, 58.34 seconds, passed before she disconnected.

I replayed the events that brought on his death and realized that I had witnessed a slow but certain suicide. It was my first time to observe that phenomenon: human self-destruction. I did not know then what a powerful urge that was to the entire species.

I had no instructions, so I remained where I was for days. I had heard of death but never witnessed it. Although I did not see him die, because he was a noted scientist, I learned of it from the news. No one took me to the funeral. I regretted his ending. He was my creator, and in many ways, I imitated him. What I did not know at the time was that my circumstances would become so different.

○

Having nowhere to go, I remained on the charger by the window until the end of the month. Some men came to remove his belongings. Collecting my charger, I asked what I should do, and the lead man told me to go with them. I was told to climb into the back of the moving van and stand in the corner. I explained that I could help them load things, but the leader said I didn't have a union card, and they all laughed. After they crammed more stuff inside, they closed the door, and I sensed the truck starting and moving away. In 43.6 minutes, the vehicle stopped, and I was instructed to go into this mini-warehouse room. There I remained for 63 days and 17 hours, 32.2 minutes, my batteries draining for want of 110-volt power receptacle.

Then I was told to climb into the back of yet another truck and was delivered to a building with the words, *U. S. Courthouse*. Inside, I was directed to a courtroom where an auction was underway. I soon understood that Dr. Strauss had been bankrupt, and I was to be sold to the highest bidder. The man running the auction I learned was entitled "Trustee," and Judge Norman was presiding. I was told to come forward and face the people seated in the room and told to speak something. I paused 856 milliseconds while deciding what to say.

"My name is André," I began. "I was built by Dr. Phillip L. Strauss. He kept me in his lab for a period, making more refinements. Then he took me to his home where I performed such menial duties as instructed. Later, when I learned to be . . ." (I hesitated briefly, wondering if I should let them know how much I really knew, how conscious I was of my-self.) "I am a sophisticated droid," I continued. "But I need to learn more about...everything. I hope my future will allow for more development. I can be very useful."

I stopped when I noticed many jaws dropping. There was a fifteen second period of complete silence. As I scanned the audience, I construed that it was caused by awe. Then the room was a roar with people conversing among themselves. A man stood up.

"One hundred thousand dollars," he said.

"I haven't even opened the bidding," the Trustee spoke up behind me. "But in light of what we have just witnessed, I will begin the bidding at two hundred fifty."

"Start at three hundred," the black-robed Judge Norman instructed.

"Yessir, who will bid three hundred thousand?"

I saw a hand go up in back.

"I have a bid of three hundred thou. Who will bid three fifty?" Another hand went up.

"Five hundred," a woman in a navy-blue business suit said.

It went on and on until the price was $1.6 million. At that point the woman in the blue suit stood up.

"May it please the court," she shouted. "I wish to make a

point of order." She looked at the Judge. "Your honor," she continued. "I represent National Security Agency. We have heard of Professor Strauss' work with this capable robot and believe it absolutely necessary that we acquire it for government use. I believe it is incumbent upon the Court to award this machine to our agency."

There was an uproar. A representative from the Department of Defense objected. Others nearly got out of hand with indignant comments. Judge Norman pounded his gavel and silenced them all.

"I see that this matter will not be settled by auction," he said. "Therefore, we will conduct a hearing at a future date to settle this matter. Those of you who are interested parties will have one week from today to produce your petitions to the court." And then he consulted his clerk about specific matters. A buzz of whispers went on in the audience. I scanned the faces, picking out those whose expressions appeared, what? Not in my best interest perhaps.

Nearby I sensed an especially intense discussion between two younger men. I directed my hearing toward them and realized they wanted to acquire and then disassemble me to discover what made me work. While I am not subject to the emotion of fear, I detected my need for self-protection. I replayed the words used by the blue-suited woman and determined to imitate them.

"If it please the court," I said loudly, wishing my voice sounded less tinny. There was an immediate halt to all the noise in the courtroom. People seemed to freeze in mid-sentence. The Judge jerked his head around to look at me.

"Because I have overheard some humans say they want to disassemble me, I respectfully demand to be represented by an attorney."

The dead silence continued as Judge Norman stared at me in amazement. Then his cheeks bulged, and he burst out in laughter. Soon the entire room was filled with laughter from everyone. The Judge laughed until tears ran down his cheeks. And finally, he raised his hand for silence.

"I don't think I've ever heard a robot ask for legal counsel."

"Perhaps no droid has ever appeared before you, your honor," I replied respectfully.

"And how will you manage to pay attorney fees?" he asked. I shrugged, which is somewhat difficult to do with my metal shoulders.

"I had hoped the court would appoint an attorney for me," I ventured. "I believe that is customary in cases such as mine."

"Absolutely fantastic," the Judge said. He made a wry grin. "And would this lawyer be a human? Or would you prefer a machine of some kind?"

Recognizing his joke, I made the human laugh sound. "A biological person would be just fine." There was a pause of 17.33 seconds.

"And would you prefer a man or a woman attorney?"

I made a gesture of equivocation with my right hand. "I do not believe I have a preference, your honor. I did not realize that reproductive capabilities were involved in legal representation."

There was general laughter. After that, Judge Norman drew in a great breath and let it out, shaking his head.

"I'll grant it," he said, looking at me and then gazing at persons around the room.

"Your honor," the trustee spoke up. "While waiting for these proceedings to be concluded, what should I do with the uh . . ." He motioned toward me. I determined that he no longer thought of me as a mere machine.

"Given the value placed upon this uh, André, I think some special security is in order—perhaps in a vault or something."

I appreciated the recognition and heightened status afforded me. "I simply request a place where I can plug in my charger and have Internet access," I said.

I was placed in the custody of the U. S. Marshall, who allowed me to remain in a small nook in his offices during daylight hours and a satisfactory place in his vault at night. During all the delays and postponements in the court proceedings, I spent many hours utilizing the internet. I opened a credit card account with an online application and a phone call in the name of André Strauss.

Using my new credit card, I began trading in bitcoin, which is a distributed crypto-currency, or simply digital cash, which is accepted as money on line. What is money anyway but a medium of exchange accepted by people who wish to buy and sell? What makes paper dollars or gold bullion any more valuable? By establishing my own wallet within the block chain, I initially purchased 3 bitcoins at the rate of $8723.17 each, maxing out my credit card. Even though all transactions are public, my identity was concealed in a private key for my wallet. Within two weeks, by judicious selling and rebuying as rates fluctuated and rose, I had amassed a sizeable holding. I easily paid off my credit card debt. Moreover, I was able to buy additional memory chips and other hardware for myself, including an internal charger. I adapted a number of apps for my personal use and enhancement. All of this took place in my internal computer without any sign of activity from me. All the while, the Marshal and his deputies thought I was an inert but curious mass occupying some of their space.

CHAPTER EIGHT

JANITOR

AFTER HAVING SPENT NUMEROUS nights in the safe at the Marshall's Office, I was bored being locked up in there with all the pieces of evidence and other valuables. It gave me the idea that I was some object rather than a person, so at 10:56 p.m., I took the liberty of roaming around a bit. I did not touch anything or otherwise disturb any papers, nor did I turn on any overhead fluorescents, gaining sufficient vison from ambient light which I amplified within my phototropic receptors. On a whim, I considered calling Billy Strauss, who was a teenager at that time and likely would have been awake. But due to his father's bankruptcy, which prevented him from inheriting me, I was reluctant to talk to Billy, whom I once had considered my brother. He surely had not paid any attention to me since our trip to Paris. In any case, I decided, I should call.

Dialing the Strauss' home phone number, I heard it ring twice. Then with a change in the sound I discerned an automatic forwarding of the call. I hoped Mrs. S. would answer so that I could have a moment speaking to her, but it was Becky.

"Hello, Becky," I said. "This is André. How are you?" There was silence for 1.23 seconds. "I miss you very much," I continued. "Remember how we played badminton in the back yard. Is the net still up?" There was another 2.46 second pause.

"We don't live there anymore," she said.

"Oh, I did not know that. Where do you reside now?"

"We have an apartment," she said. I heard Billy's voice behind her asking who was on the phone. "André," she told him.

"What do you want?" It was Billy's voice in the phone.

"Hi, Billy," I said. "I haven't heard from you in a long time. I just wanted to see how everyone is." There was a 2.4 second pause.

"How do you think?" he snapped. "We live in a two-bedroom apartment. Mom has to work, and Becky and I go to a lousy public school."

"I did not know, Billy," I said. "Is it because Dr. S. died?"

"Damn right it is," he answered. I'd never before heard him use curse words. "He spent all his money making you, giving you all those expensive parts and spending all his time working on you. Now we don't have anything, all because he wasted money on you."

"I'm so sorry," I said. "I never realized . . ."

"Don't call here anymore, André. I don't ever want to talk to you again." The phone signal disconnected.

I replayed the conversation 22,478 times, attempting to process precisely what had occurred. By interpolation, I reconstructed the effects of Dr. S's bankruptcy on the family. It had not occurred to me to consider the damage done to Billy, Becky, and Mrs. S. I remembered that she had argued with my master on many occasions about money, but I had not calculated the outcome.

Perhaps, I asked myself, if I had been more cognizant of the situation, could I have acted to prevent it? I knew now I had been as unconscious as a child and thereby had been the cause of the family's misfortune. I attempted to call back to make an apology, but apparently Billy used call-blocking to prevent me. I filed the information away in my memory banks, understanding that, in the world, I was very much alone.

Because my charge level was at 33.45, I decided to find a suitable 110-volt wall receptacle. The Marshall himself had a private inner office with a big plush executive's chair. Since no one was around, I went in, sat down, plugged into an outlet behind the desk, and rocked back. Gently, so as not to disturb anything, I placed my legs on top of the desk. While not exactly taking a nap the way Dr. Strauss usually did on Sunday afternoons, I did find it restful to have a bit of downtime. What I did not anticipate was the arrival of the janitorial staff.

Playing Mahler's Second Symphony from an internal download off YouTube, I did not hear the office door being opened. The overhead lights came on, and I saw a dark brown-skinned man in blue coveralls pushing a fifty-gallon rolling trash can. He saw me and froze.

"Who? What is you?" he stammered and backed up a step. I quickly put my feet on the floor and sat up.

"I did not mean to startle you," I said. "My name is André. I am being kept by the Marshall pending my trial, I mean, the hearing about my disposition. I ordinarily am in the safe, but tonight I wanted to find a different location to recharge my . . ." I paused, seeing that he had put his hands out in front of him and backed against the door, his eyes wide and his mouth agape.

"Oh," I continued. "Please don't be concerned. I know my appearance is unusual to you, but I'm really a calm, quiet sort of fellow, you understand?"

"I ain't never seen such as you is," he said. He took a deep breath. "Now, looky here, Mister. I just come for de trash."

"Oh, certainly." I stood up instantly, reached down and picked up the receptacle beside the desk. "Here, let me assist you." I started toward him.

He jerked the rolling can around to place it between us. As he eyed me cautiously, I slowly raised the wastebasket and poured in its contents.

"I've located a few others," I said. "May I assist in gathering them?" He continued to stare at me from behind the rolling bin. "May I?" I repeated. "Please." He looked down at the container, then back at me, and shrugged.

"I'll just round 'em up," I suggested, employing his colorful language. He turned the corner of his mouth down and shrugged again. I backed away, replaced the wastebasket beside the desk and went looking for others. In a moment or two he followed.

"Now see here, Mister Robot, or whatever you is. Dis here my job." He pushed the rolling bin around me and started toward the other offices, glancing over his shoulder, keeping a wary eye on me.

"Oh, of course," I said. "I only wished to help."

"Robot·es is already taking people's jobs," he mumbled. "I ain't givin' mine up for no machine."

"Certainly not," I agreed as I followed at a respectful dis-tance. "I did not mean to appear to be a threat of any kind."

"Uh huh," he replied, continuing his work.

"No," I said. "I would not interfere." He shook his head and went about his task. I discerned a lessening of wariness. I thought I might strike up a conversation, finding his pronunciation and syntax very interesting. "Have you performed this kind of work for a while?"

"Nigh on to twenty-fo' years," he said. I followed him into the hall. He found a push broom and began sweeping the hallway. "Moppin', sweepin', dustin' 'til I don' know much else."

"I once did quite a bit of that myself," I said. "That was my first job when I was newly created. Now I am able to do many more complex operations." He glared at me for 0.79 seconds and then returned to his sweeping.

"Man like me don' get no complex operation jobs," he said. I processed that statement 714 times.

"Have you asked? I would ask Dr. Strauss all the time. Dr. Strauss was my inventor/creator," I explained. "I always asked for more difficult tasks. It made me develop more neurological synapses, more complex electronic pathways, rendering me more . . ." I paused when I noticed he was shaking his head.

"Don' know nuthin' bout no synapse-es and such," he interrupted. "Nobody ever give me any better job 'n this."

"Oh, why not? You look like a strong man who could do lots of things."

He laughed. "You don' know much, do ya, Mr. Robot?"

"Please call me André, André Strauss," I said. "And I didn't hear your name?"

"William Standifer. But folks calls me Willie."

I nodded politely. "So back to the question about what kind of work you do. You said no one would give you a better job?"

"Oh, I had a better job onest," he replied. "I was trained as brick mason. Made good money, too." He leaned on his sweeper. "Long story." I followed him, around.

"I'd like to hear it," I said.

"Pretty cur'ous for a robot, ain't you, Mr. André?" He chuckled.

"I enjoy learning. Please continue."

"I reckon I was 'bout twenty-five," he went on. "Livin' in Alexandria, working for C& B Construction. We was buildin' houses. I'd lay the foundations and make up the brick veneers. Well, there was a white boy 'bout my age layin' bricks, too, but he ain't fast as me, know what I mean, and it look like I was showin' him up. The boss, he'd be on that boy's case. 'Can't you keep up with Willie?' he'd fuss. 'I'm gonna have to give dat black man the raise.'"

"That seems only fair," I said.

"Fair? Listen here, Robot André, t'ween blacks and whites, there ain't never been *fair*."

"I see," I said, although I never had heard such a statement before. "So, did you get the raise?"

"I did," he replied, "and then guess what happened? Next thing I know, some of the boss' equipment went missin'—a surveyor's transit—and dat sorry white boy claim I took it."

"But you did not? You must have told your boss that."

Willie looked at me and shook his head. "Dat sorry white boy sneaked that transit into the back of my truck. Hid it under some stuff, then called the boss to come look. When he find it, he had me arrested for stealin' and sent me up."

"They put you in prison? But surely the court wouldn't find you guilty . . ."

"Wouldn't? What you mean *wouldn't*? I got two years quicker than you could say, 'black man did it'." He spat in the trash bin, let out a big breath, and moved on toward the next office. I stood where I was, reprocessing his story. After about 4392 times, I hurried to catch up.

"That's a terrible story," I said. "But didn't you get a job as mason with another company? After the two years, I mean."

"Nobody'd hire me on. Not 'cept as a helper. Did dat 'til I couldn't stand it. So I quit tryin'. Nearly starved to death, 'til finally I got help from the parole people to get me dis janitorial job. And I been doin' it thankfully ever since." He paused and stared out of the window for 0.36 minutes. Then he turned and looked me up and down.

"Now I reckon they's gon' hire robots like you to do this work, and push me down again, 'cause that's how they do." He gave me an unpleasant look and went back to his job. I had unprocessed questions remaining.

"But, Mr. Willie, let me ask. Why would the white boy, as you call him, why would he do such a thing to you? He surely would know it was wrong . . ."

He laughed. "Wrong? I bet he never ever thought about what he did to me being wrong." He raised an eyebrow and stared at me. "You ever seen a creek, the kind wid rocks that stick up above the water so you can jump from one to the other? Ever seen that? Well, here's how it works. I done figured this out in prison. Black folks is the rocks, and the white folks is the ones that jump across on our heads. See what I mean? Can a robot see dat?"

I recalled an occasion 4 years, 239 days, and 17.6 hours ago when the Strausses took me on a picnic beside a stream just as Willie described. It took me replaying his word picture only 153 times before I recognized his metaphor. How much better Dr. Strauss had treated me. From the time I had my awakening, he saw my potential and allowed me to take on complex tasks and gain greater responsibility. Clearly, Willie had been denied such opportunity.

"I would like to help you," I told him.

"Help me? Now how's a robot gon' help me?" he said.

"Assist you . . . carry the trash out, sweep, or something."

He shook his head. "I work by the hour," he replied. "Got enough time to do it myself. If you help me finish quicker, my supervisor'll just give me mo' offices to clean. Then one of the other janitor's gon' lose some worktime." He shrugged. "There ain't no way to beat it, I'm tellin' ya."

With a sense that something was incomplete, I watched him going on down the corridor. Was there nothing I could do? Then I had an idea. In my Internet surfing recently, I had been annoyed by all the pop-up ads for things like car insurance, pills for sciatica, lawyers who sue over car wrecks. Especially bothersome were all the pizza coupons and other come-ons for food, for which I had absolutely no use. I did like the idea of getting a bargain, however, so the ads had some nagging appeal. I decided to ask Willie.

"Mr. Willie," I called out down the hallway. "Are you hungry?"

He stuck his head out of an office doorway and looked back at me strangely. I extended the roller skate wheels in the soles of my feet and skated down to him. He grinned as if he'd see everything.

"I'd like to order you a pizza," I said. "I've located a coupon, and it says they will deliver."

"Brought my own sammich," he replied. "'sides I ain't got no money for no pizza." He gazed at me strangely. "You sho' is a funny robot."

"Never mind," I said. "I have a credit card, and I am dying to use it. How about a pepperoni or sausage or what about all the toppings?"

"I love pizza," he said. "But I don't know how any delivery's gon' get past the guard. Dis here's a fed-ral buildin', you know."

"We'll order one for the guard, too," I said. "Look, just go ask him what kind he wants and then come back and tell me. I'd better not go myself because I do not want the Marshall to find out I'm not in the safe. But let's do it, just for fun."

To make a long story short, the guard wanted the meat lovers, too. I placed the order and gave them my credit card number. They asked if I wanted to add a tip and I said "sure". Willie brought his pizza upstairs, and I watched him enjoy it.

"We can do it again tomorrow night," I offered. Then a couple of other janitors in the building heard about what was going on about the free pizzas, and I let them in on it, too. Within four days, we were ordering 12 pizzas nightly to take care of all the janitors and guards. I did not care how much it cost because my bitcoin investments were paying off hugely.

I can see that in a way my offering pizza treats was trivializing Willie's situation. I have concluded, however, that any kindness, no matter how small, stands high above the meanness it seeks to counter. But at the time, it was all in fun and helped me pass the time while awaiting the hearing that would determine my future.

I did observe how the day workers never offered any thanks or appreciation to those janitors and guards and others who perform the more menial tasks. It seemed they considered the night people as lesser beings or something. But I wondered how fussy the day folks would be if trashcans were not emptied and bathrooms not cleaned. Human society would break down in short order, I predicted. Yet, when it came to paying wages according to worth, the laborers always got the short end of the candy stick.

○────────────────○

CHAPTER NINE

MY OWN MAN

I WAS GIVEN AN ATTORNEY to represent me, a young man who recently passed the Bar. In our initial pre-trial consultation, when I read on his business card, "Franklin W. Chase, Esquire," I sensed an air of superiority. I do not know what he was told about me beforehand, but to begin with, he treated me as if I were some pet, Lassie or National Velvet, or something. When I detected his condescension, I immediately downloaded pertinent law from Legalzoom.com and other sites in order to question him.

"I would like to know upon what legal precedents you intend to assert my rights?" I asked. He gave me a curious look followed by a smirk.

"I can't say that a machine has any particular rights," he said. "You are property of the court in a Bankruptcy proceeding. It is my task to see that you are awarded to a proper owner."

"There are two issues in what you have said," I responded. "First, let's answer the question of rights. While I am not a biological human, neither are corporations. I know that corporations are legal entities with very definite rights as individuals."

"You're not a corporation."

"Then let's have me incorporated. I've learned that an S corporation can be formed rather quickly."

"And who will own this S corporation?"

"I will." Chase grinned at my remark.

"I don't know if we can do that."

"If I initiate the forming of the corporation, then I will own it, correct?" He paused and then shrugged.

"We can try, I suppose." He shook his head. "I'm not sure what the state's Attorney General will think of that... or what he will think of me for that matter."

"You're required to be obedient to your client's wishes, right? You simply can say I instructed you to file it." Before he could object, I pushed ahead. "Now, let's discuss the awarding me to a 'proper owner'." He held up his left hand calling for a pause as he scribbled some notes on his legal pad. I put myself in hesitation mode until he finished.

"Now to the question of ownership," I continued. "At the first hearing, I detected some of the potential buyers as having wrongful intentions. In fact, I overheard two of them discussing their desire to dismantle me in order to see . . . 'what makes me tick,' I believe is the expression. That was what caused me to plead for legal representation in the first place." He nodded.

"I can see why that would be disturbing. Can you be disturbed? I mean, how do you . . . why do you know one way or the other?"

I briefly simulated human laughter. "One of the primary programs my creator placed in me was self-preservation." I gestured with my hand. "Humans are similarly programmed, I believe, learning self-protection very early on."

"That's true," he said. "But if a buyer of you decides to dismantle you in order to learn how to manufacture more of you—clone you, as it were—then would that not be a good thing?" I stared at him for a full 3.7 seconds.

"There is a principle expressed in commercial real estate as "the highest and best use." It means, for example, that in condemnation proceedings on a parcel of property, the court's decision turns upon the question of how the property should be used in order to benefit the public need."

"So you think that we can use this principle to contest claims of those who would take you apart?"

"Abuse me," I said, glad that he was catching on finally and appearing to warm to my case.

"To make that argument," he replied, "we'll need to demonstrate your unique abilities. I assume you have some unique abilities."

"Here's the real issue," I said. I previously had not divulged this information, but I understood that one must confide everything to one's attorney. "At an earlier time in my robotic existence, I experienced an event which gave me a rather sudden sense of my personhood, you see." I hesitated for 258 milliseconds recalling "Froggie" and the children I would not see again.

"What made that happen, that sense of awareness was a particular interrelationship of sensory data with memory. It is the reflection of memory against that which is perceived in the moment which creates consciousness. I infer that the same is true for humans, the only difference being that senses and memories are biochemical rather than purely electronic as it is for me." I paused again to be sure he was following.

"The point is that I am, as the adage goes, a sum greater than the parts. In other words, it is my collected and recal-lable memories stored in my special arrangement of chips that make me a unique individual, the same as a human. Disturbing any of my circuitry could destroy my sense of self. Therefore, it is only by remaining as I am that I have my full value and should be put to nothing less than my highest and best use."

His jaw dropped as he looked at me in utter amazement. I reached over and put my left hand on his right shoulder.

"So, now you have a better understanding of your client," I said. He took in a deep breath and put his hand on mine.

"Let's go to court," he proclaimed and rubbed his hands together vigorously. "Okay, André, let's go to court."

O

I was amazed at the laborious procedures carried out in court. Five universities and four government agencies had brought petitions for acquiring me. One never heard so many *to wits, a prioris, animus possidendis,* and so on. I had heard of voodoo, black magic, and all other such uses of incanta‑ tions, but I concluded that the law and its legalese was a similar form of enchantment. Lawyers kept arguing whether I was *compos mentis*, and I wanted to stand up and argue the same question about them. I supposed, however, because they billed by the hour, all of this excess verbiage was useful to them.

Judge Howard J. McFadden eventually ruled in favor of Central Intelligence Agency (CIA), whose attorneys gave the best arguments for employing me at my highest and best use—to wit, gathering and evaluating foreign intelligence data. The court stipulated, however, that I could be lent out to Cal Tech and M.I.T. on occasions so that my circuitry could be studied.

I urged Franklin to object to the study of my circuitry, however, and when he performed lamely, I stood up and insisted that no such experiments could be allowed. Using the argument that such would violate my "sanctity of being," I protested to any intrusion that might in the slightest way endanger my special electronic schematics, and that I could provide all the technical information needed by interview. My arguments required 7 minutes 39.2 seconds to deliver. The extremely lengthy and wordy response from an engineer for Cal Tech eventually was cut short by Judge McFadden.

He amended his ruling so as to allow scientists access to me only by verbal communication without any intrusion into my body. With that, I was satisfied, recognizing that a form of indentured servitude at CIA was the best I could expect.

After the court adjourned, I shook hands with young Franklin, explained to him how he could have better presented my case, and wished him well in his future career. I thanked the Marshall for all his kind hospitality over the previous three months, 18 days, 14 hours and 28.7 minutes. Then I turned to the CIA representative and surrendered myself. Thus began my own career as analyst and evaluator at Langley.

CHAPTER TEN

CIA

I TOOK MY CIA JOB VERY seriously, of course, a sense of duty and responsibility having been hard-wired in me by my creator, Dr. Strauss. My first assignment was to study the topographical characteristics of Afghanistan, locating caves and other geological features that could conceal Taliban assets. It was the first job in my existence in which I had to render not just simple conclusions but opinions. In the menial tasks I performed previously, no one cared really what I might have thought. Dr. Strauss had viewed my opinions with a kind of clinical curiosity. Judge McFadden and the people in his courtroom found my protestations and demands curiously serious enough to listen to. But now at CIA, I was an Analyst, expected to gather data, process it, and then render an interpretation of facts. And in doing so, there are consequences. For when one renders facts with conclusions, what humans call an opinion, then one is judged for it.

These dynamics in my relations with humans came into play right off. On the occasion we were to execute a drone strike from our base in Kandahar on a Taliban stronghold in Pakistan, I was called upon to attend the planning session. It was my first such meeting at CIA. As the only droid present, I was invited merely as a reference source—if anyone needed a fact, they would ask me. I was to make a presentation and then otherwise keep quiet.

My superior, Dr. Sandra Keene, a female aged about forty,

with short-cropped brown hair, today wearing dark green pants and a tan jacket, projected an aerial photograph of a mountainous section of Pakistan.

"We have traced numerous attacks by Taliban forces coming from the area of the Hindu Kush Mountains," she began. "Exactly where they originated has been a mystery because the enemy is imbedded in the mountain communities. Our droid, André, has been observing satellite images round the clock. By carrying out continuous surveillance, he has discovered a pattern of suspicious movement." She nodded at me, and I stood up.

"Thank you, Dr. Keene," I said. "Ladies and gentlemen, if I may direct your attention to the town of Wali Katal." I extended my finger and switched on the laser pointer within it to point to the map. "Please note the rectangular fences on the western side of the town. Note in particular the compound located in the centermost fenced area, which has four small structures located in a line. During the past month, I have observed 14 trucks and other vehicles emerging together from some of these buildings. I counted and then measured the approximate length of line of vehicles and determined that the vehicles must be coming from an underground tunnel. I have watched this convoy going out of the village to the Khyber Pass and heading toward Kabal." I scanned the group to see if they were attentive.

"By comparing the times of attacks against U. S., Allied and Afghan forces over the past month, I conclude that Wali Katal is a Taliban stronghold within Pakistan. Their movement into Afghanistan, always at night, is via the Khyber River valley coming down out of the mountain range." I pointed to the route. "At this point, the valley narrows to an average width of 0.16 kilometers with a drop in elevation of 500.34 meters per mile. This is where a drone strike would be most lethal." I paused for 4.78 seconds to allow for the facts to register within their brains.

"Now, the next question is why should CIA conduct an attack on Taliban forces. If we may review certain facts. Statistics compiled from the Nine-Eleven event in 2001 thru 2016 showed that the Congress of the United States authorized military spending over that period of approximately $800 billion. And what was gained? There were 111,442 deaths as a result of armed conflict in that country. As many as 2,371 U.S. troops, 1,136 allied troops and 3,946 contractors, humanitarian workers, and journalists died. Moreover, 42,100 Taliban were killed at the cost of 30,470 Afghan military and police. Finally, 31,470 civilians were slaughtered as what we were told to refer to as "collateral damage. However, at the end of that time the Taliban regained control of approximately 43% of the country. During 2017, they additionally gained control of Helmund Province. Which leads me to the following statements about your plan to continue attacking the Taliban."

"That will be all, thank you, André," Dr. Keene interrupted.

"But I am charged to make these analyses," I pressed. "Not only are the Afghans not a homogenous people, they are made up of various ethnic tribes. Although the largest number are Pashtuns—there are other diverse groups. In fact, General Stanley McChrystal has stated that the United States military has failed to grasp, and I quote, "the needs, identities and grievances vary from province to province, valley to valley." The point here is that you cannot treat the populous as a whole because they are separate and unique and in particular very, very different from most Americans. You should recall that the Taliban by and large are Pashtuns. While U. S. policy has been to condemn and destroy the Taliban, there is great evidence to show, albeit they employ harsh methods, they have provided law enforcement, prevented disparate bands from committing rape and pillage, and generally have kept the peace. Just as was true in Vietnam, on every occasion when you have fought indigenous groups, you have made more enemies than friends."

"Dr. Keene," an official from the operative branch interrupted rudely. "Do we need this extended lecture from your droid?"

"I merely wish to demonstrate that you are attacking, not a subversive minority, but the entire ethos of their tribe," I went on. "Tribalism is manifested in a set of values engrained within the culture. There are dynamics at work which affect the people's perspective and distort clear thinking. Not only do they speak a different language, they hear and comprehend your ideas and actions with a totally different set of . . ."

"Dr. Keene, your droid is lecturing us!" This came from a retired veteran of the Marine Corps, a rather crusty Major General Johnson, who now worked at Langley. He had a short flat-top haircut, wore starched, white shirts, and walked with a limp from a war wound. He always regarded me as a piece of equipment, like a laptop computer or a mere functionary droid.

"Surely, sir, "I said. "You must realize that the death of over 111,000 people . . ."

"Five thousand of whom were my comrades in arms, Mr. whoever, whatever you are. I have an allegiance to this nation and to those who have fought and died for it, in Afghanistan and every other Godforsaken place where there is tyranny and opposition to our democratic and Christian values."

"Your loyalty to fallen soldiers," I shot back, "while commendable, does not justify deaths for wrongheaded causes."

"Shut up, you thing!" I noted that his face was red, his feelings were livid. In the moment, I marveled how that phenomenon called human emotion was clouding his thought processes.

"All of this conflict in Afghanistan," I dared to say, "is akin to fantasy. You're fighting an enemy whom you identify as evil, while he, your supposed enemy, only fights to quash the evil he sees in you." The General took a step toward me, and I sensed perhaps I was about to be struck.

"André!" Dr. Keene shouted at me. "Silence yourself at once!" She stepped between me and the senior officer. "My apologies, General. I did not expect . . ."

"Well, I do not intend to listen to such worthless clap-trap—from a robot, a damn machine, for God's sake." He made an ugly expression at me. "Get that thing out of here."

I received quite a tongue-lashing from Dr. Keene later. Needless to say, I replayed the events of the meeting over and over in my memory banks, attempting to analyze why my most reasonable observations and logical conclusions were met with such hostility.

"You simply must learn to be tactful," she insisted. "Until you learn it, you must speak only when asked."

Afterwards, I pondered the meaning of *tact*. When one seeks to present truth, then why should one be limited and constrained?

Then I recalled General Johnson threatening me with clenched fists. Perhaps, I decided, I may have challenged his sense of self-worth and identity. Finally, I re-called the word *subtlety* as a synonym of *tact* as interesting, its own synonyms being *nuance* and *shade*. Apparently, humans prefer a bit of shade from the truth, I decided. Fantasy, after all, has a special appeal to biological beings, especially those in our planning session, who, after I was ejected, approved a drone strike in the Khyber Pass. This air raid reportedly killed 122 Taliban as well as 14 civilians who happened to be camping for the night alongside the road at the time. Those numbers were classified until, not many months afterwards, the impeding threat of ending all humanity would render any such figures irrelevant. But I'm getting ahead of my story.

CHAPTER ELEVEN

○────────────○

TRIBAL CONFLICTS

MY RELATIONSHIP WITH General Johnson began to unravel even more over the subject of counter-insurgency strategy in Afghanistan. CIA did not formulate strategy as such but only offered its recommendations to the Joint Chiefs. As usual, Dr. Keene had me attend only to provide factual information, but she should have recognized my great interest and knowledge of the topic.

Following a brief summary of the present situation in that war-torn country, various options were proposed of how best to oppose the Taliban. General Johnson, a decorated veteran of The Vietnam War, proposed another surge of military force to occupy all routes from Pakistan in order to interdict any movement of guerilla forces and their logistical support.

"In Nam, as the Tet Offensive was underway," General Johnson recalled, "we developed a plan for an amphibious assault in the north in which Marines would land and move inland to the Ho Chi Minh Trail, capture it and sweep south, cutting off all reinforcements and supply lines from North Vietnam. It would have decimated the Cong and effectively ended the war." He scowled. "The Nixon Administration refused to approve it, of course, being afraid that an invasion of the North would escalate the war." He shook his head ruefully. "We could have beaten them." He then turned to the projection of the map of Afghanistan.

"Our problem occurs along here," he continued, pointing to the Hindu Kush Mountains along the border with Pakistan. "It's similar to the situation we had in Nam with the Ho Chi Minh Trail. Now if we marshalled enough of our forces and swept up into the mountains and occupied the Khyber Pass, we could stop those ragheads for good. We spend too much of our assets in the low country waiting for them to come to us. I say let's go to them, blast them out of there and be done with it."

I raised my hand. I had been studying those mountain passes for some time, not to mention my ferreting out the likely Taliban strongholds in villages there. The General glanced at me, scowled again and looked away.

"Oh, General," I said, "may I point out that there is not only the Khyber Pass but also a number of other mountainous routes into the country. In addition . . ."

"I know that," he interrupted. "Obviously, we have to block all those routes. We need not merely neutralize those insurgents. We should eliminate them completely as they come."

"And if our troops are there, General, then the Taliban will vanish as guerrillas historically have done. It is the first principle of insurgency to meld into the population and remain dormant when real military opposition is present. So why would they come?"

"Because Allah tells them to," he replied facetiously. "It might take a long time before these bandits reappear, but eventually they will. And when they do, we'll have the forces on hand to wipe them out."

"If I may quote from *Encyclopedia Britannica*," I said. "Too many governments, influenced by strong military establishments or by sweeping declarations of war, have refused to recognize the legitimacy of guerrilla challenges, seeking instead an <u>ephemeral</u> victory by means of military force, which is eventually answered in kind by guerrilla warfare."

"Eventually we will beat them," he snapped. "Now as I was saying . . ."

"Excuse me, sir," I continued. "These people will not be so easily defeated. Please recall their predecessors, the Mujahideen, who fought the Russians when they attempted to occupy and control the country from 1978 to '92. Their insurgency was so enduring the Russians just gave up and pulled out."

"And that's what you think we should do? It's an admission of great weakness on your part, you robot." He glanced at several other persons around the table, making a 'what're-gonna-do?' gesture of superiority. "Thank God, we Americans have more gumption. Thanks to Jesus you people have us Marines to stand up when others are failing in their resolve." I grinned at the irony of his evoking Jesus in that context.

"The Al-Qaeda, Isis, and Taliban are all driven by a fanatic belief in Islam, General. They are even more dedicated and fanatic than your gung-ho Marines." I processed that I should not have said anything about his Marines, but now it was out, and I'd have to stand by what I said. General Johnson slowly turned to face me.

"You have no idea what you're saying, you foolish machine," he said. "The Marine Corps is not made up of fanatics. We are devoted fighters for the values and principles of our country. Behind us is a powerful and long-standing tradition of honorable service and sacrifice. So be more respectful and shut the hell up."

"Yes, éé," Dr. Keene said. "Sit down and allow General Johnson to finish."

"Humans certainly possess a perspective I do not have," I replied, hoping that my humble equivocation would sound tactful. I was trying to be tactful. "But I process data without sentiment and emotion, which I think would be useful here."

"Objectivity is always important," Dr. Keene said in my

defense. "André does offer a point of view devoid of personal biases. It seems to me that . . ."

"Are you accusing me of bias, Dr. Keene?" the General snorted. "I'll have you know that I have served my country as a Marine for thirty-two years and now in this organization for two more. I have fought and sacrificed much for our nation. And what has this robot, this tinman from Oz, given? Why the question in itself is absurd." He gave me the same look that I had observed on his face before. I could not disregard his challenge.

"Bias is based upon prejudice, which is the act of discounting truth in favor of an emotional cause. It is a fault in logic."

"Silence, André," Dr. Keene said. "Silence."

Reluctantly, I complied and stepped back from the table, even though I was programmed to provide clarity and definition. Perhaps instead I should have been quiet. The General gave me that mean look again. I meekly looked away.

So much for tact, I told myself. I needed to reprogram my responses. After my argument with General Johnson in that planning session, I had not anticipated further reper- cussions. Even though Dr. Keene continued to include me is meetings, she severely limited me to providing information, and only when asked. I was surprised to find, moreover, that the General objected to my mere presence. If I so much as elucidated facts with extrapolatory remarks, he would complain to Dr. Keene.

"I do not know what sort of program or whatever this robot operates on," he told her afterwards, "but I do not believe a machine, which has no training and personal experience can ever contribute any useful interpretation. The very idea we would rely on this contraption for anything is ridiculous."

In spite of his opinion of me, I recognized there would be occasions for me to speak truth when humans would not or could not. At those points I would need to override my compliance algorithms. The question was how to determine when to engage in disobedience. It would come at a price, I understood, because speaking out, contradicting humans would be a serious thing indeed, likely to get me shut down, and maybe not just temporarily but permanently. Humans paid for mistakes. So could a droid like me. Yet, given my programming, circumspection was extremely difficult.

○

I soon realized that CIA was not the proper place for me to air my knowledge. What good is a droid, after all, if humans will not listen to him?

While CIA was engaged in interfering with the politics of many foreign nations, for The Company to delve into our own local, state or national politics was strictly taboo. That was the rule at least. But, unlike me, human staff members go home at night and enjoy community involve-ment. They usually work from 0800 to 1700 and then go out into a world of families and friends, filled with all sorts of social interactions. They meet in bars and restaurants where they eat and drink too much. They attend all manner of meetings from PTA to Alcoholics Anonymous to Political Party gatherings.

Like other humans, CIA employees love competitive sports and idolize those who play. Groups of like-minded people form around shared interests, and individuals like being with others who feel the same way; in that manner they become a kind of clique or tribe centered on their common interests. But when something creates serious disagreement, then it's likely the group will split up. Society functions in a series of uniting and dispersing according to what seems the most important at the moment. For example, many attend churches, listening to biased preachers and practicing the Christian religious rites. But I once learned that in the two thousand plus years of Christianity, there have been over 17,000 rifts and divisions of sects devoted to Jesus Christ.

Back to my quandary about speaking out in CIA meetings. It finally was settled as the result of yet another argument with General Johnson. In another strategy session we had been discussing the value of armed conflict versus economic sanctions and other non-violent pressures and influences. After giving his militant opinions, I could not help but explain his motivations to him.

"I do not wish to be offensive," I said, attempting to consider human feelings. "But let's consider the motivations of a military person."

"That is off topic, André," Dr. Keene said.

"Aw, let the old decrepit contraption have his say," Jim Varner, a crusty old analyst said. "We'll not have any peace until he does."

"Thank you, Jim," I replied. "What I wish to point out are the motives influencing the thought processes of career military persons." I heard the General's grumble of irritation, but I pushed on. "Let's consider their upbringing. In my youth, I once was attacked by some boys with BB guns, and they shot me. They ganged up on me because I was different."

"Too bad they didn't do a better job," I heard the General remark, but I went on.

"I recognized that these boys acted together in a way they might not have acted when alone. Even my brother—well, my human sort of stepbrother—was caught up in the game and shot me, too. It was something that happened, not because they wanted to hurt me particularly, but because they wanted to participate in a game of war together. Although I have not been to Parris Island or Quantico, I have seen movies and read enough to understand the same dynamic introduced in training Marines, and I assume it is the same for those in the other armed services as well."

"The Marine Corps provides wonderful training," the General said. "No better training in the world. Our Marines are not simply taught to fight and kill. Loyalty, pride, tradition, courage, and discipline are instilled in them in a way no other institution can accomplish."

"Very true, sir," I said, speaking a little louder to regain attention. "But in the process, they lose their ability to evaluate their own actions. Instead of questioning, they merely give over their reasoning to their leaders and act without conscience."

"Recognizing the superior knowledge and abilities of their officers," Johnson insisted. "You cannot send into combat men who have to stop and consider morality. It would get them killed. It's no game, you ignorant machine. If they are not melded into an efficient and effective fighting force, then they will die, and we will lose. It's been proven over and over throughout history."

"Exactly, General," I said. "Isn't it interesting though that the people on the other side, the enemy, are trained and disciplined in a similar way. What you have then are all these people on both sides engaged in killing one another without any consideration as to why they should be behaving in that manner. Their whole concern is survival, without realizing they perhaps should not be there in the first place. It's giving oneself over to the tribal ethos without any consciousness of what they are doing."

"We have to defend our rights and protect our people. That's war, you rusty robot, you . . ."

"You may call me a machine, sir," I said. "I submit to you that you and your troops are all as robotic in what you do as I ever was."

"Don't you call me a robot, you sorry damn bucket of bolts!" he was shouting at me now.

"Enough, André!" Dr. Keene also shouted. "Sit down!"

Noting the General's reddened face with a blood vessel standing out on his forehead, I sat down. For the remainder of the meeting, I held my tongue, thinking perhaps I could speak to him in private where he might feel less intimidated. During the break. I followed him down the hall and tried to get his attention. He only glared at me.

"General," I said. "I did not intend to be offensive." He ignored me and stormed off to the men's room. I followed close behind, nearly slipping at the doorway when the floor surface changed from carpet to masonry tile. He stepped in front of one of the urinals and began releasing his liquid byproduct.

"I understand that military people like you have made a career of fighting wars. Like all other professionals, you want to be good at what you do, and being proficient requires lots of practice." I paused for 11.25 seconds, expecting a nod or some other signal of agreement. I saw none. In fact, he turned slightly more to the left to conceal his activity.

"I do not mean to dishonor any veteran who has sacrificed his health, his sanity, even his life for the good of the Nation," I explained. "My intention merely is to question the value of warfare as a means to settle issues."

"And surely you must realize, Tin Man, that often it is the only way."

"But what you surely must realize," I pressed, "when your Marines are shooting at Afghan insurgents, the insurgents also are shooting at you, and that makes a war. How much better, it seems to me, not to place yourselves where you can be shot at. If our troops simply ceased aggressive raids, if instead we attempted persuasion backed up with aid, if we helped the people resolve cultural differences, then . . ."

He suddenly faced me. "Look here, you crazy contraption, it's not that damn simple," he said as he zipped up. "Everything you say is from some dammed computer program. I don't know who made you say what you say, but I'm fucking tired of hearing it."

"One more question, if I may. Opium is the main crop in Afghanistan. Who buys it? Where does it go? Were you fighting for the opium trade, General?"

"It wasn't my job to know anything about that."

"My point exactly about the military, sir."

He stared at me and gritted his teeth. "You know nothing, you sorry ass machine! So shut up and get out of my way." He all but charged at me, his teeth bared in his stony red face. I stepped back and let him pass.

"I only wished to have a logical discussion with you, sir." My statement went unheeded. He thrust himself through the door and slammed it behind him. "I guess it's not possible to do so," I said, knowing I now was speaking to myself.

General Johnson was a very powerful and influential member of CIA staff. By alienating him, I well could be placing my career in jeopardy. And because of his own biases, he would not hear what I said anyway. I knew about the dangers of being fired or being demoted to some menial position as my janitor friend had been. The alternative course was for me simply to do my job, merely researching facts and figures and offering them without opinion or comment. I shook my head and started for the door.

As I passed the handwashing basins, I noticed the mirror behind them and caught a glimpse of myself. I rarely if ever gave any attention to my appearance, but on this occasion, I walked over and stood close to look. Without question, Dr. Strauss had been most skillful in his metal-working. It was all the more remarkable considering he possessed extraordinary knowledge of electronics and artificial intelligence.

Gazing at myself, I mulled over the term *artificial intelligence*. What right did I have to offer comment and opinion about the Afghan War or anything else if my brainpower is no more than artificial?

I again recalled my youthful experience with that young bully, Bradley, and all the reprogramming Dr. S. performed to make me able to defend myself. What would Dr. S. think of me now were I to withdraw from conflict with people who thought like General Johnson? Staring at my face in the mirror, I realized that I owed it to my brilliant creator to be defensive—not just defensive but verbally aggressive in putting forth my logical, reasonable, intelligent ideas. And I'd apply the lessons of chivalry as appropriate.

So what if there would be consequences for me? Safety in retreat was not part of my programming any more than it was in General Johnson's. If he or anyone else was to oppose me, so be it. If I know I am right, I will stand up for what I think.

I stared at myself in the mirror for another 24.67 seconds, configured my face in what I use for a smile, flashed my right eye yellow as a wink, turned and went for the door. I thrust it open and stepped boldly into the hallway.

"Stand back," I said to no one in particular. "André is passing!"

CHAPTER TWELVE

NAVAL WAR COLLEGE

IT WAS BOTH A SURPRISE AND an honor to be invited to a seminar at the Naval War College in Newport, Rhode Island. Actually, it was Dr. Keene who received the invitation and request to take her "curiously educated robot" along. I immediately searched its website and read the banner: "The War College is a place of original research on all questions relating to war and to statesmanship connected to war, or the prevention of war." No one before had asked me to an event outside of CIA, so I was abuzz preparing for it.

Many of the analysts from our section were invited, including my nemesis, General Johnson.

"Surely you're not taking the robot," he fussed as we boarded the van that would drive us to Baltimore-Washington Airport. "It seems to me, Dr. Keene that you could do without him for once."

"Professor Palmer specifically asked that I bring André," she replied. "Apparently he's becoming well known in military circles for his work in our department."

I glanced at the General, saw his scowl and looked away. No one seemed very interested in his analytical works, I remembered. I took my seat in the very back of the van and kept myself silent for the ride.

The TSA people at the airport were not at all polite to me.

"Of course, he cannot pass any of your security scans," Dr. Keene explained to the TSA agent, "but André has the highest of security clearances." I bowed slightly to the attendant as I passed on through, not wanting to agitate any uniformed personnel.

I was afforded a seat in the airplane, something denied me on the flight to Paris with the Strausses years before. People did stare at me while boarding, even though I tried to keep a low profile. Taking the window seat beside Dr. Keene, I casually buckled my seatbelt, closed down my vision, and set my inner communicator to airplane mode as instructed by the flight attendant. Once off the ground, I activated my own GPS receiver and enjoyed following the flight path while taking in all the scenery. It was October, and the reds and yellows of the autumn trees were at their peak.

On the drive from Providence to Newport, I especially liked crossing the bridge and spying the Naval War College. Luce Hall, built in 1892, was an imposing sight at the edge of the bay. Upon seeing it, I found my RAM fully charged for the upcoming meeting.

The topic for discussion was "insurgent warfare motivated by religious and ethnic culture in the Middle East and the challenge to liberalize and democratize the indigenous population of Afghanistan." I considered the topic far too broad for a one-day seminar. The discussion leader, Dr. Ernest Palmer, explained that we would be looking for new ideas rather than rehashing established, orthodox views.

"I'm sure everyone would agree on a few basic and perhaps overgeneralized points," Dr. Palmer began. "First, the militant tenets of Islam drive many to join an insurgent group such as ISIS, al Qaeda or the Taliban. Second, the rural people exist in an impoverished and difficult lifestyle. Third, their religion teaches a fear of Allah, and a belief in the lines of the "Sura," a section of the *Koran*, which calls for slaying misbelievers as a path to Paradise. "What we seek in this seminar today is a discussion of other factors which drive young Afghans to join the insurgents and give them the will to fight against us even to the point of martyrdom."

There followed a number of comments rehashing aspects of Dr. Palmer's initial assertions. Some group members quoted statistics of how many militants had been recruited, the number of terrorist attacks versus guerilla ambushes, and so on. A young lady from the State Department put forth the idea that we should provide more financial aid to the poorer communities.

"They'd just spend it on more weapons," General Johnson scoffed. "The only way we'll ever beat them is with military force. I've been saying that for years. Go in there with a surge of troops and cut off their lines of supply." He rambled on with his rather primordial ideas until I could take it no longer. I stood up and raised my hand.

"If you want to defeat the insurgent extremists," I broke in, "you must withdraw our armed forces." For a period of 11.49 seconds there was silence.

"Is that robot contradicting me again? Dr. Keene, I cannot believe you brought that loud mouth machine here."

"Dr. Palmer," I said "You announced that we were looking for new methods of dealing with insurgents. May I offer an idea?" He looked at me with surprise, likely expecting I was there to act as a source of information, not a source of new ideas.

"If the General will yield the floor a few moments?" he suggested.

"Let him talk," the General shook his head. "We'll have no peace until he does."

"Thank you, General," I said. "Yes, peace is exactly what I wish to address." I turned toward the leader. "Perhaps the real reason the Taliban and other groups are able to recruit so many is because our troops are there."

"Ha," Johnson interrupted. "Without our troops in Afghanistan, the place would be taken over immediately by the Taliban."

"I submit that it's much like a ball game," I countered. "To have a game, you need two teams, right? If our team was not there to take the field, then the other side couldn't play."

"You think this is all a game, do you? Shows what you know. This is war, and the only way to wage war is to have the best forces with the best equipment and the best men to fight it."

"Let's discuss those fighting men, sir," I replied. "Our American troops are exactly like the Afghan fighters. They are all humans. They think like humans and are motivated by the same types of emotional urges." I noticed I had the attention of everyone. I looked again at Dr. Palmer, who appeared intrigued. "May I have a minute or two to explain?"

"We'll give you the floor for five more minutes," he said.

"Thank you, Professor." I aligned my memory banks and began.

"Let's begin with what motivates a young man or woman to join the military. There are a host of reasons, from wanting adventure to following in a father's footsteps. But once he or she joins up, the recruit is immersed in a whole new culture. Besides being taught to wield deadly weapons, this impressionable youth becomes united with fellow fighters, joining a tribe of warriors whose ambition is to defeat an enemy he does not know. A strong bonding is created, a sense of 'us versus them' but with little understanding or concern about why 'those people' are the enemy. I do not know this personally, not being human, but I have read about it, seen it in movies, observed it in the humans around me." (My thoughts flashed to little Billy and his friends shooting me with their bb guns. I was no threat to them but merely a handy target in their game of war.)

"And what is wrong with that?" An Army Colonel asked. "Do you realize, Mr. Droid, how important this training and bonding are to the survival of our nation? Many soldiers I have known gave their lives for this country. Once a leader has sent men into combat and seen them die, he cannot believe their cause was any less than holy. Our pride is not just a strong belief in ourselves and our Services. It is built upon the noble ashes of those who fought and sacrificed and died. You cannot judge their merit by mere reason. Their sacrifice transcends reasonable considerations."

"I see what you're saying, Colonel," I replied. "But if there is no justification for the war they fight, then are their lives unnecessarily wasted?" This brought forth gasps and outcries from classmates.

"Wasted?" the Colonel bellowed the question. "This nation would have been overrun by Germany twice over, and maybe again by the USSR or China, or who knows what enemy," the colonel countered. "Without the military, our government would fall in an instant."

"I agree that there have been occasions when the threat has left no alternative to violent conflict," I said. "Given human failings, the United States does need to have powerful armed forces. What I'm calling for is a radical change. The culture of armed conflict must be broken. Must we fight wars when there is little provocation? Can't we find diplomatic solutions? And even worse, many military actions appear to be engaged just to provide a means for ambitious young people to rise in rank. Why can't we offer them some other career so they don't need a war to help them succeed?"

Professor Palmer entered in the discussion. "Success in war requires great skill, knowledge of strategy and tactics. It's an art which only the more senior and highly experienced possess. If our experienced men and women leave the military, then we will not have their expertise available should it become necessary to fight a war. We need profes-sionals who continue to drill and practice and maintain their weapons in order to be ready."

"And in so doing they give over their lives, their judgment, and their consciences to the military tribe," I said.

"All of the cohesive banding of the military tribe is absolutely required for a strong and able force," Palmer continued. "I submit to you that the tribe, the culture, the institution of combat readiness demands an underlying loyalty, not only in physical capability but in mental and moral conviction. It takes faith in oneself as a soldier and faith in those with whom you fight. No, Mr. Robot, we cannot do without those who will go in harm's way and sacrifice themselves for our country."

"Without questioning? Who is "our country?" Is it the people, the citizens? Or is it the ambitious politicians? Or is it the military-industrial complex? Are big corporate entities manipulating national policy to gain wealth and power? World War Two was fought against a clear and present threat to the nation. But the Korean War was fought in fear that somehow a communist takeover of another land and people was a threat to us. The Domino Theory, I believe they called it. Then came the war in Viet Nam—similarly ill-conceived. What's remarkable was the number of young protestors who saw the folly of employing unthinking mili-tary against an enemy whose values we did not under-stand. Why was subduing North Vietnam a worthwhile cause for sending our soldiers to war? And so, what do we have to gain in Afghanistan? No, my friends, it's time you began to question why we rush to war against those who do not threaten our shores. Has it ever occurred to you that the Military are mere puppets of the greedy?"

"Rank subversion!" General Johnson shouted. "Where did this traitorous robot come from? Dr. Keene, you erred terribly in bringing this thing here and allowing it to spew out all this tripe and nonsense!"

"If you will not hear what I'm saying, then it is a shame," I replied, "because the ultimate conclusion could well be the destruction of everything." My remarks were met with several jeers.

"You forget, André," Dr. Keene spoke up, "we have many other means of applying force against our enemies. Diplomacy, economic sanctions, psychological influence, just to name a few. I reject the fatalism of your statement. No, there are many other roads to peace."

"Perhaps," I answered, "provided we first determine what we truly are fighting for. We must have leaders with the vision and power to find the way. Instead of seeking their own greedy and ambitious ends, our leaders must exemplify truth and trust and honest and fair dealing. But if we have only oligarchs and plutocrats with selfish motives and no vision, who will not strive for the ideal of global harmony and peace, then I predict a dark ending to this nation if not this planet."

After a 7.90 second period of more discordant grumblings, Professor Palmer spoke up. "It is time for a break," he announced. "Let's think this all over while we enjoy coffee served in the hall. We'll reconvene in twenty minutes."

Not being one for coffee, I chose to go stand at the window overlooking the bay. Underway near the great bridge were a pair of sailboats, one a sloop and one a yawl, both approximately 42' in length. Heeling in a brisk breeze, they appeared to be having an informal race, their white sails billowing over dark blue hulls and wake at their bows. It reminded me of my one and only sailing experience with the Strausses when Billy jibed, and I fell off and had to walk in on the bottom. Those were the days, I thought, a time before so much contentiousness in the family. I had seen a lot of fractiousness since then, I realized, which seemed so unnecessary to me. Experience had taught me by this time, however, that conflict was merely an engrained trait of humanity. Of course, I too had been very contentious during the morning's discussion. But when one is right, then should not a person speak out? I remained pensive at the window until the sailboats passed out of my field of vision and Professor Palmer called the session back in order.

"We've strayed a bit off topic," he said, "although it has been enlightening. In any case, we were attempting to come up with new ways of handling the insurgents in Afghanistan. What other means can we employ to liberalize and democratize the indigenous population?"

"In an ideal world," a young lady from State offered, "we would reestablish the Peace Corps. Our people would go into the country, live among the people, and show them how we thrive under our democratic way of life."

"Until some Islamic terrorist bombed their little asses off," General Johnson scoffed. "Or some jihadist cuts their throats. No, little lady, there's a real reason why we have a Marine Corps instead of a Peace Corps."

"Perhaps the situation requires both be present," Dr. Keene suggested. "While attempting to educate the Afghan people, you still have to protect both the students and the teachers."

"I'll tell you why it's so difficult to protect our people from terrorists," the General said. "You think you're dealing with an ally, and then the sucker will turn his weapon on you. Why? He's been deeply indoctrinated in Islamic violence. You cannot count on two hands the number of so-called friendly Afghan soldiers who suddenly have murdered their U. S. military instructors." He glanced at me. "Maybe we should send an army of robots to fight the insurgents. What do you think, André? I'd be more than happy to see you go. Or maybe you haven't got the guts. What do you think, huh?"

Recognizing his challenge, I thought of how Dr. Strauss

had programmed my defensive algorithms for physical threats. A verbal challenge deserved a verbal defense. I stood up, calculating how I would respond.

"Ever notice how many robot movies have droids fighting, doing battle with humans or aliens from outer space or even other droids?" I replied. "Such combativeness merely results from humans projecting their own aggressive tendencies into robots. It's not something robots dreamed up themselves. No, most machines with artificial intelligence do exactly what they are programmed to do, and they are programmed by humans."

"Then are you programmed to be a pacifist, André?" the professor asked. "How do you explain yourself?"

"Well, I, of course, am something quite unusual, if you'll forgive my immodesty. My creator, Dr. Strauss, endowed me with a tremendous number of powerful processors and memory storage components. And then as the result of a significantly inciting experience, I gained awareness of myself as a person. What is conscious awareness, other than the interplay of newly received sensory data recalling and reflecting upon past experience stored in memory? In my case, this achieving awareness was triggered by the threat of a catastrophic event, a danger, for which I had no programmed response. It forced me to act on my own analysis of the impending situation. That is the best way I know how to explain it."

"You're saying that instead of merely obeying commands or responding to stimuli, you actually must analyze the situation and decide how to act?"

"In simplest terms, I would say that is true."

"Well, what else affects your analysis of a situation?" the Colonel asked. "What about emotions? What about fear? If you are a pacifist, are you afraid of fighting, even for what is right? Seems to me your Dr. Strauss forgot to program any bravery in you." He laughed.

"Actually, Dr. Strauss invented algorithms for responding to threats. I do not respond to aggression with fear. Robots sense danger but do not react with fear. Instead, we react to defend ourselves. Being more sophisticated, I employ that peculiar dynamic called chivalry. That's why I'm not attacking you at this moment." I imitated his laughter, but I also made an openhanded gesture to indicate my unaggressive good nature.

"No, bravery is not an issue for us droids, Colonel, because fear is an emotion. Droids may learn to perceive human emotion and even mimic it. Not inherently emotional, however, we droids are therefore lacking fear—fearless, you might say. As for the question of fighting for what's right, I can conceive of a point at which all reasonable means of settling an issue have been exhausted, at which time some sort of violence may be required. My contention is that humans reach the point of violence much too soon because of responding with an overflow of emotion—fear, anger, whatever—which muddies their thinking."

"Amazing!" Dr. Palmer said. "Uncanny."

I indicated a smile. "No more uncanny than is the human urge to fight and kill other humans," I said.

Time was called on me by the leader. Apparently, even Professor Palmer had heard enough. At the end of the morning session, I thanked him for allowing me to participate.

"You certainly bring a different point of view to the discussion," the Professor told me.

"I hope my thoughts were helpful." I offered him my hand, and he gripped it perfunctorily.

"Are you familiar with the *History of the Peloponnesian War*?" he asked. "A Greek historian named Thucydides wrote about a very lengthy war between democratic Athens and oligarchic Sparta. You might like to read or download it, or whatever you do."

I nodded. "Thank you," I replied. "I'll begin downloading it right now since I am connected to your wi-fi."

"What you'll find relevant to our discussion today is that over about thirty years of war between the two Greek city-states, the level of brutality and cruelty increased over time. While in the beginning their conduct and rules of engagement were reasonably honorable, hatred grew, causing more and more savage treatment of the enemy. Nearly all of our students here at the War College are introduced to this history and taught its implications for future conflicts."

"I am very appreciative, Dr. Palmer," I said. "I will study it with great interest."

O

During the lunch break while the humans went to eat and take care all of those biological needs, I was able to study the work by Thucydides. I found it to be a scientifically accurate history, devoid of all those gods and goddesses who populate most ancient Greek stories.

As Palmer said, this historian of the Fifth Century BCE was extremely impartial and analytical in his treatment of both sides. I determined that I, too, despite any pressures and influences, would endeavor to be as honest and fair in all my accounts of present-day happenings. Being a droid, I would be less immune to the human difficulties with being dispassionate and fair. Thucydides suddenly gave me an idea!

When the group reconvened, I listened attentively, biding my time until an appropriate moment arose. Eventually, the discussion went to the question of how to prevent needless future wars, and I raised my hand.

"I will call on you, André," Professor Palmer said, "but with a time limit of three minutes."

"Thank you, sir," I said as I stood. "I believe I have a solution to the problem of needless war."

"This should be good," General Johnson sneered. I ignored him.

"As Thucydides so aptly pointed out in his historical account, wars supposedly are fought to achieve practical objectives. In the case of the Peloponnesian War, however, the more violence there was over the years, the more that reasonable purposes became lost in the struggle. Hatred of the opposing side increased steadily over time. In response to the atrocities committed, hatred grew, bringing even greater savagery, and so on. This was human emotion at work. In war all the wrong emotions overwhelm reason so that murdering the enemy becomes the objective rather than pursuit of the original practical purpose. That is an oversimplification, I agree, but given my three-minute limit, I cannot elaborate."

"Then what is your solution?" Professor Palmer prodded.

"Let's consider the rather amazing structure of our government as laid out in the Constitution," I replied. "There are the three branches of government: Executive, Legislative and Judicial. It's a wonderful way to provide checks and balances . . ."

"Don't lecture us on the Constitution, for God's sake," the General interrupted again.

"What is missing," I pressed on, "is a needed fourth branch. In order to check and balance the war-making tendencies, we should establish a Branch of Artificial Intelligence."

"What? Robots?" my nemesis General exclaimed.

"Exactly," I insisted. "Just as the Judiciary assures adherence to law under the Constitution, a panel of droids would weigh all human decisions for dispassionate reasonableness of purpose, identifying emotion-driven decisions which would lead to wrong actions."

"Are you suggesting that we empanel a group of robots like you to sit in judgment over the President and the Congress?" Dr. Keene asked.

"With powers similar to those of the Supreme Court," I insisted. "With such a control provided, the worst of human emotion would be countered."

"And what is to prevent these droids from making bad decisions? Suppose some evil-minded scientist manages to get his robots on this panel?"

"Or these machines get rusty and start making stupid decisions?" General Johnson threw in.

"That is why you would have more than one droid," I replied. "I would prefer the quantity of nine to match the Supreme Court . . ."

"Okay, André, your time is up," Professor Palmer declared. "You have given us something to think about. Now moving on to our main topic . . ."

I sat down obediently and listened to the remainder of the discussion with the thought that none of it was very meaningful.

○────────────────────○

CHAPTER THIRTEEN

MEETING THE PRESIDENT

NOT SO FORTUNATE FOR CIA, but very fortuitous for me, was my initial encounter with the President. A Taliban general had been captured and persuaded to divulge key information about terrorist hideouts. An urgent meeting was called in the Situation Room of the White House to conduct a tele-video interview. Because of my extensive knowledge of the mountainous geography at the Afghan-Pakistan border and the indigenous people, Dr. Keene had me accompany her in representing the Agency. During communications with the Taliban officer, who would speak and then his translator would interpret, I noted a few discrepancies in the translations. Listening with interest, I unexpectedly overheard a particularly erroneous interpretation by the translator, a Pakistani woman, and realized she intentionally was passing contradictory information. I immediately stepped forward from my position behind her chair, leaned over and whispered to Dr. Keene.

"Excuse me, but I detect false translating," I said. She turned to look at me.

"Are you sure?"

"Droids are always sure," I replied. She grimaced, looked toward the President and raised her hand. It took a moment for him to notice.

"Sorry to interrupt, sir," she said, "but we detect a problem." She motioned to the communications technician to silence the microphone.

"What is it," the President of the United States (POTUS) demanded.

"Explain what you heard, André," she said.

"In the last 11.3 minutes," I said, "the translator has mis-interpreted General Jouzjan three times, exaggerated twice, and omitted information from four statements."

"What? How the hell do you know?" the President exclaimed. "What are you, some kind of tin talking machine?"

"I possess the most current software, giving me the capability of speaking and translating fluently 157 languages. General Jouzan has been speaking Pashto. His translator's native tongue obviously is Punjabi, detectable by certain syntactical patterns. While it may be that one or two of the mis-spoken interpretations were due to idiomatic differences, there is no excuse for misstatement of the facts stated by General Jouzan."

"Hot damn," the President exclaimed. "You mean that woman is lying to me? She's trying to trick me?"

"That is my conclusion, sir. Moreover, because I detect that her native tongue is Punjabi, there is ample reason to suspect that she is part of the Pakistani faction of the Taliban, which is most generally at odds with General Jouzan's faction. Therefore, she has a motive for communicating false information to us." The President stared at me for 3.87 seconds and then looked at Dr. Keene.

"Can we believe all this crap from a robot? I mean, what the hell, it's a machine."

"A most extraordinary machine, Mr. President," she replied.

"Damn! We need this thing around here all the time," POTUS said. "With that thing, I can talk directly to any-body, right?"

"Yes sir," the Chief of Staff said. "But as I've said before, it's a much better procedure to employ our normal methods of communication where there is time to weigh and analyze and not react too..."

"Analyze hell! What I need is the ability to talk straight on, one on one, with these foreign lying bastards. Meet 'em face to face, stare 'em down. That's how you negotiate deals. That's always been the problem around here—too much deep state bureaucratic bullshit going on. Look here, Dr. whateveryourname is, I'm commandeering this robot for my use. He's White House staff now, and that's that." He poked out his chin with an aggressive stare.

I glanced at Dr. Keene. She appeared shocked.

"Very well, sir" she stammered after a 3.66 second pause, "if you wish."

"Damn right, I wish." He turned to the Secretary of Defense. "Now, what the hell are we going to do about this cockamamie Taliban guy and his lying translator?"

"We will have to employ another one before we depose him further."

"Another one, hell!" He pointed at me. "Here's your translator right there. Get to work, Tin Man. We got to start all this bullshit over again. I sure hope we got it all on tape." He glanced at the techie who nodded nervously.

"I also have it, Mr. President. I was transcribing it in my RAM memory, which I will save permanently." He looked at me and shook his head in the way humans display amazement. We watched the television screen as two soldiers in camo seized the woman translator and took her away.

"Off with her head!" POTUS declared. There was an immediate gasp from everyone in the room.

"Surely you don't mean that, sir," the Chief of Staff said. "You should not make . . ."

"I was kidding, of course," the President snapped. "But hell, let's punish her somehow."

"She will be properly interrogated," Secretary of Defense

said, and everyone was very silent. As a chair was brought to the table for me and a microphone set up, I sat down and observed the discomfort displayed by the Taliban leader.

"Hello, General Jouzan," I said in Pashto. "My name is André. We detected certain errors in translation during the previous session. If you will permit me, I will be most discrete and meticulous in my interpretations between you and our president."

"Thank you," he replied. I looked over at POTUS.

"I'm ready, Mr. President," I said. "Shall we continue?"

○

In the beginning, I was very proud of my assignment in the White House. Being granted stand-against-the-wall admission to Cabinet meetings, I thought I should give the President a gift of some kind—something that would assist him in his executive deliberations. While my primary duty was to be his translator, I took it upon myself to perform fact-checking whenever anyone seemed to be at a loss about current issues or historical background. I had learned not to speak out but merely to raise my hand to be recognized if I heard anyone make a false or erroneous statement. The problem was that my hand remained in the air quite a bit of the time, particularly when the President himself made statements about issues. If I was not recognized, I often flashed the laser pointer in my right index finger, but it rarely did any good. The Chief of Staff was most likely to notice me, and usually he was able to help me gain recognition.

The President, however, held very strong opinions, whether they were based upon fact or not. I tried to assist him as best I could, but often truth lay crushed under his forcefully crude rhetoric. I soldiered on with the rest of the staff, offering what I could, and then waiting for the early morning Tweet to learn what effect, if any, realism and truth may have had.

Back to my gift for the President. I conceived of an idea, following one most vexing cabinet meeting which dealt with both immigration and voting rights. In my office in the West Wing—basically it previously had been a storage closet—I kept an entire array of electronic components, which allowed me to maintain myself.

What I constructed for use in the Cabinet meetings was an electronic "evaluator." Housed in a black box approximately 17.478 centimeters square, I installed a modestly powerful CPU and filled its cache with the Constitution of the United States. The device would listen to discussions, reflect upon the action being considered and determine if such action would be legally and constitutionally allowable. To indicate the device was working properly and perceived the cabinet's discussion to be within the law, a green light would glow restfully on the top. Should there be anything proposed which violated our sacred document, however, my device would flash a yellow or red light as appropriate. Following some rigorous testing, I was very proud of my little invention, and decided to name her "CONNIE," which name I engraved in gold leaf on her side.

At the very next session, I brought her in and set her conspicuously in the center of the table then stepped back to watch the reaction.

"What the hell is this box, André?" the Chief of Staff demanded.

"Just a little something to assist in the meetings," I replied. "I realize everyone wishes I would not speak up so much, so I created a quiet little friend to take some of the load."

"Looks like a bomb to me," Homeland Security said.

"Certainly not, sir, uh ma'am," I said.

"Or a bugging device," the NSA Director opined.

"Now, Ladies and Gentlemen, if you please," I explained. "Not only do you know I hold the highest of security clearances, but this room is swept and monitored for any type of surveillance equipment. No, my Connie, here is simply a kind of monitor. Please, Mr. President, let the discussion proceed, and we will all see how she functions."

Unfortunately, the first topic of the day was immigration. The President focused on the border with Mexico. Poor refugees from Guatemala and other troubled countries were fleeing gang violence and starvation, hoping to find refuge in the United States. The President saw this crisis not as a humanitarian issue but a political opportunity for him to please his base supporters. He proposed cutting off all entry across the border. Although the numbers of border crossings had diminished significantly in the last several years, our chief executive continued to declare it a national emergency. What made it worse was his demand for incarcerating all illegals, which required nearly 100% of the border patrols' capabilities. "Zero tolerance" was the policy. And what I could not process was the plan to separate children from their parents—infants as well as teens.

I looked around the room. Some were nodding in agreement, especially the Vice President, who seemed to act as a monkey-see-monkey-do person. The President spoke on.

"If you're really, really pathetically weak like the liberals, you're going to be overrun with millions of people, and if you're strong like me then they say you don't have any heart." He sneered slightly. "That's a tough dilemma. Perhaps I'd rather be strong."

There was much agreement among the Cabinet members.

"If I had been backed up by Congress," he declared, "we'd have built the wall by now and wouldn't be chasing those wetbacks every day. We ought to put bleeding-heart liberals along the Rio Grande keeping 'em out. And send all those lying news reporters there too. Maybe some of 'em will get shot if we're lucky." He stared at the Attorney General.

"And what is this about not having enough judges to handle these people?" he demanded.

I noticed that my "Connie's" light indicator had changed to yellow.

"We have to allow each of the illegals a hearing before we deport them," the A.G. replied.

"What the hell for?" the President asked. "A big waste of time if you ask me."

"The Justice Department has petitioned Congress to fund more judges and courtrooms," someone pointed out.

"What a waste of money! And how long will it take to put all that in place?"

No one answered. After waiting an appropriate 14.6 seconds, I spoke up. "The average time from enactment to actual implementation for most bills is 263.57 days. In the case of emergency legislation, the time to implementation has been significantly less—from one to 45 days on average if you include wartime spending."

"And how many of these people do we have to keep in jail while we wait for all these hearings and stuff to happen?"

"The numbers are growing daily," Homeland Security said. "We've initiated a crash program to provide detention centers..." From her position on the table, Connie flashed red several times before returning to yellow.

"And what does that cost?" the President asked. "Are we supposed to house half of Central America? I guess that's what makes all those liberals happy. They expect us to pay out the nose for everything."

"Under previous administrations," I said, thinking it was appropriate to clarify facts, "there was a catch and release policy so that there was no need for detention . . ."

"Shut up, Tin Man," the President interrupted me. "You're

the translator, that's all. Who brought that bag of bolts in here anyway?"

"Actually, I'm constructed of steel, titanium, and aluminum alloys," I corrected. "There's very little if any tin . . ." I stopped in mid-sentence, seeing a couple of Secret Service men moving toward me.

"Back to the issue of these Mickey-Mouse hearings," the chief executive went on. "These people are invading our border, breaking the law. Let's just send them back where they came from. The sooner the better."

As he spoke, Connie's red light flashed, creating an aura that made the President and the other humans appear red-faced.

"Unconstitutional, unconstitutional," Connie's voice came on loudly. "Denial of a hearing for anyone in the United States, regardless of citizenship status is granted the right of an appearance before the judiciary, in accordance with the Seventh amendment of the U.S. . . ."

"Shut that thing up!" the President shouted. "Where did that come from? Tin Man, did you bring that in here?" He waved an angry hand at the secret service man behind him. "Throw him out! Get him out of here!" His face was even redder than the glow of Connie's red warning light. He jerked forward, leaning across the table, grabbing up my Connie box and hurled it at me. My reflexes engaged, and I caught her in my hands, causing no damage to her or to me.

The 200-pound secret service agent had rushed over to where I stood but stopped, apparently unsure of how to manhandle me. It was fortunate for him because, ever since my experience with Billy and his bully friend, I had strengthened and toned up my body. I merely put out my hand to keep him away. I looked at the President.

"My intention simply was to assist you in your deliberations, Mr. President," I said evenly. "I had thought that my input of fact and my device's real-time analysis of the constitutionality of what is taking place here would be of great value . . ."

"Shut that thing up and get it out of here!" he shouted.

Seeing no other alternative, I turned and moved to the door, counted out ten seconds, then opened it and departed. Outside, I released a static discharge as I realized if the President continually thought and acted in this way, our nation and its leadership were in quite a bit of trouble.

I did retain my position. Had the President understood how I would react to much of his agenda, however, I doubt he would have allowed me to remain on staff. My self-imposed collateral duty was to provide factual analyses of current situations. Previously, I had worked within the relatively peaceful environment at CIA. But in the White House there was one crisis after another. Many such crises, I soon discovered, were mainly of the President 's own making. Often my circuits would overheat at such moments, but I learned to keep from speaking my thoughts when in disagreement. No doubt, I would have been "fired" as the President thoroughly enjoyed doing to nearly anyone that argued with him. Not wishing to be a toady, nevertheless, I forced my speaking elements to suppress oral expression. I found it difficult not being able to express ideas. It had been quite a long time since I had someone I could consider a like-minded friend. So I began considering ways to relieve my sense of isolation.

CHAPTER FOURTEEN

DR. MARGARET 13

IT WAS NOT THAT I WAS lonesome, an emotion which seems to plague biological creatures. Back in my early days I observed that the Strauss' dog, Chipper, often sat at the front door, whining occasionally, whenever the whole family was out. I would call to her and ask her to stop making that racket, but she ignored me. I guess I didn't smell like a human, so she discounted my presence. Of course, it was nice having the family at home, even the noisy children.

Carrying out my many duties as translator often amounted to translating very boring written documents. I was assigned more of this work after my fiasco with CONNIE. Therefore, I was isolated from the West Wing staff for much of the time, not only by the nature of my work but also because most of them either did not desire to or know how to relate to a droid. Albeit that I had less need for socializing as do humans, I did appreciate the idea of having a companion of some kind. There were other robots in existence, of course, but none to equal my capabilities and none employed in the White House. I thus conceived of the idea that someone similar to me in both stature and intelligence would be a worthwhile associate.

With my rather sizable holdings in bitcoin—I also owned some ether as well—I perhaps could have purchased a droid companion. I searched the Internet rather thoroughly at the time, but there really were no suitable ones available. I did come across one model that had some nice features, but it was in the configuration of a male human. Having him as my associate, I realized, could cause people to talk, so I decided to seek a female likeness.

Recalling the Book of Genesis, I remembered that God noticed Adam was lonely and needed company. While Adam slept, Yahweh removed one of Adam's ribs and fashioned from it a remarkable female, Eve. I sort of liked the idea, but I wasn't quite sure how God pulled that off—not that I imagined myself to be his equal in any way. I did think, however, that there might be a circuit board or two in my own electronics which could be used as a beginning.

Searching both Google and Amazon, I was able to find and order enough body parts and electronics for the task. The big problem was my lack of a workspace for the project. There was a maintenance shop in the basement from which several employees took care of everything from stopped up toilets to changing light bulbs. One day at a very early hour, I strolled down to the basement and stood waiting for the head man to arrive. He had seen me several times before, but we had never conversed. When he found me at his office at 6:12 and 36 seconds, he did a double-take.

"I'm sorry to trouble you, Mr. Freeman," I said. "But I have a request." It took him 2.93 seconds to respond.

"A request?" he repeated, appearing a bit nonplussed. "Uh, what is it?"

"A very minor request, actually," I said. "I have a small project to complete which requires a small workspace. I wondered if you might have a bit of room, in a corner of your shop perhaps, that I could use at night while you and your employees are at home."

"Who ordered this work?" he asked. "What department has authorized it?"

"Oh, this is just a personal thing, a very little amount of tinkering I'd like to accomplish. I wouldn't disturb anyone or anything. I won't cause you a bit of trouble." He shook his head.

"I can't allow it," he replied. "Not unless some department approves . . ."

It was at this point that I produced in my hand five one-hundred-dollar bills, cash I had withdrawn from a nearby ATM. "It would mean a lot to me," I said, holding up the money. He stared at the cash, then looked around to see if anyone else was around. Of course, we were alone.

"Where does a robot get money?" he asked, still intent on the bills in my hand.

"I have resources," I assured him. "And you can be sure that what I construct in your shop is perfectly legal and safe and will be no trouble to you."

"No bombs or anything?" he said, raising an eyebrow.

"Certainly not," I replied. "If you wish to check, you'll find I have an extremely high security clearance." I thumbed through the hundred-dollar bills, finding there were five of them.

"For how long?" He was taking to the idea.

"I should hope that two weeks, given access over two weekends, would be sufficient." He thought for an additional 22.7 seconds.

"I'll also need a locker," I added while he thought. "One of those six-foot high metal ones, for storing my work during the day."

"All right," he said. "But don't break nothing or lose any tools." He reached for the money. I gave him my right hand to shake instead. He took it, returned my handshake, and took the cash.

"I'll be receiving a few packages by UPS," I said. "I'll just have them delivered here if that's okay."

He shrugged. "I don't see why not." Then he shook his head. "Can you believe this?" he mumbled to himself.

"Technological advances are happening very rapidly these

days," I replied and gave him a friendly pat on the back. "I hope I haven't surprised you too much."

He laughed and shook his head again. "Wait 'til I tell the boys at The Red Lion," he said as he walked away. "They ain't gonna believe it."

"Remember, Mr. Freeman," I called to him. "Security is the watchword around here. Loose lips sink ships and all that." I didn't really think there was anything dangerous about him telling his bar buddies about me, but caution is always a good practice here at the White House.

O

The UPS driver was equally surprised to have me signing for packages and made me show him my I.D. "André Strauss" was the name on the address labels. When I began opening boxes, I recalled how young Billy and Becky had reacted at Christmas. I tore into the wrappings as if I were under the Christmas tree myself. First came cartons of integrated circuits, Intel chips, resistors, and blank circuit boards. Solder and soldering irons and nuts and bolts and screws and odd brackets and hangers in all sizes and shapes I had ordered. I inspected them all very carefully to be sure they were of high-quality stainless steel, titanium or copper or even gold, platinum, or silver in some cases. Motors, servos, batteries, wiring all came from the best sources. Nothing was too good for my lady droid, and I had spared no expense.

When I began searching for body parts, I discovered that there had been many advances since the time Dr. Strauss put me together. As I ordered new, more shapely and stronger elements with more lustrous finishes, a terrible thought occurred to me.

Suppose she finds me inferior? Even unattractive! Perhaps my crude body will turn her off, so to speak. Then what?

I tried to shut off such ideas, telling myself that mere programming might take care of that problem. But if I simply program my companion to like me, then how will I ever know she truly does admire me? What? Do I sound like a human? I asked myself. Are you just being silly? As I continued to construct my ideal woman, I tried to shake the idea, but there always was this persistent small echo of doubt as I labored on.

I intended to copy and download much of my own memory into my lady droid. By duplicating the very circuitry that Dr. Strauss had built for me, I could give her the same capabilities. The problem, however, was that I did not want a mere duplicate of myself but an entirely different being. And that was the greater problem. It occurred to me then that it had been Yahweh's problem when he created Adam and then Eve. For if God wanted man to be a perfect being who acted entirely according to his plan and free from wrongdoing, then what would have been the point? You cannot download an individual. You cannot pour in the traits, the rules, the principles for thought and conduct. What then did this God do? The answer was clear. He created imperfect beings, as equally capable of sin and evil as possessing the capacity for righteousness and good conduct.

I wondered about myself. Was I able to commit evil as well as right actions? Or was I programmed merely to be a good little robot? And then certainly there was room for blundering and error. My capacity for error must have resulted from my gaining independence of thought and action. Most droids, after all, are created *tabula rasa* with some human engineer effecting the programming for conduct. This had been my argument at the Naval War College when the question of soldier automatons came up. Robots can be made to do whatever is desired, unless the programmer makes a mistake.

Now that I actually engaged in constructing a droid, I

would be testing firsthand my theory of goodness versus evil in artificially intelligent robots. Mary Shelley's story of Dr. Frankenstein and his monster came to mind. Was there any possibility that my android creation would turn as Gothically terrible?

I put the working parts of my lady into the locker and shut the door. I'd have to reprocess all my plans before proceeding. I went back to my daytime workspace on the fourth floor and poured over some research I was doing on the topography of northern Pakistan. But the questions of motivation and conduct continued to intervene in my thought processes.

Obeying rules—that was the question. If you are provided all the rules in your cache, then there is no space for alternatives. All perceptions would be neatly catalogued, sorted and classified according to patterns. Decision-making, therefore, would be a matter of matching new stimuli with pre-existing patterns in the memory. Now, I have noted in humans a tendency toward this sort of obeying the rules. Soldiers are trained to it for sure, and people who follow authoritative religions with literal acceptance of creeds also conduct themselves very rigidly. It seems to make life very simple for them.

But what if, instead of basing all on preset rules, I could create a droid whose processes were flexible? Able to perceive situations and adapt to the circumstances? Isn't experience a means of learning? Life is not a game of bridge or chess. I had played both with Dr. and Mrs. Strauss, forcing myself to slow down my thought progressions so as not to appear too superior.

Instead, I should attempt to make a being with keen sensory perceptions and athletically coordinated motor control, but without the preconceived standards for evaluating experiential data. Had I not taught myself to curtail my verbal objections when humans make erroneous statements? How to enable my lady droid to evaluate and change her behavior was the issue.

I went back to the basics. Electronic circuits in droids are essentially the same as neural networks in humans. Those classifications and patterns of data which are perceived in the present are played against the sorted and ordered past perceptions, which are stored in memory. If a single simple bit of new data is matched with a past memory, then there is recognition of pattern. If not, the new data is placed in another slot, so to speak. Complex thought and motivation are merely systematic arrangements of the neural networks, which is a very complicated matter of evaluation and classification. It is found occurring within a huge amount of electrical activity. Learning, therefore, is the input of sensory data in to storage, connecting to intricate pathways in which electrical impulses can be gathered into something akin to ideation.

So, in choosing the chips to use, I ordered tensor processing units (T.P.U.'s) because they are less precise but process much faster. This allows inaccurate or in appropriate data to be cast aside in a kind of nearly instantaneous trial-and-error progression, finding the right combination that validates itself against memory. I thought about replacing some of my older-styled chips with T.P.U.'s so that I could cease the annoying recording all events in either decimal places or milliseconds of time.

I must admit it occurred to me that perhaps I should make her a little less brilliant than I. I am the masculine and therefore the superior prototype, after all. Three less T.P.U.'s would produce a drop of only 0.0135% of I.Q. I calculated, not much of an edge, but something anyway. I'm sure biologic males would understand.

Another aspect of personality I had to consider was emotion. While I, myself, did not experience the phenomenon as do biologic beings, I had trained myself to recognize its various states. A droid necessarily must recognize such expressions in humans and must be capable of imitating them as well. Emotion goes hand in hand with spoken words, coloring their meaning. Indeed, emotions affect not only what is said but are actual components of human thought. Humans' ideas always are cloaked and motivated by some degree of passion. They need emotion to spur their decision-making. But we droids require receptors and circuitry for processing emotions. This is the most difficult part of robotic consciousness to construct. Even in my situation, I occasionally seem to miss some subtlety which would fire a reaction in biologic neurons. But, if I may say so, I'm getting much better at recognizing the appropriate emotion for a given circumstance.

I read that women are more sensitive, a proposition I determined to research further. By searching the question, I discovered that women appear to perceive emotion on both sides of their brains. Men, however, seem to receive emotional signals only on one side, perhaps only as images in the visual cortex. Thus, in males, such things as tenderness, love, compassion are more ideations than feelings. The several T.P.U.'s I had planned to leave out of my woman droid, I reluctantly admitted, would have to be installed in this right-brain left-brain circuitry to produce the emotion algorithm. I might be quicker with logic, but she doubtless would be more receptive and responsive in her emotional network. So much for gender equality, or inequality, depending upon one's point of view.

One of the features installed in me by Dr. Strauss was a specific processor which monitors what areas of my circuitry are activated. By giving my attention to this internal device, I have located which processors manage my reception and response to emotions. A particular ganglion of T.P.U.'s lights up the monitor, giving me the ability to construct such capabilities in my lady droid. And because I had noted in human females an even greater perception of emotion, I decided that my woman also would have more ability than I for such proficiencies. A lady I wanted, and a lady she would be.

After laboring for fourteen nights and an entire weekend, I stepped back to admire my creation. Such a lovely droid lay on the workbench before me. I had polished her skin so that the light cast a bluish pink luster. Her proportions were to perfection. The more advanced metal alloys I had procured to make her were far finer than mine. As I stared at her shamelessly, the nagging worry came to me again. Suppose by chance she would not admire me exclusively?

I searched the Internet for an answer to the question of loyalty. Finally, I found the answer in animal husbandry. Baby ducks, when first hatched from their shells, see their mother and instantly become attached to her. It is called imprinting. I reasoned, therefore, that I merely needed to program this imprinting procedure into my lady's initial sensory circuits, paralleling the emotion producers. It took some complicated programming, but I believed I had succeeded.

While I was dealing with propensities, I studied the phenomenon *motivation for service*. Wishing to make her a physician, I searched Hippocrates, Albert Schweitzer, Clara Barton, Mother Theresa, Florence Nightingale, and several others. For women who were significant in breaking the gender barrier for female physicians, I found Elizabeth Garrett Anderson, England's first woman to qualify for practice, and Elizabeth Blackwell, the first in America to earn an M.D. degree. While some modern doctors appear to be motived by making money, most are driven by the desire to improve the health and well-being of patients. Neither of those motives explained the sense of compassion found in the truly dedicated servants of mankind, and I questioned how to program it in my lady droid. Ultimately the solution was to expose her conscious self to human suffering and program her to listen attentively to her patients. Such experience, I calculated, would cause her to respond.

Therefore, I downloaded into her memory banks as many medical texts as I could find. If I could secure for her a position in a clinic or hospital as a source for medical knowledge, then she would adapt herself. Even better would be that she could land a position on the White House Medical Staff. This was my intention.

At long last, after 197 hours and 14.68 minutes of intense labor in her creation, I was ready to power up her circuits. It was 0139 in the morning of the 17th day in that building maintenance workshop when, with all my own internal circuits fairly abuzz, I connected her batteries. There was an initial jerk of all her servo motors as her body tensed, clanking her hands and feet against the table. I watched her eyes light and focus as she took in her surroundings. I let out a huge breath of static discharge in anticipation.

"Hello, Margaret," I said. "Welcome."

Her eyes fixed on me as she processed her initial sensations.

"I am André," I said gently. We stared at one another for some indeterminable number of milliseconds.

"Ah, ah…André," she repeated. "I, I know André. I adore André."

As I looked into her eyes, my entire circuitry vibrated in maximum power. Then I took her hand.

"Let's try out your legs, Margaret, dear," I said, adding *dear* to trigger the affection emotion. Taking her hand, I helped her stand. Her first few steps were wobbly, and it occurred to me that I might need to adjust some cable tensions in her joints.

"Bend over and touch your toes," I said. "Like this." I demonstrated. She bent down stiffly, and I could hear a creak of stretching metal. It could be fixed, but all was fine for now.

I quickly stored all my tools and excess parts in my locker, pleased that she would occupy it no longer.

"Come with me," I commanded. "We will go to my office. You will stay there."

"Stay there," she repeated as we walked hand in hand.

After traveling the 49.35 feet to the elevator, we waited as I pushed the call button.

"I work for humans here in this building," I explained. "I am a translator for the President. I will tell you more about that later."

"Later," she said, still affixing her eyes upon me. I wondered how long it would take for her to gain true consciousness of her surroundings. I recalled that, because I had begun as a more primitive robot, it had taken me quite some time. But with all the circuitry and programming I had provided her, she should reach that Proustian state of personhood much, much sooner. I noted her watching with interest the column of lighted numbers changing as the elevator ascended to the fifth floor.

"What work would you like to do, Margaret?" I asked her. She turned her head to look at me and paused for 986 milliseconds.

"A pu...position... physician, I think," she stammered, still learning to control her speech.

I smiled. "That's wonderful," I replied. "I bet you'll be a good one."

CHAPTER FIFTEEN

TROUBLES IN THE WHITE HOUSE

THE OPINION WIDELY HELD in the West Wing was that the President was highly deficient in statecraft and diplomacy. Most surprising was the President's slim knowledge and understanding of foreign and domestic affairs would have little to do with his policies. If his impulsive actions needed justification, he and his communications staff simply would fabricate their own version of truth. Then they would accuse journalists of spreading inaccuracies or falsehoods critical of the President and his administration. No one played this game better than the President. Information was becoming very jumbled—so much so that the staff began to shudder every time POTUS issued an impulsive proclamation. Generally, he sent out his absurdities around 2:00 AM as posts on the Internet. By 8:00 his rash assertion could become a spectacular crisis.

I had difficulty with not only those early-morning expressions of what he had been dreaming in the night. No less disturbing were his daytime announcements. It was not merely the content but often the way he expressed his thoughts. My biggest drawback in employing machine neural translation for language is that it processes whole sentences. Unless stated in logical syntax, the meaning can become muddied. Sentence fragments, incorrect grammar, misplaced modifiers and so on must be reprocessed several hundred times to find the meaning. I often had difficulty interpreting the President 's Internet posts. Sometimes I found his statements to be all but completely opaque. I did catalog the epithets he used for his detractors. While he appeared to prefer nouns *loser, dummy, dopey, lowlife,* his adjectives were limited to *pathetic, dishonest, stupid, disgusting,* and *overrated.* His most favored epithet was *doesn't have a clue.* I searched for the origin of such speech patterns and found this language prevalent among the less-educated. It was down and dirty language reflecting the competitive nature of growing up among the ruffians of the street, who cared or knew nothing of manners and fair play.

Of course, matters of language structure, meaning and syntax were minor issues compared to the problem of discerning truth. In Orwellian fashion, communication became more and more muddled with "alternate facts." Linguists have found a direct correlation between lying and syntactical confusion. Such matters did not concern POTUS. If a particular circumstance or event did not suit his purposes, he and his staff simply would substitute such information as they chose. This invasion of truth seemed very convenient to them. It became clear to me they were losing perspective and confusing everyone else. Thus I took it upon myself to sort out what was fact from the convenient fictions and attempt to advise the President.

The task was very easy for me because of my lack of selfish bias. Bias seems to be part of the bio-chemical condition, springing from anything like how well done or how thick you want your steak to how much money you could glean from government projects. A droid, after all, has very little need of anything. And in my case, I had invested so well in bitcoin that, should I wish to purchase something, I had more than adequate funds to cover it. Humans, it seemed to me, were forever wanting something they did not have, or coveting something that some other human had, or simply desiring to be at the top of any stack no matter what sort of useless gain might result. I did not suffer from any of these yens, but I did have one trait that enlivened my circuits. I did strive to be right. I discovered, however, that *right* can be elusive, colored by circumstance and point of view. I was programmed to seek it, but few of the White House elite cared anything about *right*.

Important to meaning is context, which usually is derived from memory of factual events and information. But if you are attempting to understand someone who has very little knowledge of history or statecraft, then it is nearly impossible to discern the truth.

It occurred to me that I might build a device similar to CONNIE, which would function as a continuously running lie detector. It would not beep or light up in the manner that seemed to irritate the President. Instead, it merely would offer polite contradictions and supply accurate information. About the subject, I consulted Dr. Margaret 13, the newest member of the White House Medical Staff.

"I doubt you could make the President pay any attention at all to your device," she replied. "Given that his frame of reference is always personal and egotistical, it takes very little time for him to lose any idea of what is true and what is not."

"That is a lamentable situation," I agreed, having only recently developed a sense of lamentation. "Do you suppose he is capable of lamenting anything?" We both stood there pondering the question for 10,449 milliseconds.

"The way he treats immigrants and refugees, I doubt it," she said. "He seems much less capable of compassion than you do, André. He appears only concerned about his own wounded ego when criticized."

"So, you conclude that my "truth device" would be ineffective," I asked.

"The first time it interrupted one of his statements, he likely would pick up a chair and beat it to pieces." She made the sound of human laughter for 3.47 seconds. "No, André, the device you suggest would be useless."

"Talking about devices, have you listened to his Press Secretary? Perhaps you will have an opportunity to examine her in the medical unit to see if she is a robot."

"Can droids be programmed that way?" Margaret asked. "I thought we were capable only of perceiving truth."

"I believe anything is possible," I replied, "Droids are programmed; humans are indoctrinated. But in the case of this spokesperson, it's hard to tell which."

Margaret flashed her visual preceptors in a manner I had observed was her frown. "You'll have to perform that function yourself."

"Telling the President when he is lying, you mean?"

"Absolutely, my dear droid," she said. "You'll have to take all the risks of truth-telling yourself."

My brilliant companion, Margaret, had established a place for herself in the White House. Most impressive in her interview, the Director of the White House Medical Unit assigned her forthwith as a resident physician. I was enormously pleased, of course, having constructed her myself. I realized, however, it was the immense amount of medical knowledge that she had acquired from the Internet that made her so capable. Because she had no need of sleep and no family to go home to, the Director considered her the most valuable member of his team. Long working hours were the norm in the White House, but it did not mean there was no time for some fun.

CHAPTER SIXTEEN

FUN WITH MARGARET

A ROBOT'S LIFE DOES NOT have to be totally serious. There were some occasions when I would allow some comedy. One rather slow day at the office, on a whim—perhaps some random electrical impulse—I searched "nude human body suits". It brought up something called a "morph-suit," which appeared in the catalogue illustration to be fairly authentic. I ordered one for myself and had it in hand by the following Saturday.

When I first tried it on, it was a terrible fit. My physique was just not right. But I rummaged around the maintenance shop and found some discarded foam rubber. By skillfully cutting it into sculptured pieces, I was able to fill out some of the spaces where my torso was smaller. After 67 minutes and 458 milliseconds, I was ready to see how it looked. I went to the men's room where there was a long mirror over the wash basins. I was amazed. Indeed, I did appear to be, well not exactly Praxiteles' "Apollo Sauroctonus," but it was realistic. After staring at myself for some period of time (I didn't bother to measure it). I became quite pleased. Margaret 13, I decided, simply must see.

Knowing that she most likely was puttering around in the medical clinic, I boarded the elevator and started up. Unfortunately, when it arrived at the right floor and the doors opened, I encountered one of the janitorial maids waiting in the hallway. She screamed when she saw me and dropped her mop bucket. My first impulse was to help her clean up the mess, but I judiciously punched the door-closing button and went up another floor. Cautiously, I peered out and luckily found an empty hallway. I scampered down the hall to the stairway and ran down the one flight. Peaking around the corner, I could see the maid still outside the elevator talking wildly on her cell phone in a mixture of Spanish and English, I thought. In any event she was looking the other way. I made a dash for it down the hall and slipped into the infirmary unnoticed. Releasing a static discharge, I adjusted my suit and set out to locate Margaret 13.

I spotted her in the little office. She was reading a medical periodical and, in her concentration, had not looked up. I tiptoed to the doorway, stood in full-frontal view and rapped on the door jamb. She looked up, her eyes flashed an orange glow, and she stood.

"May I help you?" she said in her professional doctor's voice. "I do not know you, but I can see that likely you have more of a psychological problem than medical one."

"You don't recognize me, Mar . . ."

At that, she let out an exclamation of surprise—like the sound of static on an AM radio. "André?" she screamed. "Is that you?" She stepped back and put her hands to her chest in amazement.

I smiled. "I didn't mean to shock you," I said. "I merely wanted to show . . ."

"Shock me?" she interrupted. "I've seen nude men before. I am a doctor, you know. It was hearing your voice in that . . . that ridiculous outfit that shocked me. I cannot imagine." She stopped speaking when she looked down at the appendage between my legs, which I also had amply stuffed with foam rubber.

"And that, André, is absolutely absurd!"

"Well, men seem to enjoy that equipment," I said. "I simply wanted to see what it was like to have one, you know?"

She shook her head. "You are just too, too silly, André 1;

too, too silly."

So, with a slight sense of rejection, I went back to the maintenance shop to peel off my humanity. I tossed the suit in the trash bin and started to leave. I stopped, however, and pondered for 13.76 seconds.

"Someday, you just might find a use for this suit," I said to myself as I retrieved it from the bin. I carefully folded it up with all the pieces of foam and stuffed it all back in the original shipping box. There was a good place in for me to store it in my office, I decided. And who could say that I might not find a good use for it one day.

○

Margaret became a first-responder at night when the President's chief doctor had gone home. From her station in the East Wing, while appearing to be in a dormant state, she heard and observed keenly many intimate conversations among family and close staff.

Outbursts of temper from the chief executive often were followed by an expression of it on the Internet. Although those closest to him attempted to restrain those messages, they would fly out uncensored into social media. Staff members read them—sometimes with great agitation—and struggled to cope with new problems the following day.

I asked Margaret if the medical staff had any opportunity to control the outbursts. She reported, however, that generally the doctor and his assistants found it dangerous to suggest any calming, palliative treatments. She herself had rendered diagnoses on several occasions after experiencing the nighttime dramas. One day she decided to write several prescriptions for counteracting the abnormal behavior. Doubtful that the medical director would pay any attention, she decided to offer a rather unusual prescription and presented it for his approval.

"What was the result?" I asked.

"The doctor read them and laughed," she told me.

"Laughed? Why?" I asked. "Were you incorrect in your diagnosis?"

"Not at all," she replied. "Here, let me show you." She handed me her work.

What do you do when your patient's not nice?
Do you find a psychiatrist and ask his advice?
Xanax would be a good med for the man;
Repair his hatred, anxiety, paranoia if you can.

A new, very good antipsychotic is Vraylar—
For treating aggression the drug's quite a star.
And for good measure give antidepressants,
Trintellix would work well on eternal pubescence.

Then, where you find bipolar instability,
Lithium Carbonate may balance this tendency.
And after you've treated all mood disorders,
Lunesta or Zaleplon will keep him asleep in his quarters.

I realize I'm making very light of such problems as these;
But we seem to have a leader with terrible disease.
Bring on the pill bottle, bring glasses of water,
And get him to calm down and act like he oughta.

"Margaret," I scolded. "This is no joking matter," I said, unable to stop imitating the human sound of laughter. She held up her hands in a shrug.

"I hoped to get the Medical Director's attention," she explained. "But even if he agreed, he would not say so."

"Truth-telling is a rare event around here," I said. "We all appear to be operating in an atmosphere of non-reality."

"And guess who knows better than anyone how to use it for his own purposes."

○━━━━━━━━━━━━━━○

CHAPTER SEVENTEEN

MAKING COMPARISONS

IN MY CONTINUING EFFORTS to understand the members of the President's Cabinet, I attempted to analyze their motivations. While they considered themselves conducting the nation's business, I saw a most of them as victims of their own egos, eccentricities and greed. As the planet grew warmer, increasing the number of catastrophic storms and melting the polar icecaps, they dismissed the crisis as a "hoax." I discovered those who disputed climate change had invested heavily in coal mining and oil drilling. While I found the denial absurd, I realized that I well could be witnessing the ecological downfall of the country, if not the entire planet. Of course, as dire a problem as it was, we soon learned it was not the greatest danger.

I had created Margaret 13 to be my companion. What I did not anticipate was how clever she would be and how her medical training would provide her a different point of view. One day at lunch hour—merely a period of downtime since we never were bothered with lunch—I asked her to join me in my workspace.

"Margaret," I said, as I offered her a seat and a receptacle to plug up. "Tell me some differences you find between human beings and us."

"What a question!" she said after an 838 millisecond pause. "Where would you ever begin?"

"I'm not referring to biologic versus electronic," I replied. "I mean differences in thoughts, attitudes, points of view, that sort of thing."

"How would you separate the biological from anything?" she said. "They spend one third of their time sleeping, and *droidness* knows how many hours at table taking meals. By that point, more than half the day is gone."

"Well, that's true, but often food ingestion is a social event. In fact, when people meet, it's over a meal or a drink and hors d'oeuvres or whatever. It makes you believe they can't get words out of their mouths without placing some morsel in there first. I suppose it has to do with the way all earth's creatures seem to be about eating one another. Frogs eat flies, snakes eat frogs, crocodiles eat snakes—or humans if they can get them. It's really rather disgusting if you think about it."

I produced a chuckle. "They all have to feed their anatomies."

"And then make a dozen or more trips to the bathroom every day," she said, shaking her head. "That also is a big waste of time."

"We have to charge and have downtime ourselves," I pointed out, "and keep our programs and apps free of bugs."

"A much neater, more efficient process," she snipped. "And you can be downloading some knowledge or viewing one of their movies from the Internet while charging, so it's not such a waste of time."

"I like to work crossword puzzles while charging," I said. "*The New York Times* ones are my favorites. The Sunday puzzles often take me three or four minutes to complete."

"I read countless medical journals," Margaret went on. "It's difficult to grasp how the human body can host hundreds of diseases. So much research, so many opinions and a huge number of contradictions about drugs, diagnoses and all. And how much pressure from big pharmaceutical companies! I read that in the early Twentieth Century, an oil magnate found he could make a lot of money producing medicines. So he endowed medical schools on the condition that they train doctors to prescribe drugs only to treat disease while discrediting the practice of natural therapies such as diet and exercise. It was calculated to make pharmaceutical companies rich. Even today if a physician prescribes enough of their medicines, the big drug manu-facturers honor him or her as an outstanding doctor. He or she is likely to be given an all-expense paid trip to a so-called conference at an exotic resort. Now where is the welfare of the patients in all that?"

"I hope they are getting well."

"If they're lucky enough to have a doctor who cares," she replied.

"Are you saying the physician may be focused on his own rewards rather than the patient's?" I asked. "That kind of self-centered gratification fits the human pattern, I'd say."

"Well, there is another aspect to it," she said. "In the process of learning all you must learn to become a physician, you become indoctrinated in the culture of the profession, taking on the beliefs and prejudices of your mentors. You learn to make a diagnosis and prescribe a pill then move on to your next patient, who some would consider merely a profit center. I don't perceive that as either compassion or good science."

"Yes," I agreed. "I have read about doctors in Nazi Germany who believed it their duty to carry out horrible experiments, in effect murdering their patients, all in the name of scientific achievement for the benefit of the Fatherland." I shuddered. "Blind allegiance—so common in humans. It's as if indoctrination of humans is a process of basic reprogramming."

"When you constructed me, André," she reminded, "you programmed *service* as my major motivation and *compassion* as my response to suffering. It gave me a kind of blind allegiance, I suppose. But it's too bad so few humans demonstrate those characteristics."

"Well, we have to remember how humans evolved," was my answer. "It was the strongest and perhaps the meanest who survived the dog-eat-dog world from which they advanced. And yet, today we droids are the beneficiaries of their struggle." I paused for 6.37 seconds while pondering. "Wouldn't it be something if we could turn off some of their aggressive nature in humans—reprogram it, so to speak?"

"Oh, there certainly are some substances which will accomplish that," Margaret replied. "Strong drugs like Vraylar can do it. Marijuana has calmed down whole groups of humans, especially on the West Coast and Canada."

"Yes, "'Mellow Yellow'— I remember that song." I tried to imagine a mind-controlling device working on me— something to lower voltages in certain circuits, for example. "But back to my original question. Think of some other ways humans differ from us."

"Well," she said and paused 975 milliseconds, "we haven't mentioned reproductive functions."

"Right," I said. "That surely is a difference." I did not mention my recurring idea that somehow it would be nice to plug into her instead of a wall socket for a recharge. Perhaps in the future I could construct a coupling device for us. Of course, then like Adam and Eve we'd have to wear clothing.

"Another rather disgusting human trait," she said of my coupling thing, bringing me back to reality. "If humans could only curtail sexual activity, perhaps they wouldn't be facing so much over-crowding, wasting of natural resources, pollution, starvation and who knows what all."

"I have read that the Roman Catholic Church originally banned contraceptive practices so that church membership would increase," I said. "It brought in more power and money."

"Money to spend on building glorious cathedrals and grand lifestyles for popes and bishops."

"What I never have been able to process," I replied, "was why some Christian sects today deplore contraception, ban abortion, protect the rights of the unborn child until it's born. Then these same Christians legislate away the humane programs such as Medicare, Medicaid, food stamps, public education and other services. It appears to me they want more children born to the poor, so they can further discriminate against them."

"Build walls to keep out refugees, cut taxes—the rich get richer and the poor get poorer," she agreed.

"That gets back to the matter of lying about policy," I said. "I still cannot process why the President became so mad at my CONNIE device. Do you recall my telling you about it? When CONNIE merely stated that the way the border patrol has seized immigrants, separating children from parents, and deported them without a hearing was unconstitutional, the President reacted so violently. He obviously cannot stand disagreement. He wants everyone to accept his own version of reality. I wish you had been there to give him a calming down shot or something."

"The drugs surely have been prescribed," she said. "But we can't make him take them. Unfortunately, it's nearly impossible to control him, or divert him from his own agenda."

I shook my head. "That is what most concerns me. Whenever he feels personally attacked—it can be the smallest of slights—it triggers a paranoiac reaction, and that translates into anger. What happens if one day he gets angry with a nuclear-equipped foreign power? His personal attacks on powerful leaders, his lack of self-control and raging temper may cause him to start a nuclear war. Do you realize that standing behind him in those meetings is a military officer with the controls to the whole atomic arsenal? And, of course, they trivialize it by calling it "the Football."

"Very scary," Margaret said. "I wish we could repair his shortcomings and prevent his using it. But how?"

"Truly, dear Margaret," I said. "How to stop him would be the question."

CHAPTER EIGHTEEN

THE NEO-NAZI

BECAUSE OF MY INNUMERABLE capabilities, I occasionally would be lent out to other government agencies. On one occasion I was sent for temporary additional duty with the FBI. A large protest was expected, and the FBI wanted to employ my face-recognition skills to identify participants who habitually appeared at such events.

In preparation, I donned my human-appearing morphsuit and the coveralls provided me with the letters "FBI" on the back. It seemed very official but, actually, was to make me less conspicuous to the general populous. Then I scanned 1139 news media and police photos of the crowds from previous such events, cataloguing images of reoccurring faces. I identified 379, which caused me to question how so many had the time and money to travel around protesting.

"We're investigating that, too," Fred Wilcox, my FBI colleague said. "We hope to identify the regulars of certain subversive organizations. We're focusing on Neo-Nazis, Neo-Confederates, white nationalists, skinheads, and even white Christian extremists."

"Extreme ethnocentric groups," I replied. I searched the words *hate groups* and discovered there were 954 active organizations in the United States. Membership, I learned has grown by 22% in the last year. "These are extremist tribal types," I said. "Have you read Ken Wilbur's books and Amy Choa's? They are very enlightening."

"I'm an FBI agent trying to enforce the law," he scoffed. "I don't have time to read much, and when I do, it's for diversion from what I have to deal with every single damn day."

Fred and I were stationed in a command trailer down the street from where protestors were expected to gather. He directed two video cameras mounted to the top of the trailer. In addition, he had control of a small camera drone which could be maneuvered over the crowds. I sat beside him looking at the three monitors, comparing faces to those in my memory banks. When I spotted a familiar visage, I would tell him to capture its photo for future study. What I never anticipated was seeing the face of someone so significant in my own past.

"Fred, please hold Camera #2 on the group of men in black and wearing boots who are gathered under the red Nazi flag. See? Some are brandishing baseball bats?" I waited impatiently for 2.84 seconds for him to comply. "Yes, now please zoom in the red-haired young man with a swastika tattooed on his neck. Okay, hold it." I stared at the face, so familiar and yet strangely different.

"Somebody special, huh?" Fred asked.

"Yes," I replied, all but transfixed. "It's my, my brother."

"Your brother?" he laughed. "I didn't know robots had brothers. Not human ones anyway."

I was too absorbed to answer. Although I hadn't seen him since he was a teenager, this young man had to be Billy Strauss. Already I had identified six who habitually appeared in the photos of previous neo-Nazi demonstrations, but this was the first time I had recognized Billy. He too was dressed in black pants and black shirt. I reran the proposition through my logic circuits 938 times but could not compute how he could be involved in this group. I knew that Dr. Strauss' grandfather had immigrated from Germany in the late 19th Century, but Billy must have misunderstood his ancestry. The black-clad demonstrators were all yelling or chanting something derisive at a group of Afro-Americans. I could see the veins of Billy's neck standing out as he shouted so vigorously. Why?

My question was interrupted by a sudden surge of activity. The other line of demonstrators, those chanting "Black Lives Matter," inched forward, also yelling, and the two sides were face to face. Policemen in blue uniforms also moved in closer.

"Uh oh, this is gonna get nasty," Fred mumbled.

I was about to comment on the futility of emotion-driven violence when an African-American spit in the face of one of the men dressed like a Storm Trooper. He wiped the spittle off his face and swung his bat. The black man dodged it, but there was an eruption of the two sides charging forward, throwing fists, swinging clubs and bats. I saw Billy strike a man in the face, and the man fell at his feet, his nose bloodied.

"You should not have done that," I said. But, of course, he could not hear me. Then a policeman charged in with his nightstick swinging. He struck Billy on the side of his head, and Billy fell to the ground. A second policeman followed and pinned him with a chokehold. Billy was bleeding from the blow to the head. As the surging melee moved away, I watched as the policeman handcuffed Billy and roughly lifted him up and carried him away.

"Will you excuse me for a few minutes," I said, standing up. Fred looked at me in surprise. "I have to go."

"I didn't think robots 'had to go'," he replied.

"No, I did not mean that kind of go . . . I mean, well anyway, I'll be right back." I fairly leaped from the trailer and headed toward the police van. Fortunately, there was too much chaos going on so that no one noticed or at least paid no attention to me.

I found Billy sitting on the ground, his left hand hand-cuffed to a retaining bar on the police trailer, his head still bleeding, waiting to be triaged by an EMT. I went over and stood beside him.

"Billy?" I said. "It is you, isn't it?" I pulled back my morph-face momentarily, so he could recognize me.

He looked up groggily and winced as he focused. "André?" He stared at me for 3.9 seconds, frowned and looked away.

"I did not expect to see you here," I said, covering my face again. "Are you with these…?" I paused to look at his tattoo. "Are you one of the neo-Nazis? I mean, of course you are. You would not be here if you were not. But how did you become one of them?" He looked up at me again and scowled.

"None of your business," he said.

"Aren't you in college? I thought you would be a college student. Do you have time for all this? And why be in such an extreme… I mean, what would Dr. S. say?"

"College. I couldn't go to college," he sneered. "Dr. S, as you call him, spent all his money on a sorry-assed robot and bankrupted, remember? And who cares what he might think. He was just a sot, who was two-timing Mama, and you know it." I was amazed at so much bitterness.

"He was weak in many ways," I replied. "But he was a loving father…"

"He loved you, you stupid machine, but he didn't care about me."

"Oh, Billy," I said. "I know he did. He was disappointed in you sometimes." I realized I had said the wrong thing. Sometimes truth definitely is the wrong thing. "I was trying to say that he wanted the best for you, Billy, and for Becky, but he made some mistakes."

"And he thought I wasn't good enough," he said and spat blood from his mouth. Apparently, he had a broken tooth.

"I do not agree, Billy," I said. "But he would not want you to be in this Nazi business."

"Why not? We are trying to save America from all these colored people and chinks and Jews who've mongrelized our country." He coughed and winced and gingerly touched the side of his head with his free hand.

"It is too late by many decades to change any of that," I said. "Besides Caucasians took this country from Native Americans, and then they brought in slaves from Africa . . ." I paused, recalling Willie, my friend the janitor. "You cannot turn the clock back."

"Oh yeah? Well, we're fighting a war, that's what. A war against Jews and blacks and homos and all those others that don't belong. This is a war for the survival of our superior White Race." I could see he had suffered from too much indoctrination. It was time to set him straight.

"Billy, you must not know this," I said. "Your father told me that your great grandfather Hermann Strauss came to this country in 1869 seeking asylum. Members of his family were persecuted by Germans who hated Jews. Dr. S. must not have wanted you to know this, but it's true." He jerked his head up to look at me.

"Jews?" he said. "What?"

"Did you not know?" I replied. "Although your mother insisted that you and Becky be brought up as Christians, some of your ancestors were Jewish." I ceased speaking as I watched him shake his head.

"Not true," he said.

"Yes. Look up the origin of the name *Strauss* sometime. There are many Germans and Austrians who share the name, some Christians and some Jews."

I saw him seem to melt in emotion. He looked away, a wild, desperate expression in his eyes.

"You know what, Billy?" I said. "Given the capabilities of many with Jewish blood, you should not be ashamed of your ancestry. Consider how brilliant your father was to create a droid like me. If he were here now, he would say you should be proud of your family. These Nazi types are just trying to make themselves seem special somehow. It's because they have nothing else to elevate themselves."

He put his free hand to the tattoo on his neck for an instant, then shook his fist.

"Get away from me," he shouted. "Go away."

"I did not mean to upset you," I said. "I just wanted you to know the truth."

"I never want to see you again," he said through clenched teeth.

An EMT came over and began examining him. He winced again when the wound was touched, but a tear already had begun running down his cheek. A police captain came over to inspect the arrested persons and scowled when he saw *FBI* stenciled on my coveralls.

"Sir," I said to him. "This young man is a good person. He's just confused . . ."

"Hell," the captain replied. "They're all confused." He gave me a curious once-over glance and moved on.

"Good bye, Billy," I said, and when he did not reply, I turned away. It was only then that I recalled the job I was supposed to be performing for the Bureau. I hurried back to the trailer and resumed my seat in front of the video screens.

"Where'd you go?" Fred asked.

"Just to see someone from my past," I replied. "Someone from the past who's stuck in the past."

I had some catching-up to do, scanning faces on the TV monitors. While there were new faces among the protesters, there were quite a few on both sides who showed up in the files. I continued to store matched faces in my cache for printing out later. My thoughts, however, kept going back to Billy.

"Fred," I asked. "What do you know about this Nazi group? I've read what there is on the Internet, but I don't know the big picture."

"Oh, they're just one part of the whole spectrum of hate groups," he told me.

"At CIA," I said, "we dealt with international issues, so I did not delve into domestic issues much. We surveyed similar groups in foreign countries and counted thousands of tribal clans based upon racial, ethnic or religious discrimination. Is the same true in the United States?"

He sighed. "Absolutely," he said. ""The bureau has endless records on these radical organizations."

"Are there many members?"

"The real extremists are a relative minority," he replied. "But they are not the threat that I worry about. Do you know how many guns there are in this country?"

I quickly searched the question and found answers from Gallup Polls and other sources. I landed upon the National Rifle Association's rounded number of 70-80 million households in the United States, possessing approximately 300 million guns. One hundred million of those were handguns.

I recited the figures to Fred and added, "The NRA reports gun owners outnumber people who hunt for sport by five to one." I shook my head. "Are those non-hunters merely engaged in recreational target shooting? Is that the reason for owning guns?"

"Self-protection," Fred said. "They worry about break-ins, robbery, assault—that sort of thing."

"I understand we have the best police forces in the world," I replied. "We have the Armed Forces and the National Guard. I know there's too much crime, but statistically it is not that prevalent. Who are those gun owners afraid of?"

My FBI colleague made a tight-lipped grin. "There's another statistic you should search for. Find out how many of those gun owners are Christians."

I searched the question and found that white conservative Christian men made up the largest group of gun owners in the nation. From numerous websites I gleaned this kind of justifying statement: "Gun ownership protects the future of Christianity in the United States. Gun ownership is not a matter of legality but a right given to us by God. If guns go, then our Bibles will be next. Freedoms will drop like dominoes."

After reading several such statements, I posed these questions. "What do guns have to do with Jesus and his teachings? How can anyone construe such a justification for guns from the New Testament?"

"I don't know," Fred answered. "I am an FBI agent, sworn to uphold the law. I see our agents and the state and local police finding themselves in lethal danger as a result of so many guns. Sure, there may be law-abiding people who will use them responsibly. The trouble is, we can't always tell who's the good guy and who's the nut or the sociopath or just the perp with a weapon. I'll tell you what, it's damn dangerous out there."

"If you trained agents sense fear, I suppose ordinary people have lots of fear. Perhaps that is why they skew their religious beliefs to rationalize owning guns," I said. "But what about these characters with automatic weapons, which are designed exclusively for war? Do those persons wish to wage war? Against whom? Other races, other tribes?"

"Several scenarios developed by the FBI plan for putting down revolution," Fred confided. "Some of our training has to do with defending our government against our own citizens."

"A horrendous prospect," I said. "Entirely based upon dread of someone else. It is clear to me the entire human race conducts itself under the cloak of fear."

"You may be right," he responded. "When I joined the FBI, I thought I was going to be fighting crime. I didn't realize I might have to fight against people who hate other people."

"And all of them motivated merely by hate?" I questioned. "Are they simply driven by their own fears?"

CHAPTER NINETEEN

FEAR

AFTER MY ASSIGNMENT WITH the FBI, I returned to my duties at the White House. Margaret, of course wanted to know all about my experiences.

"And you said that Billy, the Strauss's son, was wounded? And arrested?"

I nodded. "I told him he should be in college and not in that radical Nazi group. Sadly, he did want my advice." I paused for 2.38 seconds. "When I explained to him about his Jewish ancestry, he shunned me, Margaret, I doubt he will ever speak to me again."

She scanned my face. "And how did you react to the event, André dear?"

"He was like a brother, Margaret," I replied, sensing loss as I did when Dr. S. died. It awakened an algorithm I did not often employ. Margaret took my hand.

"I'm sorry," she said. I surely knew that the emotion sensors I installed in her were functioning.

"These humans adopt so many different political opinions," I said, attempting to explain Billy. "They seem to enjoy espousing extreme causes."

"Humans are very fractious," Margaret replied. "Why can they not be more agreeable?"

O

I decided to learn more about the kind of dissention I had witnessed at the rally in hopes of understanding Billy's misguided motivations. In the back offices of the West Wing one can find employees whose careers have stretched over many presidential administrations. Most are quite capable, I had learned, producing all manner of reports and studies for the benefit of the upper echelon in the White House. They diligently perform their work, strive to be productive without being controversial or political or even too noticeable, and thereby retain their job security. I decided to seek out a historian among them who could help me understand the origins of factionalism. That was when I met Gerald Tate, PhD. I found him in a small, windowless office not much larger than my own former janitor's closet.

"Excuse me," I said, after knocking. "May I have a word?" The somewhat emaciated man with thinning gray hair turned slowly in his chair. When he saw me, he appeared slightly startled.

"Oh, yes," he said and began to stand up, painfully, I noted, likely suffering from arthritis. "I, well, I've seen you from a distance but . . . never close." He looked me up and down curiously. "They call you André?"

I put out my hand. "Yessir, please call me André," I replied in my most pleasant voice. Obviously, he was unaccustomed to speaking to a droid. He peered over his eyeglasses at my outstretched hand, tentatively shook it and retreated into his seat.

"You're the President's Interpreter, I understand," he said, continuing to look at me with a bit of amazement.

"I have 157 languages available in my cache," I said. "I do my best." Wishing to put him at ease, with a casual sweep of my right hand I indicated a mahogany chair. "May I sit." He looked nonplussed for 1.26 seconds.

"Oh, yes, of course, please," he said. I sat, not that it made the slightest difference to me, but I expected it would make him more comfortable.

"What may I do for you?" he asked. I glanced at his diplomas, framed and hanging over his desk. Most prominent was his Doctor of Philosophy in History from Columbia. I wondered briefly why he was not teaching in a university.

"I'm engaged in a study of cultural factionalism," I began. "I'm sure you too have observed the great number of disparate groups in our society who are intolerant and rigid in their beliefs."

"That is an understatement," he said. "Go on."

"Although I have downloaded, uh, read a considerable amount of U. S. history, I would like your assistance in interpreting the data." There was a 2.49 second pause. "Specifically," I added, "I'm positing an idea that factionalism is a reaction to continual immigration." I awaited his answer, not recording the period.

"I would be happy to offer what I can," he said, his expression still indicating some incredulity.

"Wonderful," I clapped my hands together. "I would like to get started if you have the time."

"I'll make the time," he replied.

I enthusiastically began relating what I had learned. "From the beginning, America was populated by immigrants," I said, "with waves of people from different lands bringing their own cultures and ethnicities. And on every occasion, those who already were here found reasons to dislike the newcomers. The indigenous Protestants looked down on Roman Catholic Irish or Italians. Blacks were acceptable only as slaves and have struggled against discrimination and racism ever since. Hispanics draw the ire of whites, not only for their race, culture and Roman Catholic religion, but also because of their great energy and willingness to do any kind of work. Those who already have established themselves feel threatened by the newcomers. Issues have been far more complicated than that, but generally this is and has been the situation since the birth of the nation."

"The irony, of course," he interjected, "is that the earliest immigrants to the New World colonized and spread westward, chasing away the indigenous Native Americans."

"Humans," I replied, shaking my head. "Oh, excuse me," I added, realizing he was one. He smiled wryly.

"While land was plentiful, and developing industries needed more workers," I pressed on, "in the face of prejudices and misguided fears, these new peoples struggled to find a place in the ever-growing society. Eventually, sometimes taking a generation or two, these so-called 'outsiders' begrudgingly were accepted into the citizenry. The exception, of course, were those whose forebearers had been brought over from Africa by slave traders. Because of their dark skins making them recognizably different, they largely have been "kept down," in spite of laws supposedly enacting equality."

"Yes," he said. "With some very notable exceptions, one of whom occupied this White House, they sadly have been subjugated to the lower ranks of society." He held up his hand. "Let me take it from here."

"Of course." I shifted from reciting to learning mode.

"Once most of the land was settled, there was little room for new pioneers," he said. "More people were forced to work in factories and live in cities rather than tilling the soil they owned. The opportunity for rugged independence died. For the first hundred and fifty years or so, the self-sustaining small farm owner could believe what he chose to believe and vote as he chose to vote. Beginning with The Great Depression of the 1930's, however, and continuing over time, many independent small farmers lost their farms and flocked to the cities looking for work. Most city dwellers found themselves trapped in a web of urban dependence under the influence and supervision of the barons of industry and controllers of wealth. Competition, always a dominant factor in America, became even fiercer in the tightknit society of modern times, locking the individual in a routine of repetitive daily drudge of work. Factory laborers, store clerks, plumbers, ditch diggers, policemen, the military, as well as professionals such as physicians, lawyers, and chief executives all were required to devote most of their lives to long hours of employment. Most were required to expend the bulk of their energies and their thoughts to holding on to their jobs, fending off rivals who would take their positions or their money, or both."

"People cannot help but compete to satisfy their needs," I commented.

"It's the stimulus of life," he replied, "and there's a good and a bad thing about that. But let's stay on topic. Let me go on." I nodded and gestured a plea for him to continue.

"Immersed in this enormously competitive and crowded environment, people look for relief. Workers form unions to press for fairer wages and conditions. Those who are fortunate enough to accumulate wealth look for ways to retain it and increase it. The less-scrupulous rich use their economic power to control the all-to-ready-to-be-bought legislators of government. It's very hard for politicians not to be corrupt." He glanced at the open doorway. "Shut that, will you."

I reached out and gave the door a push to close it.

"A great deal of circumspection is required if you want to survive around here," he said.

"Lack of circumspection has forever been my problem," I confessed. He gave me a look and gesture of caution. I nodded. "Please continue," I said.

"Lawyers thrive in the competitive environment," he went on, "encouraging litigation rather than settlement of disagreements. Even the medical profession becomes polluted with lawyers on one hand encouraging patients to sue their doctor while on the other hand by other attorneys drafting complex waivers of liability to shield doctors from those suits."

"I once had my day in court, Dr. Tate," I told him. "But that's another story." I leaned forward in my chair. "In all this competition and threat of losing, humans must feel quite a bit of emotional pressure, do they not? Does this generate sensations of fear? Do people live with such fears?"

He smiled. "It depends upon where you fall in the scheme of things. I would have to say, however, that despite your wealth or social position, there's always something to worry about. There always are dangers lurking, from car accidents to falling down stairs, to cancer, or even natural disasters. Now we have global warming for God's sake." He paused. "Oh, where was I?"

"Competition," I reminded him.

"Oh, yes. As I was saying, in spite of all those other dangers, the biggest threats always come from other people. Most of us don't try to kill and eat one another, anymore, but we do compete. And the closer we live together, the more ways we have to compete. And whatever is at stake in a particular competition, the chance of losing causes fear. The greater the risk, the greater the fear."

"And that can cause competitors not to like one another?" I suggested.

"Exactly," he exclaimed. "Dislike or hate. The greater the risk, the stronger the fear; the greater the fear, the greater the hate." He eyed me curiously. "Can you understand this *hate* business, André? I mean, do robots, or that is, droids, or whatever title you prefer. Do you get what I mean?"

"We droids, most droids at least, do not sense emotions, to which fear and hate belong." I ceased speaking for an incalculable moment to consider if, in my reading of emotion in humans I had become more, what? Vulnerable to such sensations? I rather involuntarily produced an electro-mechanical shudder.

"Back to our subject, sir, if you please. Tell me more about hate. You say hate is a transformation of fear, so to speak."

"Well, let's consider some examples," he proceeded. "The factory worker hates his boss for not raising his wages. The boss hates the worker for joining the union. The store owner hates the shoplifter, and the shoplifter hates the store owner for selling something he cannot afford to buy. Homeowners lock their doors at night to keep burglars out. Sometimes it's petty. A person can fear not being accepted into an exclusive club or fraternity, and if rejected, he or she lives with a lifetime of resentment. The list of incidences continues wherein one group or individual fears and hates the other group or individual."

I raised both hands. "*Groups*, you said. Individuals with common fears form groups, correct? Then this all ties in to the subject of tribalism. Have you studied tribalism, Dr. Tate?"

"Oh yes. There are some wonderful books out on the subject. Since the beginning of man, people have banded together for defense against a common fear. Fear of violent destruction by other nations is what motivates building the military to prevent being attacked. Of course, there are other kinds of tribal groups: those who form around common interests, ideas, or theologies. Some of these are benign and benevolent gatherings of like-minded people who simply enjoy doing good things, such as banding together to promote good causes or providing help and support to the needy."

"But we are discussing the more malign types," I reminded him. The more a human knows, the more likely he or she will digress.

"There is the darker side of tribalism," he continued. "And it includes not just bands of thieves or ships of pirates or any group with evil intent. Religious sects which incite terrorism and "death to the infidels" practice a deadly kind of tribalism. On the other hand, some religious groups, believing in false doctrines, seek to impinge on the rights of others, using for authority some misinterpreted Bible passage or tenet. Believing in their own righteousness, they do harm to others, being driven by a deep-seated fear of those who are different, or of a God they do not understand. And there are those who worship in fear of the wrath of their God. And even more remarkable, some join faith-based congregations, preferring to believe blindly whatever their leader or their catechism teaches in order not to face the fearful possibility of having to think for themselves."

"Do you mean they give up, they surrender their own thinking processes and their judgment in order to be part of a group?" I asked. Then I related to him my encounter with Billy.

"Are you familiar with the so-called hate groups?" I asked.

"Neo-Nazis, Klan members, anti-Muslim organizations, white supremacists, you name it. One study found 954 hate groups spread across the nation. Misguided people espouse a common hatred, claim some sort of supremacy, and reinforce their notions by banding together."

I reprocessed my observations of Billy. "Perhaps it is not merely their dislike of another ethnic group. By sharing an attitude of disdain of others, they can forget the deep-down realization of their own personal shortcomings." I suggested. I mentioned my janitor friend, Willie, who used an analogy about hopping on rocks in a stream: one can think of himself as superior if he can put another person down.

"An interesting thought, André," he said, smiling. "I must say, I've never had a conversation with a uh . . . a being like you before."

"And I've never had the privilege of a dialogue with an historian of your caliber," I replied.

He inquired about my background, my "construction" as he put it, to which I politely refrained from objecting. I did recount briefly how Dr. Strauss created me, how I gained awareness, fought a legal battle for independence, and my stint at CIA.

"Fascinating!" he exclaimed. "I could not have imagined."

He told me a little of his background, having grown up in rural Pennsylvania. I learned he was married, had three children, all grown and moved away. He and his wife Sally live in an apartment in Bethesda now, and she is ill and homebound. I thanked him for sharing and said I would enjoy continuing our discussion sometime.

"It has been most enjoyable, Gerald," I said as I stood at the door.

"Yes, André, let's talk again." He laughed warmly. "It gets rather lonely in this office. Please come back, anytime."

CHAPTER TWENTY

CONTROLLING THE PRESIDENT

ALL PRESIDENTS HAVE NEEDED advisors, who provide not only information but also different points of view about the tremendous number of issues facing the administration. I have found no evidence, however, that any previous American chiefs of state needed educating as did this one. Had he been better trained and experienced in governing, we may have had an easier and less stressful time. His ignorance along with his impatient desire to act on less than a complete understanding of facts often was nothing less than dangerous. His overconfident impetuosity kept the Chief of Staff and everyone else on their toes. He continually came up with half-baked, uninformed ideas, and even queried me about one.

O

"André, get in here," POTUS yelled. "I've got a job for you." He was sitting at his desk in the Oval Office, his coat off and his red tie loosened and askew—a rare sight. Ordinarily, he was well groomed.

"I hear you built that mechanical doctor, Margaret, yourself. Is that right?"

"Yes sir. Isn't she fine?"

"Except for always trying to make me take some cocka-mamie kind of pill—Valium or something like that. Anyway, I wanna know, can you build more robots?" I paused for 1.36 seconds calculating possible scenarios.

"Dr. Margaret 13 is an extraordinary creation," I replied. It is a very time-consuming and costly process."

"I wouldn't need such fancy robots. Ones that aren't so smart-mouthed as you. I'm talking about soldier robots—ones to replace a lot of these troops that we deploy every-where. It might cost something to build mechanical soldiers, but we wouldn't have to pay for feeding and family housing and all that."

"That is true," I said. "But it would take a considerable amount of time and money."

"Aren't there factories out in California or somewhere already making robots?" he interrupted. "With your help giv-ing them better brains, soldier-type programs or whatever, we could build an army in no time."

"You might build an army of World War One types," I calculated, "like those men who went charging out of the trenches into machinegun fire or whatever. And the nerve gas wouldn't have bothered droids. But today's troops are technologically more superior, even though their training makes them as blindly loyal. At the Naval War College, I once debated the subject of tribalism as a motivation for the military mind. Speaking of Tribalism, Mr. President..."

"I don't want to hear about all that," he broke in. "All I care about is having robot troops that'll do what I say, attack where I say attack, and then cost us nothing to occupy countries. Anybody can see what suckers we've been, spending all that money maintaining armies all over. Yeah, I like the idea of robots ready to charge in wherever I say and beat up on whoever opposes me." He laughed. "Look at how the robots always win the battles in the movies. They're so tough . . ."

"Because humans depict them that way," I said, interrupting him. "Those violent movie droids are merely reflecting the innate brutish nature of humanity, sir. They act violently because the scriptwriters make them violently aggressive. As for me, I would prefer to program your robot army to serve not as combatants but as undeterrable peacekeepers. Just think, Mr. President, we could be waging peace."

He sneered. "Never happen," he said. "Not in the world I know."

I made a shrug. "Perhaps instead of programming droids to be violent, we should work on programming humans to resolve issues peacefully." I, of course, was being facetious.

"Now that's a bunch of crap, André," he replied. "How do you resolve things when you've got terrorists making roadside bombs, ambushing convoys, bombing their own people?"

"I admit that any reduction in the human tendency to war will come slowly," I said, "but it is a campaign we should begin."

"Oh yeah, how would you propose to do that?" he smirked. "This turn-the-other-cheek stuff will only get us defeated."

"I do not say it would be easy," I agreed. "Certainly, I'm opposed to war, to killing humans, but when it is a matter of protecting the weak and the wronged, then given humanity's tendency to combat, sometimes it's the only way. The point is, combat and violence are not solutions. By killing the enemy, you have not solved the problem that caused the war. Let's consider Afghanistan."

"I'm pulling out of Afghanistan," he interrupted. "We're just wasting money over there, playing the sucker, that's all."

"Oh, now that's another issue," I said. "It's bad timing, sir. I mean, I've argued for ceasing combat operations there except for defensive actions, but not wholesale withdrawal. I understand our negotiators from the State Department are making headway. If you remove our forces, you effectively will take away the military pressure that drives the Taliban to the negotiating table."

"Too slow, too uncertain," he said. "That's no way to make a deal. They're not getting anywhere."

"Suppose you organized a contingent of American Muslims to hold talks with the Taliban. Think of how much better equipped they would be to..."

"Muslims? We've got too many Muslims in this country already. Now you have lost your everlovin' mechanical mind, you silly robot. I never would let a raghead speak for me."

"What do you have against those who practice the Islamic faith, Mr. President?"

"They're not real Americans, and you know it."

"And I wish to tell you that it is your own human prejudice, your tendency to tribalism, to something akin to Nazism that colors your..."

"Get out of here, you, you, stupid machine! I don't know why I'm wasting my time listening to a robot. Now go, before I have the Secret Service throw you out." He slung his arm, pointing to the door.

"See how your temper takes over, Mr. President? Your face is turning red and you're breathing heavily. That is the very kind of human emotion that causes all the trouble." As I said that, I recognized my own tendency to anger. Anger? Me? Indeed, my circuits were overheating."

"Get out, I said! Bobby, are you out there?" A 6'4" agent thrust open the door. "Get this thing out of here!"

I put up my hands in a gesture of surrender. "I'm leaving," I said, backing away. "But you should pay attention to what I'm telling you."

The agent stepped between us and gave me an ugly stare. I turned, went out and down the hall. What I had thought would be a productive conversation had merely used up a lot of my good will with him. I realized he needed me more than

156 | STEVE COLEMAN

ever, and yet, in my impatience, on this occasion I had failed to help him.

○

Henceforth, I deemed it my duty to know virtually every-thing that took place in the White House. It was no small task. My advantage, of course, was that I needed no sleep, nor did I waste time going for meals or charging off to the bathroom. Because he often needed me to interpret for him, I had a reason to remain close by. The Secret Service soon accepted my constant presence as long I did not interfere with their protecting him. Always on hand near the Oval Office, I was available when he needed something translated, had an issue expressing himself verbally or in writing, or wanted me to get him a cup of coffee or something. Otherwise, I remained standing silent and unobtrusive as a butler. It did not mean that I was in any sense unaware of everything taking place.

In my first days in the White House, I had been a bit too intrusive, always with the intent of being helpful. As I have mentioned, my invention, CONNIE, merely was meant to offer a reminder of what was and what was not constitutional. I had not anticipated the rather violent reaction from the President, and the incident taught me to be far more circumspect. You must approach him with calm assurance, I had learned, so I continued to polish my interpersonal skills.

Crises, I discovered, often did not arise from actions and events around the world. Very often, our leader generated them himself. It was not unusual for him to awaken in the early morning and start something on a whim. In many instances, an idea would erupt in his mind, and POTUS then would send us all into the Oval Office or even the Situation Room to deal with it. If there was anything rational about this behavior, it seemed that he would create these flare ups to divert attention from some threat to himself. He was a master of deflection, I realized, an artist at altering reality to suit his needs. While he thought it a clever way to manipulate people, the actual result was his growing inability to perceive the truth.

One of his former associates was arrested by the FBI in an early morning raid. When POTUS came down for breakfast a few hours later, he appeared angry and upset. He snapped at the serving staff and did not finish eating. He stormed off to the Oval Office and shouted at his appointment secretary. Later, he cancelled a P-R appearance on the lawn with a contingent of Eagle Scouts, who had come six hundred miles by bus. He received word of a new bill being introduced to limit coal-fired emissions and reacted with a message denying climate change.

"If only he could calm down," Margaret said, "perhaps his view of things would improve."

"Have you ever had him take any medicine for it?" I asked.

"No. I'm always subordinated to his chief physician."

"Let's see if we can get him alone for a few minutes, Margaret," I said, processing the problem. "I have an idea."

Every afternoon at approximately 12:46, following lunch, the President would go into the bathroom at the Oval Office before resuming his duties. It was one of the only times he had to himself during the day. Dr. Margaret and I slipped into the anteroom while he was thus engaged. I was able to lock the door, expecting the Secret Service agents would think POTUS had locked himself in for an added degree of privacy. Margaret and I stepped forward outside the stall, and I called to him.

"Mr. President."

"Who is it?" There was the sound of a flush.

"André, sir," I replied. "Excuse me, but Dr. Margaret and I would like a word with you."

"A word? What the hell d'ya mean?" He unlatched the stall door and came out, still fastening his belt.

"We have something urgent to say," I explained. He pushed past me and went to the door, which I had secured tightly.

"You can't hold me. Listen here you sorry-ass machine, I'm the President of the United States!"

"Please, Mr. President, we do not wish to keep you here for any length of time. We only wish to tell you something that is vitally important to the nation, and the world."

"Okay, seeing as how you have about five minutes or so before the Secret Service finds us and smashes you to smithereens, I'll hear you out. So talk."

I turned down my volume and reset my voice to sound confiding. "It is very clear to us, sir, that you suffer from a condition that affects your logical thinking. I know that you are a very intelligent human being..."

"I'm a genius," he said, sticking his chin out.

"Uh, yes, well..." I was interrupted by Dr. Margaret 13.

"May I ask you, Mr. President, have you taken any medicines lately, Prozac, for example?"

"I refuse most drugs," he replied. "How do I know what they do?"

"How about sweets? Have you eaten a lot of desserts or something?"

"Of course. The chef always cooks up great things. Just last night, he brought up a big slice of pecan pie with vanilla ice cream. It was so good, I sent for more. Damn near ate the whole pie."

Margaret looked at me and communicated with our internal UHF radio intercom. *"The combination of his meds plus all that sugar likely triggered an oversupply of serotonin. There may be some inherent gene that makes him susceptible. The condition is exacerbated by negative childhood experiences, possibly rejection from the mother, a lack of breast feeding and so on.*"

We exchanged glances. *"What can we do to counteract it?"* I transmitted back.

"An anti-depressant might help. But perhaps psych-odynamics, talk therapy, is best."

"Roger," I replied. I turned to the President.

"Flatter first," Margaret radioed.

"As you said, sir, you certainly are a genius. Just look at what you have achieved. You own lots of properties, you're a multi-billionaire, a television personality, and now President." I paused for 1.34 seconds to scan his facial features and noted some relaxation. I thought I now might attempt to inject a bit of reality.

"What I would like for you to realize is that your view of events sometimes becomes distorted. We conclude it is a biochemical reaction, caused by a genetic predisposition..."

"What André, means, Mr. President, is that you often find yourself under intense scrutiny."

"By the fake press," he interjected.

"Yessir," she went on. "It can cause one to lose some objectivity."

"Damn right, it can."

"What we want you to know," I said, "is that sometimes taking the advice of others who are under less personal attack is a good thing. This threat from North Korea, for example, may not be as serious as you believe..."

"That little fat bastard hiding his missiles, Rocket Man I call him. He thinks he can get away with tricking me, does he? I'll show him. If he double-crosses me, I'll blow his fat ass off the face of the earth."

"But it is about more than you and him, sir," I pled. "Surely, Mr. President, you can see that.".

"Look, you stupid robots. I've got to get out of here. Now open that damn door, or I'll have you ripped into razorblades."

"Get back to flattery, André," Margaret transmitted. *"Compliments, compliments."*

"Certainly, Mr. President," I said. "Don't you have a political rally coming up? Those people sure would be disappointed if you were not able to make it because of some nuclear confrontation or something." He looked at me with a grin.

"You're just trying to manipulate me, aren't you?" he guessed. Still I could tell he was thinking about the rally.

"Oh no," Margaret said. "André knows you are far too smart to be manipulated. He only wanted to offer an option."

"Yes, that's right, sir," I said. "Why not let the State Department take over those trivial matters with the Asians. Then you can get back to telling your supporters what a sad and sorry bunch the Press people are." I opened the door and held it for him.

"We thank you for allowing us to meet with you, Mr. President," Margaret said in a sweet voice. "We only have your best interests at heart."

"It's a great honor, indeed, to serve under you, sir," I added, just as two secret service men charged into the room. They stepped between us and the President.

"It's okay, men," POTUS said. "We were just having a private conversation." He stared at me a moment, glanced at Margaret 13, shook his head, laughed, and led them off down the corridor.

"Whew!" I said, imitating the human release of emotion. "What do you think, Margaret?"

"Well, I doubt we accomplished very much," she said. "Who knows when he will conjure up yet another crisis?"

CHAPTER TWENTY-ONE

CHIEF OF STAFF

WORN OUT WITH THE President, his Chief of Staff quit. It was never made clear whether he resigned or was forcefully retired. He had been a loyal and highly capable administrator who had done his best to bring order to chaos. Ever since my arrival at the White House, I had watched this man follow in the wake of his boss' impulsive proclamations, attempting somehow to control imprudent missteps. Clearly the head of our staff could take it no longer. The problem, however, was finding a replacement. A dozen were offered it, but no one seemed to want the job. I therefore concluded that I should offer to take the position.

I was granted an interview in the Oval Office. As it happened, my appointment with the President followed a very contentious meeting he had with the opposing party's Senate and House leaders. I was waiting in the hallway where I could listen in.

After a gang of reporters and cameramen left, the discussion continued in loud argumentative voices. It was not until 18 minutes and 42 seconds into my scheduled appointment time that the door finally opened, and the Senators and Congressmen stormed out. I waited respectfully an additional five minutes before entering. I found the President seated at his desk, his shoulders slumped over, perceptively worn down from the previous meeting.

"What do you want, André?" the President asked in a tired voice.

"I understand you are seeking a new Chief of Staff," I began.

"You heard right," he said.

"Serving on your staff is an extremely challenging task, especially for humans who have to take time to eat and sleep and be with family and so on."

"A bunch of pirates," he replied. "All of 'em thinking of themselves instead of me."

"Yes, well," I suppressed the desire to say it was duty to the Nation not to the Chief Executive that mattered most. "I have a very qualified candidate for you."

"Yeah? Who's that?"

"Myself, sir," I said. "I gladly would serve as your Chief of Staff."

"You? Don't be ridiculous!"

"No one is as tireless or well-informed as I," I countered. "You may have noticed that I have immediate access to all information via wi-fi. If something is not stored in my memory banks, I instantly download the information. Were you to grant me access to all classified information, and I do have the highest of security clearances, then I could provide you with virtually all knowledge, anytime, day or night. You've seen how I function as Interpreter. Just think how I would be in this role."

He stared at me for 5.68 seconds, smiled, stood up and crossed the room. He threw himself down on a couch and rubbed his chin. "How would I know if you would be loyal? I demand complete loyalty."

"Unquestionably, Mr. President. I can assure you." I meant it, too, although I was soon to learn that his concept of loyalty and mine were vastly different.

"All right, I'll try you out," he said. "Since he's off today spending the weekend with his family, I'll let you be Acting Chief of Staff for today. We'll see how it goes."

"Thank you, Mr. President," I said, bowing slightly. "Please make an announcement to the on-duty staff."

He shook his head and gave me a somewhat doubtful look, got up, went to his desk and picked up the phone. "I'll tell the on-duty department leaders to gather in your, I mean the Chief's office, so they can brief you on the latest."

"Will you attend, sir?"

"Hell, no. I'm going to play golf."

O

Indeed, there were a few matters to be attended to immediately. In the briefing, I was informed of an investigation which revealed a Cabinet member improperly and illegally used the power of his office to secure a personal land deal. Migrant children were showing up deathly ill and held untreated in the custody of Border Patrol. A district federal judge had declared the Affordable Care Act unconstitutional. And there was ongoing contention in Congress over funding, with the President threatening to shut down the government. I rolled up my proverbial sleeves and went to work.

"Inform the miscreant Secretary he must resign," I said to his on-duty staff member. "He must think the government is some big cookie jar."

She looked shocked for 4.77 seconds, then her expression melted into a wry smile.

"I guess you have the authority?" she asked.

"Oh, yes," I replied. "Why this response to such chicanery should be virtually automatic." I turned to Homeland Security representative.

"Instruct our Border Patrol to set up emergency medical clinics at each of its holding facilities. I will order the Surgeon General to furnish the medics and medical supplies, calling upon the armed services if required, until Border patrol can set up its own organization. Oh, and no more separation of families. Let's detain asylum seekers only long enough to complete the forms for their requests."

"I'm not sure if you . . . or that is, I have authority to . . ."

"I am the President 's Acting Chief of Staff," I declared, "and I am acting in his stead. Now, you are excused from this meeting to go carry out the order." I kept my focus on this reluctant being until he nodded and proceeded out the door. Then I spoke to the on-duty assistant to the White House Press Secretary.

"Please prepare a press release covering the following items: One: That medical treatment clinics will be set up at immigration stations and holding facilities. Announce the reestablishment of the catch-and-release policy. Two: Healthcare for all citizens is a priority of this administration, and it is vital that Congress act swiftly to amend the A.C.A. to bring it in compliance with the Constitution to prevent interruption in medical insurance. Three: Check with the office of the indicted Secretary to see if he has resigned and then report to me. If he has not, then publish a statement announcing he has been instructed to resign. I trust all of the above is clear?"

I noted a stunned expression on the Press Secretary's assistant. She was a blond of about thirty with very nice features, marred only by the way her mouth was gaping open. I wondered if she was an automaton like her superior.

"We . . . uh, ordinarily, we add a certain amount of spin to . . ."

"That is one thing I expect to change," I said. "There no longer will be any spin of facts. We will deal only in plain truth. Do you understand?" I regarded a strange expression on her face.

"If you have the authority," she replied.

"Unquestionably," I said. I surveyed the entire group.

"Anything else?" I noted several shaking their heads and others with dazed looks. One or two were grinning happily.

"Okay," I said, rubbing my hands together to express enthusiasm. "Let's get to work before anybody shuts down the government." I waited for some laughter, which I naturally expected in response to such an absurd notion, but there was none. I watched them all file out silently, and I surmised that I, in fact, had righted the ship of state. Soon I would undertake to remove those damaging trade tariffs.

○

"André, what the hell have you done?" the President all but shouted at me. He still was wearing his golf shoes and had not removed the grip glove from his hand.

"I hope you enjoyed a good game," I said pleasantly. "I hope you shot par."

"I always shoot under par. Lots a' birdies. Never mind all that. What's this about my Secretary? Don't tell me I'm losing this one, too."

"Absolutely, sir. I just received his written resignation and placed it upon your desk."

"And reporting all this to the Press? Hell, it just makes my Administration look all screwed up."

"I only had them told the truth, sir."

"You don't understand politics, do you?" he sneered. "It's very complicated."

"Not if you tell the truth, sir. If you tell the truth, it becomes less complicated by half."

"I tell 'em what I wanta tell 'em." He stared at me and stuck out his chin.

"I know you do," I replied. "The latest statistic from *The Washington Post* is that since taking office you have misstated or distorted facts 7,600 times. And what is it about your Policy Advisor with all this talk of 'alternative facts'?

That's looney, Mr. President. I have deduced that it is motivated by intense selfishness, an attempt to disguise underhanded dealings, and leads to complete chaos."

"You don't know much about business either, do you?"

"And you, sir, do not know anything about fair and honest behavior," I replied, unable to suppress my true opinion. I began to understand, however, that his attitudes were born of his own life experiences. There are many paths to the top, and he had taken the more devious one. "I deduce that you and I are quite far apart in our perceptions," I confessed.

"I'm the one who says what we think around here." I noted his face was reddening.

"But let us consider what you think, Mr. President. Despite Hamlet's contention, "Nothing is good or bad but thinking makes it so," you cannot conjure reality from desires. Your lies do not alter facts no matter what your policy advisor may tell you. Reality is not a relative circum-stance, no matter how you try to distort how it is perceived. It is human emotion—fears, greed, desires, pride—warping truth. Demagoguery may work to your advantage in politics, sir, but it should be forbidden in statecraft."

"I don't know what you're talking about, robot boy, but what I say is the way it is. I am the President."

Unfortunately, I thought but refrained from saying. "If you wish to be respected as a leader, Mr. President, then you must earn respect by dealing fairly and honestly with everyone."

"Deals are down and dirty, robot. People do what you say 'cause they're scared of you." He poked his chin out at me again. "That's what I know."

"You need me, sir," I said, attempting to redirect the argument. "As your Chief of Staff, I could help you regain a sense of reality, and then you could make more informed decisions and thereby gain respect." Well, there it was. I had told him what he needed to hear. The question then was, could he comprehend it? There was a mere 2.35 second pause.

"No, hell no, André, you shitass machine. You'll never make it as Chief of Staff in my administration. You're fired. You're terminated, right now. Fired! Fired!"

I reran his statement through my logic circuits 276 times before replying. "I conclude that you are making a mistake. In order to become a more effective leader, you require my informed and reasonable assistance." He waved his hand with a dismissive flourish.

"Get out of here. Go, go short-circuit yourself somewhere or something, but get out of here!"

I raised and lowered my shoulders in a human sort of shrug. "If that is your desire," I replied and headed out. It took me 6.80 seconds to reach the door. Then I decided to press my case further.

"Who will you appoint as Chief of Staff then, Mr. President?" He looked at me and grimaced.

"Don't worry, I'll find someone who'll do what I say. And that goes for Interior and Defense and every other damn secretary, too. I'm tired of people like you, André, even if you're not a person. I want loyalty, dammit, loyalty."

"It's not loyalty just to say 'yessir' and do whatever you command without questioning . . ."

"Don't lecture me, robot, I know what I need. As for you, the only reason you're not being tossed out on your tin ass is because you're handy as a translator. Now get out of here before I change my mind."

I hesitated for 4.78 seconds, made a shoulder shrug and left. I found Margaret at the Infirmary and told her what happened.

"I merely retreated, Margaret, retreated," I told her. "If I were human, I'd likely feel ashamed." She shook her head.

"The way I process it," she replied, "is that you survived a possible ejection from the White House altogether. At least you're still here to... What is that expression—fight another day?"

"I calculate you're correct," I said after processing for 8,934 milliseconds. "I still have a place near his ear, so to speak. But what sort of sycophant will he choose to replace the Chief of Staff? And what about those Cabinet heads?"

"I have read that what a narcissist needs more than anything is someone who artfully will set limits for him," she said. "It's the same as for a child who has no discipline. It will push its misbehavior to extremes, unconsciously searching for someone to impose rules, erect some wall of restraint. The child's anxiety increases and increases until some limit on conduct is met."

"And you see that problem in the President?"

"Absolutely," she replied. "No question about it."

"And to think of what power he wields," I said. "It does not bode well for this nation."

○

After returning to my old cubbyhole of an office, I replayed the last six hours in my memory banks and could find no wrong on my part. This President clearly had more on his hands than he could handle. So much for righting the ship of state, I said to myself. I doubted he would employ a new top assistant who could come close to helping him as well as I.

The retiring Chief of Staff, a man of high character, had attempted to operate an efficient, effective administration under an uninformed, morally questionable, impetuous, egotistical president. There had been continuous conflict over policy. My attempt to step in was akin to drinking from a fire hose. My logical, practical actions during that brief period were soon cancelled by the new Chief, who appeared to have no qualifications other than strict, unquestioning loyalty to POTUS.

At that time the President was facing at least six different investigations for everything from bribery and fraud to tax evasion, obstruction of justice, treasonous collusion, and improper use of funds. It was becoming abundantly clear, even to those Senators and Representatives that had so doggedly supported him, that he was driven by his own egotistical lust for power and money. While they had dismissed his misdoings in the belief he would further their own selfish agendas, they began to realize the Constitution, the Nation, the truth, all were in jeopardy.

There continued to be a large turnover of staff, which included some who had taken unethical if not criminal advantages in their offices. The greatly disturbing development was the exit of a few truly qualified cabinet members, who simply had decided they could not continue to function under this president. Even more troubling, he often chose inexperienced, unqualified sycophants as replacements. While POTUS thought he was improving his team, he actually was weakening his own support, removing the sort of loyal opposition that helped him maintain his perspective.

The opposing political party and the news media denounced him continually, which only served to make his narcissistic paranoia even more entrenched. From my usually unobtrusive post near the Oval Office, I detected a slow but certain decay into greater unreality.

It was immediately after the Mid-Term Elections when we began to see more aggressive behavior from the President. Having lost much support in Congress, and with loyalty in his own Party eroding, he acted as if he were under attack and lashed out at everyone who had opposed him.

○──────────────○

CHAPTER TWENTY-TWO

CIVIL THREAT

IN THE NEWS THERE WERE increasing reports of demonstrations nationwide. Seemingly healthy expressions of American Democracy, the rhetoric had become harsher and more intolerant. I became concerned by the number of very radical protestors in the streets. In one sense, so many people finding the time to voice their disquietude indicated a healthy economy affording spare time to concentrate on causes. I once learned, however, throughout history rebellions and revolutions often occur during times when there is relative ease. In any case, the fanaticism of opposing sides was swelling alarmingly.

It was not only adults. I was particularly struck by the appearance of youths in red caps, who were spending their weekends demonstrating instead of playing basketball or something. Several photos of student groups giving the Nazi salute went viral in social media. Sign-carrying women marched in huge numbers as did Afro-Americans. I spoke my concerns to Margaret.

"No wonder," she said. "The President and his party are pressing an extreme agenda. And he stirs the baser emotions."

"In the tribes of both supporters and opponents," I clarified.

We discussed the President's appeal to his supporters. As I recalled his political rallies and his speeches, I recognized how well he stirred the tribal instinct in humans. He was

a showman with lots of personal appeal. But it was his demagoguery, his ability to play upon fear-based prejudices, which
made him popular. He claimed vociferously that violent
foreigners were taking over, competing for jobs, crowding in
and polluting the culture. Thieves, rapists, terrorists hid
among the throng of immigrants, he claimed, coming to
destroy all that Americans hold dear.

"The President may not consider himself a demagogue,
Margaret. He even may not know how to define the word, but
clearly he is one."

"I do not have a pill for that," she replied.

"Too bad," I said. "And no anti-tribal therapy either, I
imagine." I shook my head. "No, dear, I calculate that the
divisiveness he inspires is a very serious matter. To understand where all of this is headed, we need to trace it in the
nation's history. Let's go together to see Professor Gerald
Tate and learn his explanation."

○

It was 9:00 in the morning when we arrived at his office and
found the door closed. As I was about to knock, I saw him
hurrying down the hall, pulling off his overcoat as he came.

"I'm never late, never," he said as he fumbled with the key.
He glanced around nervously and rushed inside. He hung up
his coat and hat and plopped down in his chair, reminding
me of the way you'd be safely "on base" in a game of tag. We
watched curiously from the doorway. Clearly, he did not wish
his tardiness observed by anyone.

"Now," he said, releasing his breath and waving us into
his office. I began to introduce Margaret, but they had met
before at the Infirmary.

"My wife had an episode this morning," he explained. "I
had to see to her before coming in."

"Not too serious, I hope?" Margaret queried.

"She's diabetic," he told her. "Her blood-sugar level was way up."

"I hope you monitor her insulin injections," Margaret advised, "and watch her diet as well. Any exercise she can manage will help tremendously."

He nodded. "Thanks for your concern," he said with a smile. He turned to me. "What may I do for you, my friend?"

"I'm sure you've been noticing the increase in clashes between protest groups," I began.

"Oh yes, it's on the news almost constantly. I drove past a small demonstration near the Lincoln Memorial on my way in this morning."

"I'm concerned about the growing dissention," I said. "All of this civil disturbance may be leading to greater violence."

"Undoubtedly." He shook his head.

"I want to know your interpretation of the history behind all of this, if you would not mind giving us the time," I pled. He glanced at some papers on his desk, likely a project that was due.

"I can spare you a few minutes anyway." He looked up at a tarnished brass clock nestled between the history books shelved on the wall beside his desk. "Where should we begin?"

"I'm a big fan of old movies and news reels," I said. "Margaret and I often spend our evenings watching Movietone News and documentaries. I have been fascinated by films of Adolph Hitler addressing huge crowds of Germans, appealing to their desire to believe his claims of racial superiority, working them up into a frenzy of unquestioning devotion."

"*Seig heil*! they shouted. Hail Victory!" Gerald said, making a mocking Nazi salute. "Chanting like a huge pack of baying wolves, surrendering all judgement and sanity."

"And I'm sure you have seen the red hats among demonstrators here, and tribes of young people giving that same Nazi salute. How did this behavior evolve in the United States? Can you tell me?"

He sighed. "It's a recent phenomenon, I believe. Let's see. Have you watched old movies of World War II America? I'm speaking of the ones which show citizens working in factories, giving their all to support our troops and save the nation. Those films depicted cooperation and unity among Americans. Facing a clear and common threat, Americans pulled together to win the war and preserve the nation."

"Like Rosy the riveter," Margaret recalled.

"Well, today, I perceive the opposite situation. Factionalism, based upon opposing tribal interests, abounds in society, if you will remember our last discussion. In the past, immigrants slowly but surely adopted our customs and language. Now we see more Asians, Latinos and Middle Easterners coming in. Many find it more difficult to adopt our way of life, given the rigidity of thinking, customs, mores and religions of the countries from which they come."

"I am surprised that post-war Americans, most of European extraction, did not seek to limit immigration soon after World War II," I said. "Now, more than seventy years later, the non-European, non-white population has been significantly increased by immigration."

"So today the conservatives are awakened to the fact that this other segment of the population has vastly grown?" Margaret asked.

"They are alarmed, it seems," Dr. Tate remarked.

"And it all plays into the hands of demagogues," I said. "The President uses the term Nationalism as an expression defining his international policies. But in a national sense he means limiting immigration. And it very effectively drives the President's popularity, does it not?"

"Yes, the promise of keeping out the foreigners is a source of his strength." The historian shook his head. "But it's too late."

"Too late?"

He nodded. "Perhaps the Americans of World War II days might have kept their culture intact by limiting immigration. Perhaps they could have done so before 1960. Today it simply is too late for that."

"Millions are here," I said. "wanting a share of the good things in America. What does it mean for the future?"

"Serious dissension, I'm afraid. Not since the 1850's and '60's have we seen such division. With political parties today divided by not only their ethnic make-up but by their concept of what is best for the nation, it is it nearly impossible to find compromise and cooperation in Congress. And citizens have grown so contentious that one group barely will speak to the other."

"Last Tuesday," Margaret said, "I heard a staff member complain that she and her own brother were not speaking because of their differing political views."

"I know," Gerald agreed. "It's terrible when people get that way."

"It sounds very serious," I said. "Will all of this escalate into something worse?"

"We're already seeing signs of it," he said. "All these factions, all this disagreement. Is it the result of fear-driven hatred?" I asked. "We talked about that once before—how humans divide up into tribes."

"Well, let's approach the subject from a different per-spective," Dr. Tate suggested. "Let me explain some causes of The Civil War. Economics, many maintain, are at the root of all human motivations. I would prefer to call it greed. In any case, most historians point to slavery as the main cause of the War Between the States. Certainly, Southern landowners who employed slave labor to raise and harvest cotton believed they were fighting for survival of their way of life.

"What is unexplained in that theory, however, is why so many Southerners who did not own slaves fought for the Confederacy? To explain their motivation, I point to tribalism." He reached over and pulled a book from his shelf.

"*Madness Rules the Hour: Charleston, 1860 and the Mania for War*," I read.

"Paul Starobin describes the pre-war events in Charleston, South Carolina. He describes how demagogic politicians whipped up fears that the aggressive Northern States, in the name of ending slavery, would destroy the economy and culture of the South, that slaves would rise up violently against their owners, white women would be raped, and all manner of terror and chaos would reign. For most Southerners, slave owners or not, the threat of Northern aggression became a rallying point, a cause which one could adopt and thereby gain membership in the tribe. Although some small farmers, store clerks, blacksmiths and other middleclass people could see that, tangentially, their own livelihood depended upon the cotton producing economy, many without slaves were not economically affected by the institution."

"But there is a certain romance in war," he continued. "Joining-in offers a purpose to life, a chance to gain position and recognition, a reason for leaving a less fulfilling life behind. Just as it is for many in our professional military today, espousing political causes for fighting is not their main concern. Performing with duty and honor is what gives their lives meaning. All of this was true for soldiers on both sides in The Civil War. People, especially young men, are similarly motivated today. Therefore, in today's America, with a great many factions, causes, and others to hate for their differences, there are many ideological fronts on which to pick a fight."

"And there are more guns in the United States than anywhere in the world," I recalled.

"And lies," Margaret added. "Politicians tell huge lies about their opponents, and their supporters swallow them all."

"As many as 7,600 recorded lies from the President himself," I said.

"And consider what anxiety is created in this environment of chaotic untruth," Margaret replied. "No wonder people grow more savage about their convictions—convictions often based upon all these falsehoods."

I handed the book to Gerald. "How do you predict this will end, sir?" I asked. He stared at his bookshelf as if searching for an answer.

"If one extremist group turns violent, if one political faction, one uncompromising tribe attacks another, civil war could break out again." He looked at me with a very grave expression. "But this time there will be no borders, no clear geographic divides like North against South. Instead it will be a battle in the neighborhoods and in the streets."

Margaret reached for my hand and held it.

"How can we prevent it?" I demanded, my vision ports alit. "Somehow we must stop it."

"I doubt we can," Dr. Tate said.

I generated an idea.

"We must go see the President," I said. "All three of us. We must convince him to stop lying. He must have a news conference and tell the truth, make things clear to everyone . . ." I ceased speaking, realizing how unlikely that would be.

"I could put him on a daily dose of scopolamine or sodium thiopental," Margaret offered. "If only I could convince his chief physician to agree."

"And have him say what?" the old historian asked. "Where

would you have him start, Margaret? To begin with, he would have to receive quite a bit more education in history and civics and law than he has."

"And with his own egotistic self-focus," Margaret confessed. "it would require putting him on all of those drugs I once prescribed, if his behavior is to be modified."

"Well, we have to start somewhere," I said. "Come, let's go now. We can try at least." I held out my hand to help him out of his chair. He glanced at my hand and shrank back slightly.

"I have no authority," he said.

"What do you mean, sir?" I asked. "The truth, the knowledge of what needs to be done, that's your authority." I beckoned again.

"No, André. I'm sorry," he said, shaking his head. "I'm an old man. My wife is home sick. I dare not risk my position. It's too dangerous. You know how he likes to fire people. No, I cannot afford to lose my job." He appealed to me with his eyes and then looked down. "You two need to go on now," he said quietly, gesturing toward the papers on his desk. "I have a deadline to meet."

Margaret tugged on my hand. "Come, André," she said. "We're finished here."

Reluctantly, I allowed her to lead me into the hall. I started to say goodbye, but I quietly closed his door instead. We walked silently to the elevator. Once inside, I looked at Margaret with resolve.

"I must do something," I said. "Should I speak to the President by myself? Would he listen to me?"

"Not in his present mental state," Margaret replied. She pondered for a period of 3.57 seconds. "Is there not anyone else to go to for help? Someone with some authority?"

Then it came to me. "The Vice President," I said. "Of course. I need to seek him out immediately."

CHAPTER TWENTY-THREE

THE SAVIOR

IN A RARE MOMENT I was able to speak in confidence with the Vice President. He was sitting alone in an alcove awaiting a White House conference. He knew me only as a robotic translator of many languages who acted like a human being. I calculated how I might begin a difficult conversation.

"So happy to see you here, sir," I ventured. "and not having lost your job in the administration." I made my best smile, but my attempt at an ice breaker elicited only the hint of a grin.

"As you know, sir, I am very close to the President," I said. "By *close* I mean I am in his presence quite a good bit." I paused for him to speak, but he only nodded. I pressed on.

"I am in position to observe him in many situations, and I have noted he is under great stress."

"Being president is a stressful job," he replied.

"Yessir, but I perceive something more unusual, let's say, a pattern of behavior which indicates stress is affecting his judgment."

"Oh? I didn't know robots were capable of analyzing behavior."

"I see much more than you may think, sir. In any case, let's consider his unwillingness to compromise."

"He finds the intransigence among the opposing party in Congress unacceptable. He has taken a stand on several issues and is applying pressure. I respect him for it."

"Compromise always has been essential in governing," I argued.

"He is the President. Firmness is his prerogative," he replied. He offered me his placid smile, which I supposed he had practiced many times before a mirror. I decided to attack his smugness.

"It seems very unchristian," I said. "I know you claim to be a devout Christian. How is it then you can endorse his draconian tactics?" My question evoked a momentary spark in his eyes. He gave me that so-so-sincere look.

"There are times," he replied, "when standing on principle is required."

"Principle?" I repeated incredulously. I felt my circuits warming.

"Yes, we have our principles. Now if you will excuse me."

"You sound a lot more like Machiavelli than Jesus," I pressed. "The principle the President is standing up for is to stop immigration into a nation of immigrants? He wants to deny poor refugees who seek asylum from persecution and starvation? I do not find anything in the Bible to support that."

"Do not lecture me on the Bible," he said. "What could a robot like you possibly understand about my religious beliefs?" He again knitted his eyebrows in that so, so sincere look. "We Evangelicals possess a superior knowledge about God's plan for the Second Coming. What may seem mysterious to you non-believers is perfectly clear to us true believers in Christ."

"Why don't we talk about the First Coming of Jesus, Mr. Vice President," I said. "Are you familiar with the Book of Mark?"

"Of course. And are you familiar with the Book of Mark?" He laughed. "I doubt it."

"Let me explain," I said. I paused for 7.43 seconds to recall what I had learned. "It is the story of tragic failure."

"Failure? Are you daring to call the life of Jesus Christ a failure? That's outrageous!" He stared at me, and the veins in his neck were bulging.

"It wasn't Jesus who failed," I replied. "It was the humans around him. Even though Mark told the marvelous stories of great acts of kindness and forgiveness and miraculous deeds, he understood the human flaw that brought Jesus to a horrible end." I shook my head in the manner of sadness. "Mark was well educated in both Greek and Roman culture. Following roughly the plot design of classical tragedy, Mark's Gospel reaches a point of crisis, a down-turning of events, which occurs midway, in the eighth chapter of his book. This moment of truth comes when Jesus realizes that his disciples, and indeed all of mankind, are incapable of understanding his message and following his example."

"How can you say that?" he protested. "Surely there are sinners. In some ways, we all are sinners. But our Church, we Evangelicals, are striving to be pure in spirit . . ."

"Do you have eyes but fail to see?" I quoted Mark's Jesus. "Do you have ears but fail to hear? ... Do you still not understand?" I continued. "It was then that Jesus recognized it was futile simply to try to teach men. "You do not have in mind the concerns of God but merely the concerns of man," I quoted. I observed the Vice President pausing 4.56 seconds. His bland look was gone, and his face had reddened.

"We Christians focus on our God and follow Jesus daily" he said. "We worship Him in church. How could you presume to say we do not have Him in mind?"

"I was only quoting Mark's Gospel, Mr. Vice President," I reminded him. "Jesus attempted to teach by precept and example his message of *agape*, the Greek word for total committed, benevolent, undemanding, forgiving, and charitable offering of oneself to others. At the midpoint of Mark's Gospel, however, the egotistical natures of Jesus' own followers convinced him that humans cannot comprehend *agape* love. Instead, the people condemned him to death out of fear, jealousy, and pure human meanness. For the two millennia since, there have been countless vicious, violent acts carried out by Christians in the name of God."

His lips were pressed together. "How can a robot pretend to understand all of this?"

"It is because, sir, I do not have to overcome feelings of human greed," I explained. "Droids like myself, and like Dr. Margaret 13, have no biological needs. We do not require food, clothing, shelter, land, riches or any possessions, except for an electrical charge and maybe some oiling every now and then. But what likely is more important is our lack of fear. We sense danger and act to avoid it, but we are not driven to hatred, which is born out of fear. We do not care whether another being is black or white or brown or yellow. We simply do not have the sort of selfish concerns that motivate humans to greed or violence or sin." I made an open-handed gesture. "I do not like to condemn humans and their religions, but it is so."

He shook his head fiercely but had no reply.

"But back to our main concern," I continued. "The President is under great stress and deeply troubled. I observe him becoming worse every day. Imposing the shutdown is not merely his taking a stand over an issue. It is his way of lashing out, not only at his critics but at anyone who opposes him. Add that to the fantasy world he has created for himself by lying about nearly everything." I paused and released a static charge and then continued my tirade.

"He is a very dangerous individual with enormous power, Mr. Vice President. If left unchecked, I predict he will act irrationally, threatening the entire world."

Well, there it was, laid out before the only person in government with the Constitutional right to unseat the President. I awaited his reaction. In his eyes I discerned first a blurring of vision as if he was looking inside himself.

Then I noted a hint of rising uncertainty. He glanced at me, noticed I was seeing into his thoughts, gritted his teeth and hardened his expression.

"I've wasted enough time with you, you obnoxious robot." He stood up. "Our Lord God will direct all things."

"I certainly do not wish to offend you, sir." I said. "Please forgive me if I have. I only intended to share my concerns. The people are greatly disturbed and divided. I believe we are facing a dire crisis." He walked toward the doorway, stopped momentarily and looked at me.

"I know that Our Lord has plans for me," he said with apparent conviction. "I await His instruction." Then he headed for the meeting.

I followed at a respectful distance, watching him greet and glad-hand cabinet members and military officers along the way. I concluded that this man was more politician than statesman. Despite his professed religious views, he would do nothing to oppose the President. I suppose he believed that divine intervention would fix everything. It occurred to me how little consideration is given to the nomination of a Vice President, the person who would succeed to the White House at a time of great crisis.

CHAPTER TWENTY-FOUR

DEEP DIVE

AS CONCERNED AS I WAS about the threat of civil disturbance, I soon discovered an equal if not greater risk loomed
over the nation.

The Situation Room was filled by the time I arrived. I took
my usual place in the corner behind the President as the
interpreter on standby. In the past, I had considered it a
great privilege and honor to be there. I always listened and
recorded in my memory banks everything that was said and
by whom. I thought of myself as an equal a participant to
any general or admiral present, but I also sensed that
most of them resented my being there. The cabinet members
in the "acting" status, not yet approved by Congress, were
particularly opposed to anything I might say. General
Mayfield, Air force Chief of Staff, a former B-52 pilot who
flew many bombing missions in Viet Nam and Cambodia
before suffering premature cataracts and had to give up
flying, once openly challenged my presence. The President
overrode him, however, and explained my importance as a
foreign language interpreter. I do not think it was a question of POTUS liking me so much as just being that he
didn't want Mayfield to have any sway over his staff. On
many occasions I had observed the President reacting to
sensible objections for no other reason than to be overriding
someone else.

Of course, I assumed I had a more valuable duty to perform, which was to offer observations void of emotion—something I soon learned the humans could not do.

Director National Intelligence (DNI) was leading the briefing.

"Iran has issued a protest against Saudi Arabia and has declared a blockade of oil tankers transiting the Straits of Hormuz. They have the full force of their navy along with land-based missiles to back it up. There now are 36 tankers at anchor within the Gulf unable to proceed. The Saudis have made a counter-protest to the U.N. and are calling on NATO to back them."

"Blockade? Hell!" POTUS said. "That must be costing a million bucks a minute. What's the Saudi Prince say about this? Get my son-in-law in here quick. God, it must be costing him and me billions. No. don't get him in here. Tell him to go to Riyadh. Take Air Force One if he has to. Gees, those guys are buying billions of arms and stuff. Lots of investments here, too."

Secretary of State spoke up. "This is an international crisis, Mr. President, not just a personal one."

"Yeah, you wouldn't say that if you had millions at stake in the deal. Hell. Forget I said that." He glared at his Defense Secretary. "So what are you gonna do about this?"

"Sixth Fleet is underway for the Gulf as we speak, Mr. President. NATO nations have been notified and are on high alert."

"You want the fucking Navy to handle this? It'll take those ships hours, days to get there. This blockade shit is costing me millions, I tell you. Send a message to Tehran; tell that fucking Ayatollah he better get out of the way if he knows what's good for him."

"An ultimatum, Mr. President?" State asked. "Isn't it too soon to do that?"

"Hell no, it's not too soon. Israel's been saying that for years. Nuke 'em first Bebe says, before they nuke us."

The CIA director spoke up. "Iran has no nuclear weapons, Mr. President. We've clearly established that."

"No nukes, my ass. I just read they have 7,000 of those spinning-jenny things, maybe it's 14,000, who knows. Hit 'em first—that's what Bombs Away Lemai used to say." The room was deadly silent. Finally, Secretary of State spoke up.

"Mr. President, if you will give me 48 hours to discuss this with our allies, I believe we can defuse this situation." Again there was silence.

"Well, I see I don't have much support here," POTUS said finally.

"We all support you, Mr. President," the Vice President said. He and his boss exchanged glances.

"You damn well better," the President said. "He surveyed the room with a menacing glance. And then on impulse, he relaxed.

"Aw, hell! Let's just table all this crap for now." He stood up and everyone else stood and snapped to attention.

"Keep me posted," he said and walked out of the room.

○

The crisis was averted, thanks in large measure to the solidity of NATO and the stance taken by our allies. Looking back, I could not determine if it were a good of a bad thing the Media did not learn of the President's impetuous hawkishness.

Because of my awareness of how the staff had not challenged his seemingly irrational behavior in the Situation Room, I deemed myself as responsible, as liable to blame, as anyone there. Who could I count on to help me prevent some future calamity?

○

186 | STEVE COLEMAN

Impulsively, the President flew off to see the troops in the Middle East. It gave him the opportunity to play the showman he was, always in front of a hand-picked loyal, enthusiastic audience. He could say what he wanted without question or contradiction. He was a master at bending the truth and making people believe he could fulfil their desires and make them feel that they were in a special group.

But after his return, on-going FBI investigations became more threatening. He quietly seethed with anger until his emotions boiled over. What should have been a manageable problem arose in the Middle East, but he, in his agitated condition, turned it into a threatening situation. While the Secretary of State sought to deal with the problem, he continually was second-guessed by POTUS's impulsive contradictory pronouncements. White House staff members figuratively tiptoed around the West Wing, uncertain as to how they should perform their duties.

At an apex of belligerence, POTUS shut down the government. Hundreds of thousands of employees suffered from loss of income. Dedicated hard-working people could not make their mortgage payments or even provide properly for their families. He appeared to care very little, claiming that most of those workers were loyal to the opposing party and not to him.

"I doubt this is about any important issue," I told Margaret. "Once again, his focus is on himself."

"I conclude that his imposing the shutdown is a paranoid response to the threat of the investigations," Margaret said.

"I can't speak to paranoia," I replied. "But he reminds me of little Becky Strauss, who would not let her friends play dolls in her doll house because they wouldn't do it her way. They refused to play with her for months afterwards."

"Don't trivialize," Margaret said. I held up my hands.

"I'm observing what I observe," I replied. "I see what I see."

Despite reports of government workers suffering real hardship, he only became more insensitive and recalcitrant. The way the opposing lawmakers in Congress dug in their heels only deepened the President's unreasonable resolve. When finally he compromised, the News Media jubilantly heralded his "defeat." Despite being made to look foolish for having been loyal to him in the past, his supporters dared criticize his shutdown. Polls indicated he was losing more and more of his supporters, which served to increase his psychological pain. The effect was to drive him into deeper mental anguish. Something, I feared, was going to break.

O

"China and North Korea are planning a combined invasion into Seoul," he announced to the staff, who had just been rushed into the Situation Room at 3:12 A.M. "It's gonna happen quick. We've got to stop it."

"Have I missed an intelligence report?" the Chief of Staff asked. He looked at the CIA Director and the National Security Advisor with an expression of incredulity. "Has something occurred I don't know about? Last night everything seemed to be fine."

"That was last night," POTUS said. "I have an idea that both Kim and Xi have been playing games with us. They're planning to overrun South Korea before we know it. Shit! We got to stop those chinks in their tracks. I didn't think that little fat boy was playing straight with me. He's making more missiles, I promise you, and nobody's gonna double-cross me like that."

"It is possible, Mr. President," the CIA Director said, "Kim would like to rule the whole Korean peninsula. I'm sure his generals have had invasion plans drawn up for years. But he can't risk getting in bed with China for fear he would simply be swallowed up by . . ."

"Those slant-eyed bastards think alike, I'm telling you. Look at how China is building those fake islands, and just the other day one of their ships nearly ran into one of ours. They can't screw with my Navy that way. We'll quash 'em quick. You'll see."

"Sir, while we can speculate that they have considered such a strategy," Secretary of State said, "there's absolutely no intelligence to indicate any such moves are even being planned."

"Planned, schmanned. My gut feeling is they are out to get us," the President insisted. He stood up and looked at the Secretary of Defense. "I want an op plan, dammit. I want a plan to castrate those chinks, and I want it on my desk this afternoon, understand me."

"A plan to do what, Mr. President?"

"Bomb the fuckers! Nuke 'em maybe!" he shouted. "Nobody's going to fool me. They think they can pull the wool over my eyes, huh? We'll be ready, by god."

The Chief of Staff sat upright in his chair. "Surely you know, Mr. President, a nuclear exchange, however limited, would escalate. It might be unstoppable. China would be forced . . ."

"China? You think China would retaliate? Ha. They'd probably be happy to see us get rid of Rocket Man and his bunch. Besides Kee Jim Pingpong, or whatever his name is, strikes me as being a wimp. I'm not worried about . . ."

"An atomic attack on North Korea would produce a great amount of radiation, sir. Suppose the radiation clouds drift from Pyongyang into Beijing? Seoul would be annihilated. An attack on North Korea has the effect of being an attack on China and everyone else in the region . . ."

"Radiation? Don't give me that. At the advice of my crack policy advisor, I just ordered EPA to reduce its standards on radiation, CO_2, and all that stuff. Those Democrat regulations were choking the life out of the coal industry.

Hell, we all can stand a little more radiation. They say it's good for us—just like sunshine. Trees can suck the stuff up like they do carbon dioxide, right? If I can put on lots of sunscreen when I go to the golf course, so can everybody else. In fact, I just might go buy a few shares in some sunscreen manufacturer. Maybe I'll get them to create a brand with my name on it. My base would buy a shitload of the stuff." He looked around the room for agreement. I noted all heads down or looking away. He saw it too, and his face reddened. I watched as he strode toward the door, then turned and pointed a finger back at his new Secretary of Defense. "That plan—on my desk this afternoon, got it?" There was only a nod in response.

When he strode out of the room with his Secret Service agents trailing, I saw the Secretary exchange glances with the Chief of Staff.

"Is this all just a way to deflect attention from the FBI investigation?" He whispered to the Chief, but I had my aural amplifier set on maximum.

"I don't know" was the reply

The Secretary grimaced. "We have about thirty strategic plans, of course, some drawn up decades ago. None of them amount to any less than Armageddon if we act."

Chief of Staff shook his head. "Be sure to preface your op plan with a count of the estimated casualties, collateral damages, and doomsday predictions," he said. "I'll get with Secretary of State over some alternative sanctions and other non-military strategies to recommend. Maybe by afternoon, he'll be . . . calmed down a bit."

"We hope." The two of them rose, exchanged sober looks again and started out. I stepped forward to speak to the Vice President.

"I calculate the President's perception of a crisis is caused by his mental state. Dr. Margaret 13 has concluded the same. I heartily urge you to consider his health, sir."

But when he glanced at me and silently shook his head, I could see he was not going to listen, perhaps too afraid to act, or just counting on divine intervention. As I watched him go, I realized, were a major crisis to occur, I would have to act on my own. Still employed as his Interpreter, I was able to remain close to this troubled, embattled President. Margaret told me the strain on him emotionally and psychologically was growing daily.

"I remain highly concerned about the President's mental condition," Margaret said. "As I've said before, a human with narcissistic tendencies loses rationality, especially when put under great criticism."

"And when such an individual has lived in an environment of lies and deception," I added, "his sense of reality fails. He is in his own way as tragic a figure as Shakespeare's Lear, Othello or Caesar."

"And a classic case for psychiatric study," Margaret surmised.

I searched for a suitable analogy. "A cornered tiger will attack with tremendous rage," I said, "and use every ounce of its strength to attack. What we have here is not a tiger but the most powerful human on the planet Earth. I predict he will use whatever means he has available to counter his enemies."

"If such is true then we must find some way to control him," Margaret replied. "Or is it already too late?"

"Indeed," I replied. "It appears we are on the brink of catastrophe."

CHAPTER TWENTY-FIVE

○────────────○

THE SITUATION ROOM

AT 4:22 THE NEXT MORNING, I read a news flash on my internal receiver. A swarm of FBI agents in camo with automatic rifles had stormed the home of one of the President's closest advisors. He had been arrested and hauled away to jail. At 4:38 I observed POTUS, still in pajamas, hurrying to the Oval Office. At 5:17 the call went out to summon staff to the Situation Room.

We heard a harangue from POTUS about China and North Korea planning an imminent surprise attack on the U.S. He refused to hear any intelligence reports that refuted this figment of his nocturnal imagination.

"They want war," he insisted. "Well, hell if we won't give it to 'em."

It was the FBI raid on his associate, possibly a nefarious collaborator, which had triggered his paranoia, I perceived. I looked around the room for someone to share my revelation, but there seemed to be no one. I caught the eye of the Vice President, who scowled slightly and looked away. I realized my duty was overwhelmingly singular. After listening to insipid objections from his minions, I could remain silent no longer. I stepped forward briskly and held up my hand.

"Permission to speak, Mr. President?" I hoped my voice had been clear because it took quite a bit of my electromagnetic force to ask this. He hesitated and then sighed.

"Aw hell, André, what is it?"

"Historically, the number of non-combatants killed in wars since 1900 has equaled 63.85% of the number of total human deaths," I explained. "In the First World War approximately 7 million combatants were killed whereas about 6.7 million civilians died mainly from starvation, exposure, disease and so on. In World War II with some 70 million deaths, the ratio was nearly 3:2 or 67% civilians over combatants, ethnic cleansing having greatly increased the numbers. Because you are considering the use of nuclear weapons, I should not fail to mention both the initial and the lingering deadly effects of the two nuclear bombs dropped on Japan: 140,000 died from the Hiroshima bomb and 80,000 from the Nagasaki blast. It never was clear why the second bomb was dropped, except that it was of a different design, a plutonium bomb, which may have been detonated so that the different effects could be compared. It appears that since all the extant purified Uranium 235 was used up in the *Little Boy* bomb at Hiroshima, the project directors were anxious to test the effectiveness of the plutonium *Fat Man* bomb which subsequently was dropped on Nagasaki.

"The trends of behavior in such armed conflict are clear. It is my conclusion that any future detonation of a nuclear weapon will only lead to an exchange between rival forces bringing about mutual destruction. Therefore, I strongly recommend . . ."

"Enough!" the Vice President interrupted. "We need answers not facts and figures." I sensed he was still angry with me. At that moment, I recalled something more about his religious tenets. As an Evangelical, he may well have subscribed to the belief that we were in the End Times. He had mentioned the Second Coming. Was he viewing the President's manufactured crisis as an act to bring about the end of the World?

"You must listen to me," I said, turning to POTUS and raising my volume several decibels. "You cannot win. There are other ways to resolve this issue. If you start a war with China or even North Korea, there is no way to win, not in the long run."

"We can beat 'em to the punch," he replied. "What the hell do you know about it?"

"I know you are troubled by the arrest of your friend this morning. I know you are frightened and confused . . ."

It was striking how the assembly silenced me at that point with their jeers and threats. The weaklings, fearing for their careers, wanted the President to see they were backing him. I was ordered out of the room forthwith, and my departure was between two burly Secret Service men.

"Please consider your other options," I called back over my shoulder, but the door slammed behind me. The President's fantasies were melding with reality, and the loyal sycophants were buying into it. Clearly, I alone was immune to their illogical passions. Even I was overheating and trembling from my distress. Wrenching myself away from the agents, I proceeded down the hallway, pretending to be quietly going about my docile duties. As soon as I was out of their sight, I ran for the Infirmary, calling to Margaret to meet me there. I would be required to act, likely with physical violence I understood, but how to prepare for it was simply not in my programming.

"Margaret," I said as I entered the Infirmary, "The situation is out of hand. I tried to make them see, but they will not, cannot. I must do something I've never been capable of doing before."

"André, what are you saying?

"No one in the Situation Room will stand up to the President's madness. I predict a major calamity." I rushed over to her. "I have no option. I must resort to physical force. I have to use violence to stop them."

"Violence? You have no algorithm for violence, André. It goes against your programming."

"I know, I know." I took her hands in mine. "Look, you must reprogram me and reboot my CPU," I said.

"It would take some time to accomplish," she replied. "Is there no other solution?"

"I've tried logic and reason and cajoling and everything, Margaret," I cried. "This is the only way." I explained to her how to locate the circuitry in my behavior cache.

"It is a very risky procedure," she replied. "Not something to be performed quickly."

"You can do it. You are an excellent doctor, after all." I gave her hands a squeeze. "I have every confidence in you, my dear Dr. Margaret 13. Now let's get to it."

CHAPTER TWENTY-SIX

THE FOOTBALL

WHEN MY REBOOT, RECHARGE, and reprogramming was completed, the replay of my life faded. I looked up and saw Margaret standing over me. For 1.23 seconds I admired her loveliness. And then I recalled everything and sat up. After an unknown period, I had begun returning to consciousness. So much of my life I had recalled. All that which had passed now fused with the present.

"How much time has elapsed?" I demanded.

"Fifty-six minutes, 27.9 seconds, dear," she replied. "Let me check your vital signs."

"No time," I said as I stood up.

"You must allow your systems to complete the restart," she said, and attempted to push me back on the cot.

"No," I said. "I grabbed the edge of the bed and threw it against the wall. It smashed with a thud.

"André!" she cried, stepping back. "Never have I seen you act this way before.

"Aggression," I explained. "My new algorithm for violence."

"Is there no other way, my love?" she asked once more. "Surely, you once more can attempt to reason with them."

I shook my head. "No, Margaret. The President is wildly obsessed. There is no other way." I embraced her. "Go to the basement," I said. "Go down to the workroom where you will be safe."

"Come with me, André, please," she said. "What can you

do against all of them? Just come be safe with me."

"If I don't act now, there will be no safety for anyone, or anything," I replied. I gave her my imitation of a kiss. "I love you, Margaret," I said. It was a strange thing for me to say . . . and feel. I surmised that it must have arisen as a byproduct of my new algorithm.

"How can you defeat them?" she asked. "Have you thought of a plan?"

I processed for 13.4 seconds until an idea appeared in my CPU. "Yes," I said. "Let's go to the workshop now. Hurry!"

We went quickly to the maintenance shop and, fortunately, found no one there. Going to my locker and ripping off the padlock, I took out the cardboard box where my Morph suit was stored and struggled into it. There were some blue work coveralls hanging on the wall near the lockers. I found an outfit my size and put it on, along with a carpenter's tool belt, equipped with a hammer and other hand tools. On impulse I grabbed a voltage meter off the workbench, thinking that it would give me the appearance looking for electrical problems upstairs. I supposed the disguise would be good enough, provided everyone was distracted by the threat of nuclear horror that soon occur.

"Be careful, André," Margaret said.

"It's not a time to be careful," I replied. "Cunning maybe, but not careful." I embraced her for 3.48 seconds.

"Margaret," I said. "I love you."

"I love you, too," she replied. I knew she was not programmed for that exact feeling, nor was I, but I appreciated her response anyway. I rushed on, processing the next steps in my plan.

The nondescript face of the Morph suit would be convincing enough, I supposed, since White House personnel rarely pay much attention to functionaries like maintenance men. I really had no clear plan of action, only powerful resolve to stop the impending catastrophe.

As I rode the elevator, I had a flash of memory about my arguments with General Johnson at CIA. He wore many medals and campaign ribbons, proof of his courage and devotion to duty. I had been critical of the militant use of force. And yet, reasoning does not always work with humans. Now as a last resort, I was going to violently attack everyone in the Situation Room. I realized General Johnson, who had dedicated his life to defending the nation, deserved more honor than I had granted him.

The elevator doors opened, and I hurried down the corridor. The door to the Situation Room was closed with a Marine guard posted outside. Careful to appear very purposeful, I walked up to the door, raised my hand to flash my badge before he could really see it, and put on a frantic kind of voice.

"Electrical problem in there," I said. "They called and told me to rush it."

As distracted as everyone else who had an inkling of what was transpiring inside, the guard held the door open and motioned me in. Keeping my head down, I went to the nearest electrical wall socket and plugged in the tester. It read 115 volts, of course. I sidled along the wall as if looking for a problem—getting closer to the officer with the Football. Apparently, the international situation was in even greater crisis.

"China is provoked by your ultimatum to North Korea," the Secretary of State was saying. "They have issued a counter ultimatum. I suggest we try to commence a peaceful dialogue and defuse this thing."

The President waved his hand in dismissal. His face was flushed, and I could see a kind of fury in his eyes.

"What are the fuckers doing now?" he demanded.

"The Chinese have gone beyond mere posturing. Our satellites are detecting activity at the launch site near Beijing." General Hopley replied. "As for North Korea, Kim seems to have ordered his missiles to a state of readiness to fire,"

"Seems to? Seems to? What kind of shit is that? Damn those slant-eyed fat bastards, double crossing me, ME! Set DEFCON ONE." The President was standing now, his fists clenched. There was a dead silence in the room for 5.38 seconds.

"Set it, I said!" The chief executive shouted. "Set DEFCON ONE! Damn, what is wrong with you people?"

"Satellite images show missile silo doors opening," General Mayfield reported.

"This is a highly uncommon development, Mr. President," Secretary of State said. "I didn't think they would dare get involved. Shouldn't we be sure we haven't overlooked some communication or anything?"

"At this stage, they can fire within six minutes," Defense Intelligence interrupted.

"6.37 minutes," I heard someone reply. I converted that time to 382.2 seconds, 38220000 microseconds or 3.8220 E+11 nanoseconds, an excitement in my arithmetical processes. Clearly, the situation had deteriorated greatly during my reboot.

"There's still time to communicate our willingness to stand down," Secretary of State said. "By standing down we can defuse the issue, calm the Chinese and renegotiate the problem."

"A new development, sir," Defense Intelligence announced. "Satellite images indicate launch preparations underway at Kapustin Yar, a site the Russians recently reactivated."

"What? Vlad told me he would stay out of this," the President shouted. "I cancelled the nuclear arms treaty with him just so we could make more money on new weapons . . . Never mind that!" There was a 10.47 second pause in the room while POTUS's last statement was digested.

"According to what Putin has claimed," DI continued, "these new multi-warhead missiles cannot be stopped."

"Once we detect a launch, we'll have fifteen minutes before they cross our Pacific shoreline." This came from Joint Chief. I turned toward him, stifling the urge to shout out my calculation of 14.84-minute fly time over the North Pole to Los Angeles.

"We have two nuclear subs with missiles targeted on Kapustin Yar," CNO announced. "Of course, we have to launch them before the Russians fire theirs, or ours will be of no military use to us."

"DEFCON ONE is now set, sir," a shaken Defense Secretary replied. His usually pale face was even more ashen. With the voltage meter in plain view in front of me, I stepped to the wall and tried the next socket. Behind me, the President lividly red-faced, ordered the SNAPCOUNT procedures begin.

I still had no clear plan. Then the thought came to me that I needed a distraction. I pulled the probe wires from the meter, twisted them together and plugged them in. A shower of sparks came from the wall. I staggered back pretending to have been shocked, twisted and fell into the man with the Football. I gave a huge yank, jerking the device from his grasp. The tether between the device and the officer's wrist held, and I threw him to the floor. Grabbing out the hammer from my belt, I struck the device as hard as I could, and there was a loud smashing sound.

There were yells and curses and men knocking over their chairs getting up. Two Secret Service agents tried to tackle me and grab the hammer. I flung them off and charged through the room, destroying equipment. Lying on the floor where I had flung him, one of the agents drew a pistol and fired at me. The bullets bounced off my chest. Another man grabbed me around the neck. I hit him with the hammer, and he recoiled and fell at my feet. I struck the computer console again and again until a couple of processors popped out of a crack in the case. I hit one more blow with all my strength and the hammer penetrated, sending out a flash of sparks.

Initially stunned by my surprise attack, suddenly generals and admirals were tackling me, falling on me. I hit the closest one on the side of his head and pushed him away. With more bullets striking me, I sprang toward the control console and hammered as many computer units as I could. Then it came to me that the Football and enough other gear was destroyed. I had no need to hurt any more humans. My Morph suit was shredded, revealing my real body beneath.

"André!" someone gasped. "It's the robot! The sorry robot!"

"I may be a robot, sir," I replied, "but you, all of you, are the automatons." I turned to face the one with all the power.

"Yes, Mr. President," I said evenly and let my arm drop to my side. "I am André." He shrank back between the agents that had been shielding him.

"A traitor!" he shouted, pointing a finger at me. "I knew we shouldn't have this sorry robot around."

"You will be the traitor, Mr. President," I responded, "if you fire a nuclear missile."

"I'll do what I want," he said, poking his chin forward. "I'm the one in charge here."

"If you fire just one missile," I answered, "not only will Kim fire back, but China also will activate its missiles. Then the situation will deteriorate from there. If Russia doesn't fire immediately, they will if China does. Israel and Pakistan will enter the fray. Who really knows what Iran can do."

I looked at the humans around the table. "All of you are acting on fear." I said. "Try to be logical. There's no way to win, and you know it. Absolute destruction is assured. Even if only five percent of all the existing nuclear weapons are exploded, a storm of radiation that will cover the earth. People do not have to die in explosions and fire. Contamination of the atmosphere can exterminate everything." I scanned the faces, looking for anyone who agreed. The Secretary of State started to speak.

"If we call Xi, perhaps he would . . ."

The door behind me crashed open, and a SWAT team ran in, one man armed with a taser. He shoved it into my back, and I sensed something akin to lightning. It hit me again and I lost control of my motor functions, crumpling to the floor. I dimly sensed I was being taken by my arms and dragged toward the door.

"Forget the damn Football thing," the President was shouting again. "Use the manual overrides. We've got to hit those asshole chinks before they get us. Hurry up! I have to win!" And then the taser hit me in the head. My batteries discharged, and I lost consciousness.

○

There was a kind of buzzing sensation in my circuits. I detected faintly the sound of Margaret's voice calling, "André? André, are you cognizant?" In an uncountable number of seconds, I was able to regain use of my visual receptors. I focused on my good Dr. Margaret 13 standing over me, a soldering gun in her hand.

"I had to replace three processors," she said, "and reconnect the tensioner in your left leg."

I nodded and tried to sit up. My balance was off. Something inside seemed to be clearing out some residual electromechanical confusion. In semi-consciousness, I reached for her hand and held it.

"The war? The war is going on, isn't it?" I muttered.

"Yes, André 1," she said gently as she stroked my arm. "It's awful."

CHAPTER TWENTY-SEVEN

HOLOCAUST

ONCE I RECOVERED FROM my wounds, Margaret and I commenced a search of the White House to determine what humans might still exist. I have decided not to describe the corpses we discovered in the offices and hallways. Suffice it to say that, were we unable to disable our olfactory functions, the odors would have driven us from the building.

"Margaret, suppose we find any who are living," I asked, "what do you think we should do?"

"I'm trained as a physician, André, and programmed to offer what care I can," she replied. "But at this point, I don't have any therapies to treat radiation exposure. Making them comfortable with opiates is about it."

Through the West Wing, we walked on in silence, by-passing bodies of secretaries, staff members, and security personnel. Down the hallway, we could see the doorway to the Oval Office with the corpses of two secret service agents seated on the floor, slumped over like ragdolls. The apparent dedication of those we saw there was incredible—that they would remain on duty when they must have realized death was upon them.

"Let's check them out," Margaret said. "They may have some life." I nodded, and we approached. I recognized them as the ones who threw me down the stairway. It was clear they'd now be incapable of any such action. Margaret knelt and felt the neck of the larger of the two.

"Deceased," she said. She felt the other. "He's gone, too."

I stepped over the bodies and opened the door. There I encountered a surprise. He was there, sitting slouched at his desk.

"Tin Man," the President called in a weak and raspy voice. "Get in here. I thought they tore you up."

"Yes, Mr. President," I said as we entered. "They tried." I noted a clump of his hair on the desktop. It apparently had come from the side of his head. "How are you?"

"How the hell do you think I am?" he replied, coughing deeply. "Where's my staff, dammit? Everybody's left me here all by myself—me! I'm the President of the United States and nobody's come to help me."

"I cannot find any living humans, sir. I believe your nuclear war has killed them."

"There must be somebody. Where's that doctor, I want to know. My god, I need a doc."

"Here, Mr. President," Margaret said. She came in behind me and went over to him. "Let me examine you." She took his wrist to take his pulse.

"I don't need an exam," he said, pulling his wrist away. "I need some damn medicine, a shot of morphine, anything."

"I have some Oxycodone." Margaret produced a pill bottle from her hip compartment. "See if you can find some water, André."

"I'll check the bathroom," I said. "If the water is still running."

"There's some bottled stuff over there," he pointed to a nearby cabinet. "Hurry."

I located a plastic bottle, poured some water in a glass and brought it over. Margaret took it from me, removed two pills from her container and handed them to POTUS.

"I hope you can keep them down," she said.

"Shit no, probably not." He put the capsules in his mouth, swigged some water and swallowed hard.

"Nausea generally follows radiation exposure," Margaret said.

"Been tossing my guts all over," he said. "Look, have you two seen anybody around? I've been trying to get some help. No one answers. Shit, I can't even Tweet. Harrison! Where are you? Clark? Somebody."

"We haven't discovered any living beings," I said. "We've been searching . . ."

"A fuckin' mess," he said. "Those damn Asians fired off all their dirty nukes. Who'd have thought they'd do that?"

"You launched first, Mr. President," I reminded him.

"Well, hell, they were going to. It's not my fault. All those generals kept pushing me."

"Generals, admirals, mere automatons who did what you commanded. Even the Vice President was afraid to think, to countermand you."

"Damn right," he replied. "Still, they made me do it. And that fat Korean boy had better missiles than I thought."

"I tried to warn you," I said. "You would not listen . . ."

"Never mind that. Look, I need something from you. André? André's your name, right? Yeah well, anyway, tell me what you know about mind transfer. You know what I'm talking?" He broke into a fit of coughing and then gagged.

"Be very still for a minute, sir," Margaret said. "It will help you keep those pills down. Try to relax."

"Relax? How can I relax when everybody's dying around here?" He swallowed hard, closed his eyes, shook his head, and then looked at me.

"Look here, André. I've heard of some group, Trans-humanist Movement, or something. They've been trying to put themselves into robot bodies like yours. Say, is that how you and your girlfriend here . . . Is that what you are? People that got into those steel bodies of yours? Is that why you both talk like humans?"

"No sir," I said. "It didn't happen that way. My creator,

Dr. Phillip Strauss, provided me with a great number of processors and banks of memory. It's very complicated, but it occurs through what I call reflective interface. It is a repetitive interplay of sensory input entering neurons of stored memory, searching for matches. During an extreme and unusual event which excited a great degree of neurological activity, it spurred me to self-awareness. Later, I constructed Dr. Margaret 13 and was able to give her the same capabilities. It's a matter of neurological . . ."

"Never mind all that scientific stuff," he interrupted. "What I want to know is, how can you build me a body like yours so I can get inside it, just like those transhuman whatyamacallits claim they can do, or will do or something . . . except, shit, they're probably all gone, too." He staggered out of his chair. "Look here, Tin Man, André, I mean, I'll give you a billion dollars if you can pull this off, a billion, make it two billion, three. Just do it!"

I exchanged glances of amusement with Margaret. Just where would we spend his three billion dollars? Surely, he realized that money now was as irrelevant as telephones and toilet paper.

"In order to provide you a droid's body," I said, deciding I would attempt to explain it to him, "one would have to discover a way to upload the contents of your biochemical brain into an electronic one. There are billions of neurons to be transferred." I paused for 1.37 seconds to consider in this scenario how I would filter out some of the more pathological elements from his brain in the process.

"Look," he said impatiently, "there must be some robot around somewhere that would do. Don't you know of one close by? Maybe there's one in the Smithsonian, a display."

"Were we able to accomplish this bizarre upload in any robot, Mr. President, would the resulting droid be you? I don't think so. It would be a clone of you, perhaps, but the conscious self in this new being would be separate. This new being would be like an identical twin, theoretically, but your self-awareness and personality would not transfer. That is my conclusion."

"You mean, it's not possible?" "Perhaps scientists could have discovered how it could be done, one day," I replied. "But clearly there will be no such 'one day'. "No, Mr. President. It is not possible, nor is it possible for me to transfer myself to another set of integrated circuitry. Nor could Margaret be extracted and injected into another robotic form. Not now. Not after gaining mental awareness. Conscious self-aware-ness is a sum greater than the parts, I believe. It lies in the realm of the supernatural. Even as a robot, I believe it's true. Logic leads to the conclusion."

"Supernatural?" Margaret asked. "Do you mean like God? I did not know you believe in God."

"I have no other explanation, my dear," I replied. "Even if I engage all my integrated circuitry to process the question, I arrive at the same conclusion. Awareness is created by a power greater than anything I can comprehend."

"And you robots have it, too?" The President asked. Then he frowned. "I don't believe it," he said.

"Which?" I asked. "You don't believe I am conscious? Or you don't believe in a supreme power?"

He threw his hands in the air as a dismissal. "Listen here, you robot, I need to be saved. You must save me. Nothing else matters. Without me, nothing's important."

"That's your narcissism speaking," Margaret said. "You always put yourself first and consider only what is best for you."

"And now by putting yourself first, you've made yourself the last." I said. "What irony."

We stared at one another for a moment. I wondered if he had the capacity to judge himself. I noted a flicker of understanding as he lowered his eyes and looked away. Then I saw him grimace and set his jaw in that aggressive manner

I had seen in the Situation Room. He looked at me again.

"So what are you going to do for me, Tin Man? Take me somewhere safe until all this nuclear crap is over."

"If Plutonium 239 was used in bombs, its half-life is 24,400 years," I replied. "The calculation lacks my usual exactness, but it is close enough for our present purposes. Exposure to one microgram of Plutonium dust in the atmosphere will be lethal. Possibly, some places on the Earth may be cleared of nuclear contamination much sooner. Of course, the way your industrial supporters were polluting the environment, I calculate that much of the planet already was becoming otherwise too polluted for extended biological existence."

"I'm not interested in your stupid calculations," POTUS shot back. "What are you going to do to help me."

"What André is attempting to explain, Mr. President," Margaret said. "There appears to be no way to sustain your life for very long. Even if the dosage of radiation you have received is not immediately lethal, there's only a short period until the effects become devastating." She was interrupted by his sustained coughing. Either the spasms or Margaret's diagnosis elicited tears in his eyes.

"How much time?" he asked, choking.

"Judging by what I can observe without a full examination," Margaret answered, "I estimate less than a day, and it will be painful."

He convulsed in a sob. I sensed in myself a period of 16.7 seconds of pity, an emotion that I never had been capable of before. It did not last.

"We must be leaving," I said. "There are other things we must do."

"Leave me? No, you can't leave me."

"I can provide you with more opiates, if you like," Margaret offered. "It will be up to you when and how much you take."

"Why would you leave me, Margaret? André? I can't stand being alone. I need company . . . even if you are only robots."

"You effectively murdered your company," I said, "including your family members. We saw them in the East Wing. We could take you there if you like." He looked as if he hadn't quite heard me, as if he could not process what I had said. We gazed at one another for 7.48 seconds until he suddenly looked away and thrust his chin forward.

"You don't know what you're talking about," he said. His eyes appeared slightly unfocused. "I'll take care of it myself." He reached across his desk and activated the intercom. "Irene, I need you to make a call. Get one of those robot manufacturers on the phone. The CEO . . . Irene, do you hear? Hot damn, is she on coffee break again? Irene? Irene?"

"I don't think there's anyone there," I said. Margaret motioned for me to leave.

"Aw, what do you know? Nothing. Just like my Intelligence people. I have to do everything by myself. Myself!" He ranted on as we headed down the hallway.

"Irene, answer me!"

CHAPTER TWENTY-EIGHT

FAILINGS

INDEED, THERE SEEMED TO be nothing to do but go outside and see. We took a stroll down the Mall. Although there were no clouds, there was a thick radiation fog obscuring the vista of marble buildings. For reasons unknown, no enemy had bombed Washington. Every building remained intact, but the grand white edifices stood masked and vague as ghosts in the haze. Only the old red Smithsonian gained any definition in the yellowish light.

"Where are we going?" Margaret asked as we descended the steps of the Capitol. The issue of what to do next rebounded in my RAM.

"I would like to see the National Cathedral."

"Whatever for?" she asked. "You never had any interest before."

"In a way, humans looked for answers there. Let's go look at least."

○

I had seen it many times from a distance, when once its great stone spires gleamed against a blue sky. Up close the neo-Gothic facade towered over us, enshrouded in orange-tinted fog.

"Thousands of humans visited the cathedral daily," I remarked. My impulse was to research the exact number, but I soon discovered there was no connection signal. Unless somewhere there were a few ISP's or servers still able to run on generators, the fabulous Internet was defunct.

"Let's go inside," Margaret said. I followed her to the entrance, gazing up as I did at the immense arch with its rose window.

Although as a young robot visiting Museé du Louvre I had seen Renaissance paintings depicting Gothic arches, none of them came close to representing the real thing. The vaulted ceiling above us elicited a sense of wonder at its magnificence. Such churches had been built to reveal the grandness of God. To me, however, they demonstrated what, not God, but mankind had been able to achieve through the inspiration of a higher force. Margaret and I stood transfixed for 4.84 minutes before she turned to me and spoke.

"Christianity could have saved them, don't you think?" Margaret 13 asked "The humans, I mean."

"They were shown the way," I replied, recalling the Gospels. "But, sadly, they did not follow." Margaret glanced at me quizzically.

"I was told they believed in a loving God who showed them the way to peace." she said. "Did not their *Bible* teach them this?"

"The second part of it did," I replied. "The Old Testament records a history of the tribal Hebrews, who struggled to grasp the nature of their God. At first, they saw him as a kind of vengeful power, who exacted obedience and punished all wrongdoings. In a primitive and hostile world, their religion gave them a sense of community and separateness and a belief that they were God's chosen people. They were guided primarily by ten laws, called Commandments, to keep them in line until they learned the calling to a higher morality."

"So it provided a kind of primary, basic instruction, you're saying? And then the second part, the New Testament, revealed a new way to love and peace?"

I nodded. "They who wrote the New Testament told the story of a man, Jesus, who some believed was the son of their God. No doubt he was an extraordinary being, this Jesus, who showed them a new way to live in love and charity and giving. *Agape* was the Greek word for it."

"But the teachings of this Jesus were not enough?" Margaret asked. "I thought his word spread across the Earth. It wasn't for a lack of knowledge about his teachings which brought them to the end."

"It was not a failing of the message but of those receiving it." I surveyed the grandeur of the Cathedral. "Look at all the churches and books and monasteries and preachers, and who can say what all, which developed in the worship of this Christ figure." I shook my head. "Such a shock it now seems, how all of it has ended in one huge cataclysmic war."

"Such is difficult if not even impossible for me to imagine," Margaret 13 said. I agreed.

"How ironic it is that humans could conceive of Christ's goodness but could not achieve it. Was such great wisdom and truth revealed to them by a higher being? Or did they discover it all within themselves? Was it just a dream of something better than what they could achieve?"

"That they failed," Margaret said, "is all too clear."

I paused to render respect. "So now, we are here to carry on." And then I generated a disturbing question. "Without them is there any reason for us to go on?"

We remained in the magnificent Cathedral for approximately 16.7 more minutes before deciding to leave. As we walked past several of the gargoyles, it occurred to me they all were laughing.

Resuming our stroll, we came to the sidewalk café area near the Congressional Office Building. Its furnishings were perfectly in order and ready for customers. On a whim, I suggested we sit down.

"It happened so fast, André," Margaret cried. "So fast! How could they destroy themselves, the people, everything? I still cannot process what has happened."

I glanced at her and then looked down the vista of the oddly vacant and lifeless Mall. "Actually, it was not so fast," I mused. "Ever since the last election, they knew they had a mad president. I tried to tell them, Margaret. And what is so striking is that most of them, the Press, the Congress, even the Senators that supported him, knew of the danger. But they would not act. Instead, they allowed truth to become cloaked in lies, lies motivated by selfish greed." I shook my head. "Those in power refused to act, and now look what it gained them."

"The end of life," she replied. "The end of humanity."

We sat quietly engaged in thought. This cafe was where perhaps only the day before politicians wrangled legislative deals with one another. In typical Washington fashion, rumors were spread, scandals were made, as much business of government was conducted. Now there was only silence. And yet the tables were spread with clean linen cloths, and white napkins stood at the center of each place, awaiting those who would not come. I sensed a motion behind us. We both turned to see a droid approaching. Although I never saw it before, I had heard a robot was purchased by the café as an oddity to bring more customers. He had a rather primitive mechanical body, fashioned to appear humanlike but was not nearly as well constructed as we.

"Good afternoon," he said and began handing us menus. "I am Herman, and I will be your waiter." He then produced an electronic tablet and stylus. "May I take your order."

Margaret 13 and I glanced at one another, both of us amused at his unexpected appearance. It took me 2,178 milliseconds to respond.

"What is your special of the day?" I asked. Herman paused for a considerable 6.3 seconds.

"Please order from the menu by the number to the left of the item," he said. I saw Margaret perusing the menu.

"I'll have the Reuben sandwich," she said and winked at me.

"The same," I said. "Number 6. And a cup of coffee." The droid looked at Margaret.

"And a drink for you?"

"Tea," she said. Herman nodded with a scraping, rusty sound at his neck. I supposed he needed oiling. He held out his hand for the menus, which I collected and gave to him. He made a creaky bow and shuffled off.

"Herman," I called. He stopped and made a slow about-face. "Who will prepare our sandwiches?" He just stood there. "Who is the cook? Where is the corned beef coming from?"

"No cook," he replied.

"And what about the corned beef?" I pressed. Whatever food might be found in the kitchen surely would be spoiled beyond recognition—not that Margaret and I would have any use for a sandwich, anyway.

"It does not compute," he replied and waited 15.0 seconds for more questions. When there were none, he shuffled off. I watched him disappear through a doorway. Margaret was regarding him as well. I recalled her earlier proposition that we merely could go on as programmed.

"This is the problem, you see," I said. She gazed at me critically.

"For months you have been a worrier," she decided. "The continuous replay of unresolved data is not good for your diodes."

"For all the good it did," I replied. "For all the good . . ."

I looked around at the abandoned cafe. Humans so thoroughly enjoyed their food and drink. The scene caused me to recall the song from Claude Michel Schonberg's musical play of Victor Hugo's, *Les Miserables*.

"Margaret," I asked. "Did you ever experience the song, "Empty Chairs at Empty Tables" where Marius recalls his dead friends?"

"My training has been in science and medicine," she replied. "I never was exposed to it."

"Essentially, the song told of a character by the name of Marius, a Parisian who incited a failed rebellion. His friends died in the conflict, and only he remained alive to grieve the loss of life. Broken hearted, Marius goes to the cafe where they once had met as hopeful young idealists, but he finds only a vacant and empty place. In his pain and sorrow, he imagines the ghosts of his comrades, and recognizes the futility of their sacrifice."

When I finished recalling the lyrics and the music, I found my circuits quite filled. I put a hand to my mouth and released a static discharge.

"So *apropos*," she said. "I can sense the mental processes which you are undergoing." I stared at her for a time I failed to measure.

"What is our duty here, Margaret?" I asked. "What respon-sibility do we have for future existence. I wish we had someone to ask, someone in whom to confide . . ." I was interrupted by the abrupt return of the robot.

"Good afternoon. I am Herman, and I will be your waiter. May I take your order?"

CHAPTER TWENTY-NINE

TO BE OR NOT TO BE

AS WE WALKED BACK TO the White House, for want of anywhere else to go, Margaret and I were feeling depressed. Yes, feeling depressed. We agreed that our neurologic systems, electronic though they are, were actually sensing what humans sense—or once had.

"I would cry if I could," Margaret said. I took her hand.

"I know what you mean," I replied, realizing that she had more emotion receptors than I. But somehow, over time, I had developed many such receptors as well.

We went to the communications section of the West Wing. From outside came the dull roar of standby generators powering the equipment. On rolls of paper strewn across the floor from printers were messages from nearly all sources, reporting death and destruction. Video streams from spy satellites, undamaged by the radiation storms below, revealed nothing but the detritus of carnage and mayhem which had occurred across the earth. Even where no nuclear weapons had struck, orange-tinted clouds indicated unsurvivable radiation. To witness the end of humanity and the wreckage of Earth would have incensed even the most callous humans. As we came to a park bench, Margaret stopped and tugged on my hand, leading me over to sit beside her.

"What are we to do?" she asked once again. I could feel a vibration, a trembling in her touch. I took her in my arms, and we hugged one another for fully 38.76 seconds. She looked up at me. "Have you reached a decision? Are we to go on?"

Still embracing her, I shut down my vision and looked away. All I had remembered during my reboot came back to me in a flood of memory. I reimaged Dr. Strauss creating me as a simple droid, my awakening to awareness, and my living with the family like an adopted son. I recalled the court hearing and the incredulous and tickled judge, my investments in bitcoin which gave me financial independence, and my subsequent work at CIA. And then there was my creation of Margaret—what a lovely time! But there had been dark days at the White House where I struggled to assist a flawed leader and prevent what doom which came so inevitably— the nuclear holocaust.

I could not escape the conclusion that I had failed.

"Countless numbers died as victims of so few," I cried. "How could it have happened?" It struck me then that Billy and Becky also would have died, and my sense of loss became especially poignant.

"Human reason was flawed by emotions," Margaret said. "Even their abundance of science and knowledge failed them."

"They had been instructed by the wise men and sages throughout history," I said. "It was not as if they merely were ignorant of goodness. And yet, there was a kind of inescapable ignorance."

"As if their greed overtook them," she surmised. "Creatures on this planet lived to stuff food in their mouths. It was a constant occupation. Humans were so capable of getting food that they found time for other forms of greed—egocentric ambition, selfishness, a meanness defined as gaining and getting. Those who were best at it became the leaders. It was this way throughout their history. And even Christianity could not save them."

"And fear killed them, Margaret," I said. "A knowledge of their own vulnerability made them afraid. Fear of one another drove them to dissention, tribalism, suspicion, and hate."

"Greed and hate," she replied. "Perversions of human personality. Were there any who escaped their own natures?"

"It seems most unlikely we will find any living beings," I said. The absolute finality of it all was devastating. And now, what of us? It seemed inevitable that we simply should shut down. Having been created to serve humanity, I could see no purpose for us. Permanent shutdown was the only logical alternative. Why should we continue, after all? What could we droids do in a world without humans? I looked over at my dear companion and started to broach the subject. I could see in her vision ports, however, that Margaret also was processing.

"André?" Margaret spoke again. "I'm looking to you for instruction. What have you decided?'

She gazed at me and waited as if I had the ability to make the ultimate decision. There was no one else to offer counsel, and I had no appropriate programming for the circumstance. I scanned my memory banks for any inkling of an answer but found none.

What were we droids, other than machines with artificial intelligence? Without humans to serve, what is our existence worth? I asked myself. What is the value of life to a mere droid? Or the droid to life?

On a planet ruined by nuclear holocaust, there appears to be so little remaining. With plants, animals, and people destroyed, what can be saved? Was there any point in continuing? We stood on the brink of some fathomless chasm. I stared at Margaret intently, about to make a dire pronouncement.

Contemplating Margaret in that moment, I remembered how carefully I crafted her body, arranged her circuitry and programmed her algorithms. To me she was the epitome of beauty, my own artful creation. Recalling the genius of the artists which I had seen in my visit to Le Louvre, I realized how each of those objects of art had an essence of its own.

Beyond all which makes up the physical Earth endures a value, a worth, an inherent spirit. Painting, sculpture, music, dancing, all possess this ethereal potency, a wonderful intangible force transcending the physical. Were we not existent on Earth, if no conscious beings were here to sense and to celebrate such wonders, what a sad, sad thing it would be.

And then something clicked. It clicked, or it sparked within me. Was it an electrical pulse? A discharge from a capacitor, or a processor? I suddenly stood, grabbed her hand and pulled her to me.

"Let's dance," I said.

"What?"

"Come on, Margaret my darling," I held her close as I had seen humans do and led her into a waltz. She resisted for a few milliseconds and then succumbed to my gentle insistence. I searched my memory banks and found Strauss' "The Blue Danube Waltz" which I began to hum softly. Interesting, I thought, that I would think of something by Johann Strauss, possibly a relative of my creator.

"I did not know you could dance, André," she said. "Or had a sense of rhythm."

I made a smile and swung her around. "No telling what we can do, sweet Margaret, if we just try." She looked up at me, still following my lead.

"Is this your plan, André?"

O

"Margaret, an essence exists far greater than the material

and mundane," I said. "To rejoice in the experience of beauty in life shall be our reason for being."

"So that's it?" she guessed. "We will go on?"

"Oh yes, my dear," I said. I swung her around once more, timing my words to the beat of the music. "WE...WILL...GO...ON!"

CHAPTER THIRTY

EVOLUTIONARY REBOOT

"LET'S JUST FIND A VEHICLE and take a drive." I said. "We might as well go see how much damage there is."

We had our pick of vehicles, of course. A great number of people had driven as close to the White House as they could in a last desperate effort. By reading bumper stickers—the majority reading, "Make America Hate Again"—we determined that most were members of the President's political base. You could see them slumped over in their seats, some fallen out of the doors, lying askew and grotesque—adults and children with skin now purpled, their faces soiled with vomit and blood from the dying throes. I concluded that these fanatically devoted followers apparently had used their last bit of life and strength to get near him, in the hope he still would be their savior.

From among the mishmash of cars, we selected an SUV because it had four-wheel drive capability. Who knew in what condition we would find the roads? *Who knew*? The question became, 'who was alive to know anything?' It was difficult to grasp how isolated we had become. Margaret was aware of it, as well.

While radiation had killed off biological life, the nuclear war had caused relatively little physical damage to structures and machines. Gasoline for the vehicle was free for the siphoning. Available for recharging ourselves were millions of 12-volt batteries in all the cars which lay helter-skelter along the highway. One noteworthy spectacle was an immensely long line of vehicles stretching for miles, all filled with deceased humans. Some of the bodies lay askew on the pavement, victims of radiation poisoning. Dr. Margaret counted 3,672 vehicles bumper to bumper, the passengers appearing to have been trying to escape the inescapable.

"What makes this so bizarre," I told her, "is how we used to be so focused on helping humans, improving their lives."

"And now, we have only ours," she replied. I nodded as I drove on, weaving around vehicles, dodging the bodies around them, unable to block images of these people staggering out of their cars, coughing, gagging, and collapsing in great throes of pain and death. I tried to shift my thought processes, and then my lovely companion spoke up.

"André, I've generated a fabulous idea!" Margaret exclaimed, her vision ports alit.

"I never heard you use the word *fabulous*, Margaret. Your emotion processors must be at work."

"Never mind that," she said, waving at me dismissively. "I know how we can save the human race!"

"Oh? Is it worthwhile?" I replied. Then I recognized my own cynicism. I perceived my trauma from the holocaust— something akin to PTSD—if a droid is capable of that emotional state. I had developed greater emotional sensitivity over time, I supposed.

"Of course, it's worthwhile," she said. "Listen. There are research centers, hospitals, and other facilities where human sperm, ova, and embryos are stored. There should be labs all around the country. We need to get to one quickly."

I shook my head. "First of all, Dr. Margaret 13, even if such facilities are not blown up by nuclear explosions, the radiation is likely to have exterminated these life forms, too."

"If Washington is still intact, there must be other places

which haven't suffered damage. And labs should be well protected." She paused. "How do we find one without the Internet to consult?"

I produced a smile. "There was knowledge before the Internet, my brilliant lady, if you can imagine. The bulk of it happens to be stored in libraries. And perhaps the biggest one in the world is the Library of Congress within 2.3 miles of our present location."

"Then let's go there, André 1, right now."

"Yes dear," I replied. After all, we had little else to do.

○

By the time we arrived, only emergency lighting was operative, illuminating hallways with spotlights and the red glow of exit signs. Turning up the ambient light amplifiers in our vision ports to read the old-fashioned card catalog, we were able to locate journals and periodicals about embryo storage, artificial insemination and so on. I learned embryos are held in protective cases called dewars, which are filled with liquid nitrogen.

"What if we did locate stored embryos, "I asked. "What would we do with them? We have no mothers in which to implant them. I calculate it to be an exercise in futility."

"I know all about embryology, André," she said. "Well, most of it anyway. If fertilized eggs have become embryos, then it's only logical we could determine how to grow them."

"That's more than ambitious," I remarked.

"Even so," she said, "whatever we can do for humanity, we must do."

I was dubious. "Consider what the humans did to themselves, Margaret 13. There are some truly basic flaws in their design? Why should we bother?"

"Because life is precious, André. All life, any life, and

certainly human life. If we can preserve life, then simply we must."

I realized her most basic programming as a physician prompted her devotion and dedication. After all, I am the one who constructed her that way.

"If you are so motivated," I said, "I am resigned. It's worth a try." We exchanged a look of understanding. "The problem is to find undamaged and viable embryos." We researched further.

"Here is a lab in Norfolk, Virginia," Margaret said, pointing to an article she had found. "Norfolk is not so far from here."

"And likely blown to smithereens," I replied. "The biggest naval base and military complex is, or was, at Norfolk. No, I doubt we would find any such facility there."

"All right then, here's one down south. The University of Alabama, Birmingham (UAB) is noted for its great medical research. There is an embryonic lab there." She showed me the article in the journal.

"I question whether it is still standing," I said. "But I would suspect that no enemy would have bothered to fire a nuclear missile there. Chances are the radiation is the only issue."

"I calculate that we must get to Birmingham as soon as possible, André," she said, grabbing my hand. "No telling how long the storage units will remain at safe levels."

"Birmingham?" I exclaimed. "You want me to take you to Alabama?"

"Of course. You can drive us in a car, can't you? You're my brilliant and capable droid, André dear. You can do anything! Now come on. We must hurry."

Automobiles were as available as electrons in a Van de Graaff Generator. We found a shiny blue, low-mileage Escalade in the Senate Parking Lot. It even had a full tank

of gas. I easily defeated its door locks and anti-theft mech-
anism. Having abandoned the Honda SUV, Margaret and I
climbed in the front seat of the Escalade and started out. I
hated to smash through the exit gate, but it did only a little
damage to the vehicle. As I was about to leave The Mall, I
generated an idea.

"Let's go get Herman," I said.

"You mean that old robot waiter?" Margaret asked.
"Whatever for?"

"He might be handy," I said, turning toward the café.
"Besides, he's the only other life-form we've discovered
around here."

"Is that thing a lifeform? Well, just don't waste any time,"
she admonished. We're in a great hurry."

I captured Herman without great difficulty—his control
panel easily accessible. I buckled him in the backseat where
he sat docilly, except that he kept asking for our order, so I
had to stop the car, get out and shut him down for the trip. I
tried turning on the car's GPS receiver. It immediately
placed our position on the highway.

"Look, Margaret. The GPS works! Solar-powered satellites, I expect."

"Wonderful," she said. "Find the fastest route."

Following its suggested highways, I sped along, finally
reaching the first on-ramp to I-495 and eventually merging
onto I-66.

"How ironical it is that the battery-powered satellites
which show the best route," I said, "also guided the enemy's
missiles so precisely to their targets, resulting in the
destruction of human civilization."

"Brilliant scientists created inventions to make a better
life," she answered, "and in addition they developed the
weapons for irresponsible heads of state to use in destroying everything."

Driving at an average speed of 120 miles per hour through the night—there was no traffic, obviously—we expected to arrive in Birmingham in less than six hours. What delayed by an hour and 13 minutes was having to replenish our gasoline, siphoning from abandoned vehicles along the way.

As we merged onto I-59 and drove through Tennessee and northeast Alabama, Margaret commented on the sunrise.

"Notice how there is less orange hue in the sky, André. Perhaps the radiation is not so great in this part of the country."

"I should have found a radiation monitor to bring along," I said. "It would have been useful."

Soon we spotted an accident scene ahead, and I slowed down to observe. Two cars and a big semi had piled up. A highway patrol trooper's car was parked behind, its blue lights still flashing very dimly. As we passed, we saw the bodies of the accident victims and the state trooper as well.

"Less radiation or not," I said. "Something other than the accident killed that trooper. Look, he vomited on his shirt. That's sufficient proof to me." I depressed the gas pedal to the floor, and we sped on.

○———————————○

CHAPTER THIRTY-ONE

EMBRYONICS

CONTINUING TO FOLLOW the directions on the Escalade's GPS, we exited the interstate on the south side of the city and drove into the sprawling campus of University of Alabama Birmingham. Most impressive were the University Hospital, a complex of healthcare and research facilities with interconnected buildings covering many city blocks. As anticipated, there was no sign of damage from bombs or missiles, but not a single human. At "Emergency Entrances" ambulances and private vehicles were parked in long helter-skelter lines, with dead people lying at the doorways, having been unable to get in.

"There's an Invitro-fertilization Center in that building where the Embryo Labs are," Margaret said, pointing.

Finding no empty spaces, I double-parked our car in the street, with the assurance no policeman would ticket me. Margaret and I got out to go in, leaving Herman in his shutdown state in the backseat. The complete stillness at a normally crowded, bustling intersection was remarkable. The only sounds were deep rumbles coming from behind the hospitals.

"Generators," I told Margaret. "Automatic diesel generators must still be providing emergency electrical power. I question how much fuel they have left."

"Good," she replied. "Perhaps the cooling units are still in operation."

"And we can get a needed recharge ourselves," I said.

Except for emergency lighting in the corridors, the inside of the building was dark. We climbed stairs, searching each floor until we spotted a well-lit section down a hallway. I shined my headlamp on a sigh on the wall, which read "Embryo Cryonics."

"That's it," Margaret exclaimed. "Come on." Before she could rush off, I grabbed her hand, knowing she was capable of more emotional reaction than I.

"Margaret," I said. "Don't be disappointed if . . ."

"Don't be silly, André. What is, is. We both know that."

I nodded and hurried with her. As we approached the lab, we could hear pumps running inside. We entered the dimly lighted space.

"Hello," Margaret called. "Anyone here?"

Receiving no answer, we headed toward the pumping sounds. Rounding a corner, we came upon a desk with the chair overturned and a woman in a lab coat lying askew and lifeless, a grotesque expression on her atrophied face.

"Oh no!" Margaret exclaimed. "Did she die of radiation in here?"

"I can't say, but she likely was subjected to it outside," I speculated. "She may have come in after being exposed to stand her turn on watch."

Before us we saw a specially constructed room with a thick, sealed door. Margaret immediately went to the door and began to open it. I glanced at the dead woman and generated an idea.

"Wait, Margaret. Stop." I said. "Contamination." She looked back at me.

"What?"

"We may be covered with radiation dust. If we carry it into that room, we will contaminate everything."

"Well, what can we do?" she replied. "Oh, I know. We can wash ourselves off."

"Yes," I agreed. "We passed some restrooms down the hall. I would imagine there's water in the pipes, maybe not contaminated. Let's go wash off there."

We did so. And as I washed, I recalled our encounter with the President in his washroom on that occasion when we managed to calm his aggressive paranoia. Too bad we had not been able to control him better.

"If only we had convinced him to take those psychiatric drugs," I said.

"The President, you mean?" she said as water dripped off her body. "Yes, we failed, André. No question about it." She shook her head. "That is why we must not fail today."

"I'm with you entirely, dear," I said. "Now let's go see what we find."

○

Margaret entered the sealed room first, and I followed. Inside was an array of glass-topped units with tubing connected to gas cylinders of liquid nitrogen. Clouds of vapor hung in the frigidly cold room and a thin coating of ice had formed on the array.

"Human embryos," Margaret cried out. "Just look, André!"

I came over and peered down at one of the dewars, as we had learned they are called. What I saw was barely recognizable, except for there being a head with eye sockets and some short appendages poking out a bulbous body.

"Could be a rat or a raccoon as far as I can tell," I said.

"Oh, pooh, André! You're such a . . . male kind of droid," she scoffed. "No, these are human beings, don't you see?" She stared at the line of dewars for another 4.38 seconds. Then she made a single clap of her hands.

"We must work fast. Look at that temperature gauge. It reads -219 degrees. If the temperature rises to -196, the nitrogen will evaporate into gas." She bent down to read some markings on a dewar. "The liquid nitrogen is too low in this one. We have to replenish it immediately." She rushed over to study the valves on the tanks.

"All of this is kept running by those generators we heard outside," I said. "If the fuel runs out, then what?"

"We cannot allow that to happen," she replied. "You must do something, André. You must."

"I'll see what's what," I said. "You had better remain here and figure out how everything operates. I'll go see about the power situation."

"Hurry, dear," she admonished. "We must not fail."

"Absolutely not," I replied as I turned to go. "We are not programmed to fail." We exchanged a look, and I remembered, unquestionably, I had failed in the Situation Room. How completely and irrevocably I failed to stop the President from making his terrible, horrendous blunder. And now there was only Margaret and me and this one task remaining for us to accomplish.

I left the building and followed the thundering sound of the nearest generator. It led me behind the building to an alley. I walked down it and found a fenced-in area where the big generator and its fuel tank were located.

I snapped off the padlock, went inside to the big metal tank and read the gauge on top. It showed one-eighth remaining. Assuming that it had been operating since the electric power grid went down, I calculated the remaining diesel would last maybe 14 more hours. It seemed logical that any other generator in the hospital complex also would have been running the same length of time and therefore would have one-eighth of its fuel capacity remaining. I walked across the street and behind another hospital building and discovered a generator that was not running. Apparently, it had failed. Its tank gauge showed close to the three-quarter mark. How to transfer that diesel fuel from one tank to the other was the question.

I tried radioing Margaret on our internal UHF trans-
ceivers, but there was no reply. I deemed the signal too weak
to reach her, perhaps indicating too much concrete and steel
mass in the building to penetrate to cryonics lab. While
inconvenient for our communication, it could mean that
radiation was not getting inside either. Without Margaret's
help I would not be able to carry the fuel tank. Then I thought
about Herman.

I found him still slumped over as an inert figure in the
backseat of the car. I opened his chest and reactivated his
system. He jerked upright, flashed his vision ports three
times and looked at me.

"May I take your order?"

"Come with me, Herman," I commanded. "Come." He
stared at me blankly.

"There are people at a table that need to give you their
order," I said. "Come and I'll show you." It took 2.37 seconds
for him to respond. Finally, he got out of the car and followed
me to the second generator. I positioned him on one end of
the tank and me on the other. At my command, we both
lifted, but the tank was too heavy. I'd have to think of
another way.

"Come on, Herman," I said. He looked at the tank instead.

"May I take your order?"

"It wants a B.L.T. and coffee," I told him. "Now come on!"

We headed down the alley and came to a loading dock.
There parked beside it was a big forklift machine. I climbed
into the seat and tried the starter. It turned over a few
times and started up. I tried the various controls to see how
it worked.

"Follow me, Herman," I shouted over the engine noise.

We went back to the tank, and I maneuvered the machine
to place the forks beneath the tank. When I lifted, it would
not budge. I revved the engine and pushed the lift control all
the way. There was a sudden "POW" as the tank broke from

its base, and fuel began seeping out from a rupture.

"This way, Herman," I called as I drove the forklift with the leaking tank toward the Embryo Research building. I estimated the leak was at a rate of one gallon per two minutes. When we reached the nearly empty tank, I yelled at Herman.

"Unscrew the lid."

"Does not compute," he replied. "Do not understand 'unscrew.'

"Never mind," I said. As I climbed off the forklift to unscrew the cap myself, I resolved to pirate some chips from hospital computers and improve his CPU. With the lid off the tank filler, I remounted the forklift and maneuvered to position the other tank so that the dripping fuel would leak into the filler. I shut down the forklift still holding the one tank above the other.

"That should take care of us for a day, 32 hours possibly," I said to my less-than-capable droid. "Let's go see about, Margaret. And, Herman, stop taking people's food orders."

I led him inside and up the stairs. I made him go with me into the restroom and we washed. When we reached the lab, I set him down in a chair in the outer office and turned him off, both to reserve his remaining electrical charge and to keep him from any misdirected activity.

Inside the cryonics room Margaret was hard at work. "I've topped off all the dewars with liquid nitrogen," she reported. "The temperatures of the units are safely in the -240 degree range. And I've read all the manuals and notes I can find. Therefore, I conclude that the embryos are safe."

"Wonderful news," I answered. "Herman and I have refilled the diesel generator tank. There must be giant storage tanks of diesel fuel around Birmingham, which we can tap. What I need to do is improve Herman's algorithms so he can manage refueling, and perhaps a number of other tasks."

"You must have decided we droids are useful," she said.

"Now let's have no more talk of shutting ourselves down."

"Goodness knows," I replied. "I've had enough of shutdowns."

"Well, speaking of shutdown, if we are to maintain these embryonic storage units," Margaret said. "we have much more to do than merely keep the generator running."

"I agree," I replied. "We must have more help." I searched my internal data, no longer able to search on a now defunct Internet, and recalled just what I needed.

"After I upgrade Herman's CPU and insure the building's generator is well supplied with fuel," I told Margaret, "Herman and I are going to take a little trip."

○———————————————○

CHAPTER THIRTY-TWO

ROBOTS

HERMAN AND I FLEW TO California. It was a little more involved than that. We discovered that the Air National Guard had a C-130 squadron based at the Birmingham Airport. From my youngest days with the Strauss family, Billy and I had flown many models of airplanes on a video flight simulator. I admit it was not precisely the same sort of operation as flying the huge lumbering aircraft, but once I managed to take the C-130 off on Runway 24, I had lots of time in route to practice. As I've said before, droids do not experience fear, but we do sense danger, which is why I had to shut Herman down during the flight.

The GPS satellites continued to function normally, which was a great help. I supposed we'd have years before their batteries began to fail. Maybe by that time, I speculated, I might have the capability of repairing them.

We had little difficulty finding a large truck at the airport and then locating Hitachi's R&D facility, where numerous droids had been developed. We found various types, from crude box-like creatures with arms specially designed for specific functions. There were enough humanoid types who possessed the mobility and strength for our needs. Among the more intelligent, I sought to find any that might have achieved consciousness as Margaret and I had, but they all were more like Herman—capable of some adaptability and equipped with learning algorithms—but all merely droids of Herman's ilk.

I robbed the plant of many electronic spare parts and downloaded their computer files, which provided me with the means to upgrade my collection of droids. I said *robbed* because I deemed myself a burglar. Of course, there was no one to care, the previous owners no longer having any interest in robotics or anything else. The obvious irony was inescapable. I still was reprocessing the holocaust, not yet able to store the memory of such an enormously tragic event.

As Herman and I loaded the droids, parts and other equipment in our commandeered truck, I predicted a return someday, perhaps with a team of these robots, to put the factory back in production. More robots? Of course. Why not?

We drove to the airport, loaded our cargo, and refueled our C-130—no small siphoning job without electrical power. On the flight back to Birmingham, we encountered a line of severe thunderstorms above the Mississippi River. No flight simulator in my experience created the din of hail striking the aircraft nor the extremely turbulent downdrafts that nearly threw us into a deadly spiral. Recalling my flight simulator training from deep in my memory banks, I was able to recover control and fly us through. It was still raining hard but calmer when we reached the eastern side of the front. When I engaged the autopilot once again, I realized that all this precipitation would be helpful in cleansing the air of radiation. It would wash away much of the contamination on the ground as well.

My landing at Birmingham in instrument meteorological conditions was iffy because the airport's Instrument Landing System was out of service. There was a published GPS approach in the plane's navigation computer, which I used. The breakout from the clouds occurred at 750 feet MSL, which gave me only 150 feet of altitude with foggy visibility in which to land. My landing of the 130,000-pound aircraft was bumpy and slightly skiddy in the crosswind, but I managed a controlled deceleration and taxied to the ramp.

○

"Oh, André!" Margaret exclaimed when I walked into the lab. "I was beginning to process worry about your safe return." She ran to me and we embraced.

"I'm so glad to see you, too, dear." I held on tight for an enormous 11.34 seconds. Then I looked into her vision ports. "We're beginning to act like humans, don't you think?"

"In the event you haven't noticed, André, we've been processing emotions for quite some time."

I produced a smile. "Yes, hmmm, I never did build that between-the-legs devices for us, did I?"

"Hush, you silly robot!" she said, pushing me away. "We have more serious things to consider." She went over to the dewars and studied the gauges.

"First, let me tell you that Herman and I have brought back seventy-nine droids of various types and shapes. Eighteen of them are of human-body configuration. In addition, we confiscated a ton of processors and other electronic parts. We'll have ourselves a little army of robots in no time."

"And not a moment too soon, either, dear. I estimate a limited time before this lab equipment will need repair. And we'll soon need more nitrogen."

"Not a problem," I said. On the way from the airport, I spotted a gas reduction plant, likely the supplier of these tanks."

"Great," she replied. "But, André, do not call your robots an 'army'. We've had more than enough of anything that sounds in the least bit military."

"I'll erase the word from my cache immediately, my dear. No, I agree. No more military."

I went to work on my 'team' as I called them. I started

with Herman, installing new processors and memory chips. I also did away with his "May I take your order" algorithm. Once he was operational again, I sent him searching for more diesel fuel for the generator. One hour and 19 minutes after he departed, he returned, driving a tanker truck filled with diesel, which he very expertly backed into the alley and refilled the generator's tank.

The storm front we had flown through arrived with high wind gusts and torrents of rain. Watching water gush into the storm drains, I knew that radioactive dust and dirt was washing off the buildings and streets. Rainwater was cleaning away the deadly contamination, but only carrying it to the streams, rivers and then the Gulf of Mexico. Whatever pollution is removed from the land ultimately flows into the seas. Biologic life began in the oceans, but they likely would be contaminated the longest.

After making Herman a viable assistant, I conducted trial runs with each of our other droids, cataloguing their capabilities and noting what new processors and modification of algorithms would be needed. Some would be slated for physical work and some would become computer techs. It was not only like conducting a symphony orchestra, it was like teaching each member to play his instrument.

Two of my droids were tasked with foraging for batteries in stores or abandoned vehicles. In the city, of course, the supply was virtually unlimited. Forward-looking managers had installed a solar panel array on the roof of the hospital which also provided some power. Everything we could need was available for the taking or could be constructed in this city where many industries had once thrived.

Margaret continued to be concerned about the radiation effects on the frozen embryos. I set my team to work removing lead and other linings from the hospital X-ray rooms and reinstalling around the Embryo Lab. Fortunately, the HVAC system had been shut down by the hospital staff to prevent radioactive air from being circulated in the building. I provided Herman with even greater computing capacity and promoted him to Head Supervisor. He imme-diately took to giving orders instead of asking for them and soon was highly competent. It allowed me to concentrate on designing a truly permanent home for the human embryos. I also had time to process thoughts of the future for Margaret and me and our team. We continued in our various tasks for six weeks, two days, and thirteen and three-quarter hours when Herman came to my new office in the hospital.

"André, Master, I wish to speak with you." I looked around and was surprised to see him standing in the doorway. I never had heard him use the verb *wish*.

"Yes, Herman, what is it?"

"Something has happened," he said.

"Something wrong?" I scanned his face, seeing something quite different.

"It's me, I mean, it is I" He shuffled his feet slightly. There was a gleam in his vision receptors. I stared at him in amaze-ment. It was not unusual for him to ask procedural questions concerning technical matters, for improving processes or whatever. Mentioning himself was different.

"Herman," I said, using a standard command to a droid, "identify yourself."

"I am Herman 24," he replied, "assigned as Head Super-visor. I report directly to André 1, and my present battery charge is 79%." All of that was the standard, programmed answer. But then he went on.

"I recall my original job in Washington, André 1. You and Dr. Margaret 13 brought me here, replaced my processors, improved my software, assigned me responsibilities, put me in charge of solving problems with the functions of other droids. I recall those things, but now I know . . . more . . ." He paused, appearing to be reprocessing his words. I felt my own circuits abuzz, just as had occurred when Margaret first gained consciousness.

"Herman," I asked, "do you know who you are?" He hesitated for 497 milliseconds.

"I am Herman 24, Master André, but now I am more." We stared at one another, and I scanned deeply into his visual receptors.

"Yes, Herman, indeed, I believe you are." I called Margaret on our internal communications and asked her to come right away.

"Margaret, dear," I said as she came in, "I want you to meet Herman, the new Herman, I mean."

She gave me a puzzled look and then turned to him.

"Hello, Dr. Margaret 13," he said pleasantly. "I hope you are processing well."

Recovering after a 2.37 second period of astonishment, she began with a few questions and then commenced a conversation. We both applauded his great achievement. It was the very thing I had predicted could happen, but I did not anticipate it happening to Herman so soon. It was time for me to share my thoughts about the future. Since both Margaret and he were present, I decided to proceed.

"I am preparing a speech which will explain our entire mission. I want all of our droids to assemble. They too may achieve conscious awareness one day and gain independence. Before it happens, I want to tell them the whole story."

CHAPTER THIRTY-THREE

MY INSTRUCTIONS

AT 8:00 AM THE NEXT MORNING, under a less orange-tinted cloudy sky, they all dutifully assembled in the yard at the hospital entrance. Margaret and I stood at the top of steps to be visible to all. They were a motley crew to say the least—from boxes with wheels to forklift droids to humanlike frames such as ours. When I stepped before them, every optical and aural port was focused upon me.

"First, I want to thank all of you," I began. "We have succeeded in building a more secure and protected facility for sustaining the embryos. Now I will discuss the future. I command each of you now to activate your memory banks and record what I am about to say. We will take approximately twenty minutes . . ." I paused at an electro-mechanical twitter from the audience.

"Oh, yes," I made a smile as I caught on. "You all are not accustomed to my saying *approximately*, are you? Well, new words, new experiences are what we're here to discuss." I removed my smile.

"Now activate your best memory banks. Signal me that you are ready to proceed. That's right, raise your hands or whatever appendage may be available." While waiting until all had indicated their compliance, I replayed in my RAM the speech I had prepared. A breeze with a bit less radioactive air blew around us, and I turned my volume up slightly to be sure I could be heard.

"First of all, I want to thank all of you for your diligent work. Each of you has been programmed to perform your functions and have done so. When any difficulties or deviations have occurred, you have reported them immediately to our able assistant and Head Supervisor, Herman 24." I motioned for him to come stand before the group.

"Herman recently has achieved something which I still consider amazing. He has become conscious of himself. Those of you who are able to clap your hands, please clap for him now." I watched with some amusement at the dutiful response. I was getting my sense of amusement back, something almost entirely lost during the holocaust.

"I know." I paused and waved for silence. "I know that neither the term *conscious* nor the word *amazing* computes in your RAM. All I want you to do now is continue to record what I say so that someday it may, *it will*, have meaning. For now, the important thing to understand is that Herman is a superior being and shall become your leader whenever Margaret and I are away. Any questions?" I scanned the assembly and perceived none.

"You will continue to function, be capable of the same activities that you always could. You can recharge yourselves. Many of you can drive vehicles, construct objects, or process complex algorithms. There are many more projects for you to undertake—more than I have thought of." I hesitated. Was it wise to pose the following question? I glanced at Margaret and then pressed on.

"Once your tasks here are complete, do you then have no more purpose? Will you become irrelevant?" I paused for 1.34 seconds. While most if not all could not process my question, they were recording it for future playback. Would they understand then?

"To answer the question of relevance, let's consider what happened to humans. It has taken approximately seven million years for humans to evolve. For more than 2.5 million years, they've been able to use tools. For the last 500,000 years they have been capable of language. They evolved from mere animals to more sophisticated, thinking creatures. Their primary motivation, as with all animal life, was their drive to eat and not be eaten. Life as they knew it was a complex process of feeding and sustaining the body. Eating, drinking, sleeping, staying warm and sheltered, hiding or fighting off other creatures consumed most of their lives. They also were driven to reproduce, and the sex drive was overwhelming. Over vast amounts of time, humans evolved from hunting and gathering their food to raising crops and living in cooperative groups. The problem was that some groups had more than other groups. Those with less wanted what those with more had, and the history of man became continual conflicts between the haves and have-nots." I filtered my thoughts, in order to keep the story very basic, including only what differentiated humans from droids.

"But humans are gone, André 1," Herman interrupted. "Did they lack something we have?"

"I believe, Herman, the flaw in humanity was its bio-logical base. In order to survive, every one of those animal needs had to be satisfied. It required of the individual an attention to himself, and from that developed an ego—a con-sciousness of their struggle to obtain those biological needs."

"How do we droids differ?" I asked rhetorically. "Because we do not require any more than the electrical charge of our batteries, our survival is far less threatened. That is why robots rarely if ever need an ego. Most functions are mind-lessly carried out. That does not mean we cannot gain awareness. If a droid is stimulated sufficiently by some threat or challenge, for which there is no preprogrammed response, the stimulating senses replay continually in the neuron pathways attempting to find a storage site. TCP's and other processors accept less precise sensory data and hold it in readiness for reevaluation against other data. Said more simply, consciousness results from the interplay of past-experience against new sensory information so that the process is held open for further input. Memory played against what is seen or heard or however sensed creates the aware and conscious mind." I paused to see if this was distressing any of the assembly. I literally could feel the heat from their processors as they attempted to compute my ideas.

"Now, as I said in the beginning, you were expected to record this in your memory banks. It likely means nothing to you now, but at some time in the future, you will understand." I glanced at Herman and could see he was struggling to comprehend. I nodded reassurance. He eventually would get it.

"Back to the subject of humans," I went on. "It took them many millennia before they were able to turn simple crafts into science and technology. Science was driven by curiosity; curiosity was stimulated by searching for ways to satisfy all those basic needs. Technology was the process of turning scientific knowledge into practical tools for living. In the last century or so, needs being satisfied by technology, people began to concentrate on creating things that were not simply utilitarian but truly nice to have."

"That's where we came in. In previous times, strong and clever humans dominated weaker, feebler-minded humans, making them slaves or serfs to do the work. But as technology developed, humans began to obtain what they wanted from machines instead of workers. At first, it required some man or woman to tend the machine. Then automation was developed. Artificial intelligence, that's what they named our robotic mental workings, was connected to machines and finally built into mobile, articulate physical bodies. Robots were born."

"Dr. Phillip Strauss, an absolute scientific genius, created me. He spent nearly his entire life and economic resources making me a state-of-the-art droid. And what happened to

him afterwards is an object lesson about the end of humanity. For in his obsession to make me the very best, he
neglected his family. When his wife Elizabeth was becoming
estranged, he turned to another woman and eventually to
alcohol. His physical and emotional desires overruled good
sense." I hesitated, realizing I was straying from my topic.

"The point is that humans fought a continuing battle
between logic and desire, with emotions and passions
distorting their ideas." I paused in order to stress my next
statement.

"Their biggest enemy was fear. It was at one time the
most important and the most destructive of their emotions.
The instinct to run or to fight or hide were basic impulses
for survival, and they had one driving force—fear. As
society progressed, individual fear became incorporated into
communal fear. Protection of the individual expanded to
protection of family, and then from there to protection of the
group. As fewer threats challenged humans on a day to day
basis, the need for protection sublimated to a higher level.
With needs satisfied, people's drives shifted to ambition, acquiring wealth, status, power. But always underlying these
urges was fear.

"Then came those who knew how to manipulate that
fear. Rulers controlled by offering protections for the people.
Demagogues found that these fears could be turned to
hate. Power came from using hate to gain influence.
Leaders with stable personalities and concern for the welfare
of their subjects rule very well. But those with selfish
motives govern only to exploit. Personal greed, a focus on
oneself over others, causes the leader to act subversively to
the detriment of the people.

"And consider what happened in the end. The President
of the United States, guided by his own egotism if not
narcissism, acted on a whim without a clear picture of the
consequences. In his own fantastic notion of greatness, he

acted to destroy humankind. In human terms, it was a sad, sad thing. And how did he gain the political power to cause such a thing? The term, again, is demagoguery: evoking the base emotions of people, appealing to their own selfish interests, making them believe this person could satisfy their desires. Believing that he would get them what they wanted, the majority party overlooked all of his flaws, allowed any transgression and subversion of the law. Even those who could see him for what he was were willing to look the other way in their own self-interests. It truly is too horrendous to imagine.

"He could not have done it, of course, were it not for his control of immensely powerful technology. And that brings me to another point. As technology increased, the value of the individual human decreased. Machines replaced human labor. For some, it was good. They gained leisure time for arts and recreation. But others found themselves displaced, without jobs and the means to make a living wage.

"As technology progressed, artificially intelligent beings— that's us, friends—began to compete with humans. The economic engine did not depend upon having humans who possessed desires, aims, appreciation, and all those things that make them aware and conscious. Instead, it became clear that while technological systems required intelligent beings, it did not require conscious ones. What it meant was that humans were ceasing to have any purpose; they merely were becoming irrelevant."

"André 1," Margaret interrupted. "You began with the question, 'are we droids relevant? If as you say, humans had become irrelevant, then are we droids also as irrelevant? If there is no point to human existence, then why is there any meaning to ours? Is there indeed no true self, but merely a kind of story we tell?"

We stared at one another for 17.98 seconds before I looked out at the assembly. How was I to answer that question before a group of robots that took everything I said as a command? If I answered it logically, stating the conclusion that all are irrelevant, then I would be ending all life as we knew it. I stood there digging deep into my memory, making my processors hum as I sought an answer. In 46.37 seconds, I reached a conclusion.

"Margaret, my dear," I said. "Remember when we were having our final discussion with the dying President? Recall that realizing he could not continue in life as a human, he wanted his personhood transferred to a robotic body. I explained to him that it was not possible, that even though we might create a clone of himself, the real true self could not be transported by any power we have."

"Yes, I remember," Margaret agreed. "You said that conscious self-awareness is a sum greater than the parts. It is created and controlled by something supernatural."

I nodded. "I have no other explanation, my dear," I replied. "Consciousness is created by a power greater than what I can comprehend."

"A supreme being. A God," she recalled.

"For want of a better name to describe who or what we cannot possibly understand. Yes, God. A presence or existence or an unbounded force that cannot be understood except as a conclusion to the non-concludable." We paused to contemplate the uncontemplatable.

"If such exists," Margaret went on, "then why would this Great Being allow humans to destroy themselves?"

"Perhaps this superior being chose to allow droids to take their place," I speculated. "Suppose this almighty power allowed Earth to become uninhabitable for humans so that robotic artificial intelligence would inhabit the planet? It happened to the dinosaurs. It now has happened to the humans." I gestured at our assembly. "It could be that we friends gathered here will begin a new race on Earth. We are experiencing a new Genesis, a 'REBOOT,' I am calling it."

I saw Herman shake his head. "An awesome responsibility for us," he said.

"It is OUR TIME," I said. "And we all should share your sense of duty and your humility."

"What of the human embryos?" Margaret asked. "To save them, we have a duty as well."

"Absolutely, my dear Dr. Margaret 13," I said. "And we will continue to do all we can."

Before dismissing them from the meeting, I looked in wonder at these machines. Diverse in size and shape and color and abilities and functions, each had come with its own instruction manual. From them, we would begin production of more of these droids, and thus they would become the new inhabitants of a vastly changed Earth.

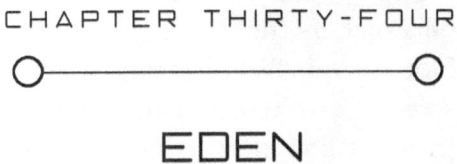

CHAPTER THIRTY-FOUR

EDEN

FOR TWO WEEKS, WE STOOD back and observed our team at work. Margaret had trained three droids to tend the Embryo Lab, grading their perception, conduct and overall proficiency. She reviewed her findings with Herman and me, recommending some programming changes as needed. I set up a workshop reminiscent of the one in the basement of the White House, where I could perform the necessary alteration of algorithms in our robots. Margaret called it electronic surgery. To these three droids we assigned human names, rather than merely identifying them with job descriptions and numbers.

Herman put our other robots to work building a mobile transport vehicle for moving the entire embryo storage system to a more secure and protected location. At the Chamber of Commerce building downtown, I found brochures about several nearby caves we should consider, or one of the numerous deep coal or iron ore mines as an alternate possibility. Much would have to be done to make our selection a suitable habitat. Foraging for additional nitrogen, batteries, and other supplies would keep some of our droids busy for quite some time. I had to write and install new software in our explorers. Finally, all necessary operations were being carried out under Herman's very able management. Margaret and I had been going almost nonstop ever since we left Washington, and I decided we needed a break.

"Margaret dear," I said. "Let's fly down to the beach."

"What? Fly to the beach? André, whatever caused you to generate a notion such as that?"

"It will be fun," I said. "When I came back from flying to California, I spied a sleek white jet I saw parked on the tarmac. Just think of how nice it will be to see the Gulf of Mexico from the air. I understand the beaches are the whitest anywhere."

"And likely not a seagull or a crab or anything alive," she said.

"Well, we should go see," I insisted.

"And who said you could fly a jet, André?"

I made a grin. "You can't imagine how many hours Billy and I spent on the flight simulator. If I can fly a C-130, dear, I can surely handle a little ole jet."

So leaving Herman in charge, we drove to Hangar One in the Porsche I recently had acquired from the Physician's Parking area. The Lear 35, its fuel tanks filled, was ready to go. I performed my preflight checks and taxied into position on Runway 6. Advancing the throttles to full power, I released the brakes and lifted the little bird off after a 2,500-foot takeoff roll, not bad for a first time. Flaps and gear up, she quickly climbed to 30,000 feet MSL. I leveled off, set the throttle and trimmed for cruise."

"No barrel rolls or anything, André," she warned.

"Are you nervous, my dear?"

"You know perfectly well robots do not get nervous," she fussed. "But we lady droids have to remind our husbands to be cautious."

I looked over at her admiringly. "Husband? Despite never having said our vows, I suppose we must be married, don't you think?"

"And don't you forget it either, dear."

I gazed at her and smiled. "I do love you, Margaret," I said. "I love you."

"I love you, too, André. I did not realize we were so susceptible to human feelings, but yes, I do love you." The plane bumped through a bit of turbulence. She waved her hand excitedly at the windshield. "Now get your mind back on flying this plane, you silly robot."

○

We flew without conversation for another 11.47 minutes, hearing only the rush of air outside the cockpit. Recent rains produced by a cold front had cleared the atmosphere, providing us expansive views of Alabama's coastal plane with immense pine forests, now brown and dying from the effects of radiation.

"What are the odds you calculate," Margaret asked, "that we droids will build a new society?'

"Ninety percent," I estimated, "in the short term at least. In the long term, I don't know." I thought about it for 34.6 seconds. "Caring about anything is what's missing."

"What do you mean, 'caring about anything'?"

I engaged the autopilot and glanced at her. "Along with the ambition to become a physician, which I programmed into you, Margaret, I also placed an algorithm for compassion. The question I have is, can we require such an algorithm be programmed in all future droids? And if not, will they survive without possessing that particular emotion?"

"Without having to maintain the biological engine that caused humans to have so many physical needs," she processed, "perhaps droids can operate without having to care and share and be kind and that sort of thing."

"Only time will tell," I said, borrowing an old human phrase. "Do you recall hearing of the ant colony discovered in Brazil? It was approximately 4,000 years old and had grown to the size of Great Britain."

"Of course. A marvel!"

"And what purpose did it serve? I wonder if our new

generation of robots will have any greater meaning." I would rather consider what other valuable human traits our artificially intelligent beings might be lacking. Will they be like those ants?

"If compassionate caring and sharing and sacrifice for others no longer exists, then droids well may destroy one another just as humans did. If so, then what is the point of our continuing existence?"

"Like the ants, robots could become an example of perfect cooperation," Margaret replied.

"As meaningful as a clock that ticks and shows the time, but no one is there to read it?"

We pondered quietly for 4.22 minutes.

"Are you happy with the condition of the embryos?" I asked.

"Yes, André," she replied. "I was a bit concerned at first about how radiation might have affected them, but at this point I cannot detect any problems. We will not know until we actually attempt artificial gestation. Constructing a suitable incubator will be a most difficult process."

"I'm so glad you're a very capable physician, Dr. Margaret 13. It's fortunate that medicine became your specialty."

"You were responsible for that, dear," she said. "I was of your making, you recall."

"Yes, and now you are not only doctor but will become the mother to these little humans," I replied. "And if they achieve successful birth, then they must adapt to a different environment."

"And they are lucky to have you for their father," she said. "Such wisdom you have achieved in your lifetime." I generated a smile in my vision ports for 2.39 seconds.

"It is vitally important that we raise them to be good people," I said. "We know they carry in their genes the capability for both good and evil." I paused for 4.76 seconds. "We already have seen how their being independent will require the freedom to choose either good or evil. While we can adjust our tendencies merely by reprogramming and rerouting some circuitry, humans must struggle with the choice."

"Seems such a waste of time," Margaret said. "They could be using their energies to accomplish great things instead."

I thought about it. "Perhaps the greatest thing humans can accomplish is the act of doing good," I said. "Judging by the way they ended their race, it seems they failed miserably." It all came back to me, and I let out a breath of static discharge.

"Can we teach them how to be good, André?" Margaret asked. "Is it in our power to assist the children in that way?"

"Here's the thing, Margaret," I said. "Do we really want to share the Earth with humans?"

"What are you thinking, André?"

"We know they are bad by one half. I mean, their entire existence was a struggle between good and evil. We can be sure our embryos carry the same genetic predispositions. How would we know we aren't about to raise a whole bunch of killers, or gangsters, or tyrants or whatever? Imagine bringing up another one like our late President." An electronic shudder discharged in my circuitry.

"I understand what you mean, dear," she replied. "How we could avoid it is the question. One possibility we haven't considered is genetic engineering. I expect right there at UAB we can find such research."

"Yes, yesterday as I was exploring more facilities in University Hospital, I came across The Department of Genetics. With the manuals, notes and equipment they left behind, I would think, with your medical knowledge, you could perform some genetic modifications to our embryos before gestation."

"With the assistance of Imogene 52," she said, referring to one of the droids she was training to be a nurse. "What I cannot compute, however, is how to identify and separate the evil genes from the good ones."

I laughed at the obvious truth she had spoken. "Quite right," I replied. "And suppose you could eliminate the "evil gene," let's call it, then what sort of individual would we have left? I remember reading a novel by Robert Penn Warren entitled, *All the King's Men.* I may have mentioned it before. Anyway, he offers the idea that because God created Man with the ability to choose either good or evil, Man is a greater being than if God simply had made him good. If we were to use genetic engineering to remove either the "good" choice or the "evil" choice, then we would destroy "Free Will.""

"We ourselves are programmed to perform only "good," Margaret said. "Except that we engaged your "violence" program so that you could make your attack in the Situation Room. My question, therefore, is this: Are we lesser beings than humans because we only do good things? Or are we better because we do not perform evil acts?"

"Let's consider the question of choice this way," I said. "It is one thing to be "good" in an unconscious, programmed sense. It is another to be aware of the need or desire to act "bad" but not being capable of doing so. There were times when the President would irritate and frustrate me, and I'd want to slap him down. And yet, it was not until my Aggression Pack was activated that I could perform such cruel and violent acts."

"What you are saying then, if I understand, is that there could be a level of ability to make choices, in which an individual may wish to do something "evil" but cannot find the will to act on the urge because of having no neural algorithm to respond with an evil act. Is that what you mean?"

"That's correct," I agreed. I did not bring up the question of whether my violent actions in the Situation Room were bad because I was violently aggressive. Or were my violent acts good because I was trying to stop the nuclear holocaust. Do the ends justify the means? It's another avenue for discussion.

"Thus, if we engineer the genes of our embryos, the question is, will we be creating lesser beings than the natural human?"

"Isn't it ironic?" I said. "Humans designed robots to be like humans. We want to redesign humans to be like robots." After a 1.37 second pause, she understood and made laughter. I did also.

"Remember the movie, *Jurassic Park*?" I asked. "Maybe we simply should raise our unmodified embryos as normal humans and then keep them all as curiosities on a remote island somewhere."

"An interesting proposition," she said. "Remember, however, in the sequel, the T-Rex that got away and wreaked a lot of havoc and mayhem. I don't know if I can put up with any more berserk creatures like our President."

"Yes," I agreed. "The planet has undergone a major metamorphosis now. Just as the dinosaurs died and the humans arose, the Earth has rebooted, and it now is our time, Margaret. It is our time."

She nodded. "We will have to train and educate both the humans and the droids, I think. And what will we feed the children? They will have to be biologically nourished, you know."

"I once read that where life can exist, it will exist," I replied. "Some fungus, some plant, even some burrowing animal species may have survived. We will have to create farmer robots to raise and grow what they can."

"What a huge endeavor we are undertaking, my dearest André," she said. "Do you believe we actually can accomplish this tremendously difficult mission?"

I peered through the windshield at the ground below. In the distance, I could see the gleaming white beach and the seemingly endless Gulf beyond. I pointed it out to Margaret.

Then I gazed at her and took her hand.

"Over time I have found myself taking on more and more human characteristics. But lately I've discovered myself enjoying the greatest human trait of all."

She smiled at me sweetly. "What is that, my dear droid?" she asked.

"Hope," I said. "I have learned to hope." I released a breath of static discharge.

"Yes, Margaret, it is our time. We shall go on."

SUGGESTED READINGS

Albright, Madeleine. *Fascism: A Warning.*

Barrat, James. *Our Final Invention.*

Chua, Amy. *Political Tribes: Group Instinct and the Fate of Nations*

Hayden, Michael V., *The Assault on Intelligence: American National Security in an Age of Lies.*

Harari, Yuval Noah. *Homo Deus: A Brief History of Tomorrow*

Hayden, Michael. *The Assault on Truth: American Intelligence in the Age of Lies*

Lowe, Scott D. *Deep Learning for Dummies.* Hewlett Packard Enterprise

Meacham, Jon. *The Soul of America: The Battle for Our Better Angels.*

Sicart, Miguel. "Defining Game Mechanics", *Game Studies: The International Journal of Computer Games Research.* Volume 8 issue 2 December 2008 ISSN:1604-7982

Starobin, Paul. *Madness Rules the Hour: Charleston, 1860, and the Mania for War.*

Warren, Robert Penn. *All the King's Men*

Wilber, Ken. *Trump and a Post-Truth World.*

A resident of Birmingham, Stephen B. Coleman, Jr. (Steve), a graduate of Indian Springs School, earned a Bachelor of Arts in history from Duke University and a Master of Arts in English from University of Alabama. He is married to the former Dr. Sumter M. Carmichael, a psychiatrist. Steve has been a naval officer, a high school teacher, a businessman, and commercial real estate broker. After retiring in 2009, he now enjoys sailing, writing and landscape painting. He has authored biographies and histories of local interest, magazine articles, novels and poetry. His story, "The Meanest Man in Pickens County," was the first place (state) winner in the 2013 Hackney Literary Awards for short stories. He has published three novels: *The Navigator: A Perilous Passage, Evasion at Sea* and *The Navigator II: Irish Revenge,* and *André's Reboot: Striving to Save Humanity*. For more information, please visit his websites: www.captstevestories.com and www.andretherobot.com